The Ghost of Grandpa Wills

Bill Tyson

White Bird Publications
P.O. Box 586
Diana, Texas 75640
http://www.whitebirdpublications.com

This is a work of fiction. Names, characters, places, and incidents are the product of the author's imagination. Any resemblance to actual persons, living or dead, business establishments, events, or locales is entirely coincidental.

Please do not participate in or encourage piracy of copyrighted materials in violation of the author's rights. Purchase only authorized editions.

Copyright©2015 by Bill Tyson
Cover by Chad Tyson

All rights are reserved. No part of this book may be reproduced or transmitted in any form or by any electronic or mechanical means, including photocopying, recording or by any information storage and retrieval system, without the written permission of the author, except where permitted by law. For information, contact White Bird Publications.

ISBN: 978-1-63363-145-8
LCCN: 2015958262

PRINTED IN THE UNITED STATES OF AMERICA

If you purchased this book without a cover, you should be aware that this book is stolen property. It was reported as "unsold and destroyed" to the publisher and neither the author nor the publisher has received any payment for this "stripped book."

Visit Bill at:

http://www.billtysonauthor.com

http://www.facebook.com/bill.tyson.505

http://www.twiter.com/@billtysonauthor

LinkedIn

https://goo.gl/UYxZeH

Dedication

To my Shelly, the love of my life. I thank God for your love.

Acknowledgements

A special word of thanks to my son, Chad, for his work in creating the cover design for this book. He did an awesome job.

Chad is a fulltime firefighter paramedic with Dallas Fire and Rescue, Dallas, Texas. When off duty and not pulling people out of wrecked cars or helping put out fires, he is a partner in a photography and video business called Studio One One Seven. Please visit their website at www.studiooneoneseven.com.

Last, but definitely not least, I must thank Evelyn Byrne-Kusch of White Bird Publications for taking on this project. My thanks to Evelyn and her team of editors for their help, their suggestions, and their patience. I have learned a tremendous amount from them. Please visit their website at www.whitebirdpublications.com.

Foreword

I love ghost stories, especially good ones. As a kid, they always fascinated me. Not the horrible, dripping with blood kind where evil always wins; rather the fun type where the good guy comes out on top in the end.

I remember fondly the old television series (in the days of black and white TV) called "Topper and His Ghosts." That was my kind of ghost story.

In the words of my heroic hero, William Watson, I can also say that I have never met a ghost I did not like. However, should I ever meet one, I do hope he/she will be like Grandpa Wills.

From whence came this story? One of my favorite pieces of music is "Unchained Melody" by the Righteous Brothers. Sometime back, while listening to the song, a vision came into my imagination, the picture of a lonely woman whose only true love had died. He had promised to return for her; she had vowed to wait for him. Decades had passed, yet she remained loyal to her vow. And from that seed, the story grew.

And so was born the story of how William Wordsworth Watson came to meet his great-great-great-great-great-great grandfather, Franklin Percival Wills, and then to discover… Well, you will just have to read the story, the whole story, to find out exactly what Will Watson discovered.

The Ghost of Grandpa Wills

White Bird Publications

The Road West

Part One

Chapter One
The Wills Ranch, Late Winter

Amelia Wills, the Mistress of Wills Ranch, sat in her power chair, pale hands trembling as she stared at the piece of brittle, aged newspaper she held. The article carried a date of more than three decades earlier. **"Three Die in Flaming Car Wreck—Infant is Sole Survivor,"** the headline announced.

A photo, dark and grainy, displayed a woman's blood-streaked face, her expression distorted by pain and fear as she thrust an infant through a car's broken window. The story continued, describing her screams, as she begged someone to save the child. It told how a police officer grabbed the child and ran to safety. Immediately after, explosion and fire engulfed the vehicle—the roar of flames failing to muffle the screams of the trapped victims. The unidentified child was the only survivor.

Amelia stared at the piece of yellowed paper for several more minutes before looking up at the two men sitting across from her. They sat watching her, without speaking.

"Where did you find this?" she whispered, her voice quivering. The only other sound was the wood fire, crackling in the fireplace.

James, the shorter one, replied in a high-pitched voice. "Locked inside a safe, down in the basement of Dad's old office building. We were clearing things out for the renovation."

"We didn't know the safe was there until last week," Jimmy, the tall one, interjected, his deep voice filling the cavernous room. "Never did find the combination—had to get a locksmith. It was in with some of our grandfather's old stuff."

"And…?" she leaned forward, her eyes moving from one lawyer to the other.

Jimmy, shifted in his chair—an antique that groaned under his weight. With a voice that could overflow a courtroom, he, now, spoke with hesitation and embarrassment. He, who could easily stare down a hostile jury, averted his eyes—unable to face the frail woman before him. "There was a stack of private papers, as well as some old journals. In one of them, he wrote about, ah…a child, a…a baby boy."

Amelia's body, ravaged with disease, was frail, but something within her imparted strength—perhaps, it was that the truth was coming out; a secret, long hidden, could, now, be revealed. She gathered herself, struggling to control her emotions. She spoke in a soft voice. "It is true, you know. I did give birth." She watched the two lawyers, wondering what their reactions would be.

"I was a teenager, not long out of high school. Oh, we wanted to run off, elope, and get married. So, we decided we would sneak off to San Antonio." Her eyes moved to the flames that danced inside the stone fireplace while she took a deep breath before continuing. "Told my parents I was going to a friend's house for the weekend. She, my friend, was the only other person who knew the truth."

Pausing to consider her words, Amelia spoke with hesitation, her eyes downcast. "He was a Marine, and he was going away, you see."

In a sudden move, she raised her head, glanced from one attorney to the other, unsure of what to say—or how to say it. Her voice firmed. "I never wanted to hide our love. I wanted to tell the whole world, but my father... Well, Papa would never have approved. He never approved of anything his precious daughter did—especially associating with Indians, much less marrying one."

Her words turned hard, tainted with bitter anger. "Of course, Papa didn't approve of Mexicans, Blacks, Catholics, Jews—or anyone else that he didn't consider good enough."

Her eyes locked onto the tall lawyer. She bit off the next few words, "But then, no one was good enough for him—or his precious daughter."

She slumped back into the wheelchair and lowered her gaze. Her fingers found the wool lap blanket, and, for a few seconds, she twisted the cloth in a knot before smoothing it out again.

Jimmy fidgeted, unsure about how to react. James reached for the antique porcelain coffee pot to refill his cup.

She straightened herself and lifted her eyes once more.

"Anyway, we had car trouble, never got to San Antonio. When we did get the car started, it was quite late, so we found a motel close by."

Looking beyond them at the low burning fire, she took a breath before continuing. "I know it was wrong. We both knew it was wrong, but we had one wonderful night." Now, she looked around, her eyes moving from one man to the other, a smile creasing her face as she remembered. "It was a really…a really…beautiful night…we had together."

Again, her voice dropped to a whisper, and she took her eyes away from them, a slight flush on her pale features. Jimmy was forced to lean closer, straining to hear.

"A short time later, he was gone—my Richard was gone—shipped out to Vietnam or some such place over there. Couldn't tell me where. It was some kind of top secret mission."

She exhaled, lifted her head, and studied the wooden ceiling beams. "Whatever it was, wherever he went—he never came home."

James lowered his cup and bent forward.

"Never saw him again…promised I'd wait… still…waiting…" She paused and took a deep breath.

Both men waited in silence.

She straightened herself, lifted her head, and continued. "I never told anyone about that night before now. No one. Not a living soul. I was young and angry, as well as stubborn— and not a little afraid. Of course, getting pregnant, I couldn't hide something like that for very long. Especially, since I was still living here at home."

Amelia looked at each of the two men, both of whom she had known since they were born.

"As you know, your grandfather, your father, and my

father—they were all friends and business partners." A frown creased her forehead. "Your grandfather was Papa's attorney for many decades. He knew all about how I had disgraced the family."

She gestured, palms upward, in resignation.

"So, in due time, the child was born. Here, at the house." She pointed. "Upstairs, in one of the bedrooms. No hospital for me because, well, then the whole world would've known about our terrible shame—the family's greatest embarrassment." Her eyes flashed with fire. She put bitter emphasis on those last few words.

The angry frown disappeared, replaced by a tender smile.

"Richard, my baby's father, was a local boy, a member of one of the nearby Indian families—the Colorado family." At this statement, Jimmy stared at her, eyes and mouth open in an unasked question. She saw his expression and replied with a soft smile, "That's right, Jimmy; he would've been your Sara's uncle…"

Gathering his composure, Jimmy asked, "Does Sara know?"

Shaking her head, Amelia replied, "No. As I said, I've never spoken about this to anyone." With the smile disappearing, she returned to her story. "Richard joined the Marines, and soon became a Navy Seal. He knew my father well enough that he wanted to prove himself—show Papa he was a real man, man enough to take care of his…his precious little daughter."

She stopped, collecting herself, before whispering. "Never came home. At least, not alive." She slumped into the wheelchair, her head dropping forward, voice quivering. "They did bring his body back, though. He was buried up in Arlington, at the National Cemetery—with all the honors.

They played taps, had a full honor guard—all that stuff. A real hero, he was—Medal of Honor and everything."

"I couldn't go." Her words were cold and hard. "Stayed home—had to act as though nothing ever happened between us—as…as if I didn't even know who he was." She raised her head and looked back at the men. The expression on her face matched the emotion in her words. "I've been up there since—to the National Cemetery—after my parents died. Visited his grave twice, wanted to go again—don't guess I ever will, now that this cancer…"

Her words trailed off into silence until she paused, catching her breath. She continued speaking, repeating herself in her sorrow. "Never came home. But, it didn't matter; none of it would've made any difference, whatever my Richard did. His skin was the wrong color—too dark for Papa's likings." She bit off these last words, one at a time, emphasizing her pain, mixed with the bitter anger that boiled within her.

Her eyes traversed from one man to the other. She beat the arm of her chair with a fist. "When the labor pains started, they drugged me, knocked me out." She bent forward again, her eyes locked onto Jimmy. "Paid the doctor off—what with him being another old friend of my father."

Exhausted by her emotions, she fell back against her pillows. "Anyway—when I woke up, they told me—told me their lies."

Her voice broke, and she cleared her throat before resuming her story. Drops of moisture formed in her eyes. "Yes, my mother and my father—my own parents—they lied to me. They told me that my baby died at birth; stillborn was what they said. Some unexplained medical complication. Deformed is how they explained it."

Her entire body shook, her voice rising in volume and

power. "They said my child was deformed; they told me my poor baby was deformed."

Tears poured down her cheeks. James pulled a handkerchief from his coat pocket and gave it to her. She accepted it and wiped her eyes with trembling hands.

"They never let me hold my baby. I never saw my baby. Never heard him cry. I—I never got to name—my own baby."

"All these years," she sobbed, shaking in the wheelchair. "All these many years, I thought my baby was dead."

She gathered her strength, looked at them and, through the tears, demanded, "Find him; find this young man."

Stiffening her back, she sat upright once again. "You bring me proof my son is alive. Then, bring him to me. I don't care how you do it or what it costs." Her fist struck her thigh in cadence with each word— "Bring me my son."

She paused again before taking another deep breath, to continue in a lower tone. "We...I...don't have...there isn't much...time. This cancer's not going to wait around forever, you know.

"Hurry. Please, hurry." The lawyers looked at each other and stood up together. Jimmy spoke first, "Miss Amelia, we've already begun the search—"

"We think he's living somewhere in the Fort Worth/Dallas area," James piped in. They gathered their coats, hats, and gloves and moved toward the door.

Jimmy reassured her. "We'll do everything we can, Miss Amelia; that's a promise."

Chapter Two
The Will's Ranch, Mid-Spring

A shiny, dark blue Hummer rolled to a stop on the white, crushed stone of the driveway. The front doors opened, and two men stepped out into the bright West Texas sunlight. Both wore sunglasses, western style, tailored dark blue suits, and expensive, handmade cowboy boots. Each placed a white, custom-made Stetson on his head.

That is where the similarities ended. Jimmy, the driver, towered a full head above the big four-wheel drive truck; James would have struggled to see through the passenger door-window without standing on his tiptoes.

Both turned and walked toward the house—an imposing, three-storied structure, constructed of hand-quarried Texas limestone, topped with crenelated battlements along its frontage and four-storied circular towers at each end. The entrance, built of teakwood and framed in blocks of red granite, stood flanked by two matching stone towers. The meticulously maintained double doors were hand carved and stood eight feet tall. Multiple windows, filled with darkened glass and framed with cast-iron shutters, frowned down from each of the floors. Altogether, it stood as an imposing edifice that cast a dark, threatening appearance.

The hot sun of late May burned down upon the lawyers, and their dark clothing soaked up its heat. James pulled his handkerchief out and was wiping his forehead before he was half way to the house. Their feet crunched into the crushed stone of the driveway until they reached the smooth flagstone that paved the entranceway beneath the portico. They were thankful to reach the shade.

"I hope she's feeling better today." Jimmy reached down to ring the doorbell. "I really hate to see her hurting so much."

They heard the notes of *The Yellow Rose of Texas* sounding from within.

"Didn't they play *The Eyes of Texas* the last time we were here?" the big guy rumbled.

James answered. "I believe they play over a dozen different tunes, including the *Aggie War Hymn*." Changing the subject, he waved a large manila envelope for emphasis. "I hope this is our man. I'm afraid we're running out of time."

"Yeah, I know. All that chemo and radiation doesn't seem to be slowing the cancer. But I feel confident we've found him."

The door chimes were still playing their tune when one of the doors swung open. A young woman, dressed in a nurse's uniform, consisting of bright green pants and a matching blouse displaying a multitude of colorful butterflies, greeted them. She had hair the color of midnight and eyes that matched. "Good afternoon, I'm Miss Amelia's nurse, Maria Gonzalez." She smiled through a set of bright white teeth. Her dark skin revealed her Mexican ancestry; however, her speech accents were pure West Texas English.

They did not recognize her. "You must be new," Jimmy said. Both of the visitors knew that the lady of the house, Miss Amelia Priscilla Annette Wills, found it difficult to keep a live-in nurse on the premises. The two previous ones left soon after arriving—claiming the old mansion was haunted.

James tipped his hat and offered a business card. "I'm James Randolph Smithson; this is my brother, James Alfred Smith, of the law firm *'Smithson, Smith, Murchison, Ferguson, Braselton, and Sampson.'* We are expected, I believe."

"Mr. Smithson, Mr. Smith," she replied. Although, her smile never faltered, her eyes betrayed her curiosity as they shifted from one brother to the other, and back again. "Please, come in. Miss Amelia is waiting for you in the library." They removed their hats and followed her into the vast, cathedral-like entrance hall, glad to leave the stifling heat outside.

The ceiling arched three full floors above them. An antique glass chandelier hung from its center, beneath a large skylight, and suspended from outsized, rough-cut timber crossbeams. Hand carved matching staircases flanked either side of the spacious hallway.

The sound of their footsteps rose from the polished granite floor to echo off the stained wood wall panels.

Halfway down the long passage, Maria stopped and held open another set of tall oak doors. Smiling, she motioned for them to enter.

"Thank you, Maria," James said. "We know our way from here." He stood smiling and holding onto the door

The Ghost of Grandpa Wills

handle.

"Are you joining Miss Amelia and me, or do you, suddenly, have other plans?" Jimmy's voice rumbled around the room.

James glared up at his brother, the smile gone from his face. "She is very attractive."

"Yeah, but kinda short for my liking. I prefer my women to be all grown up."

"Sure, like an Amazon with a gun on her hip-"

A terse command from within the library interrupted their argument. "You two, stop your fussing. Get in here, and close the door behind you." With hats in hand, they obediently stepped through the doorway.

The room they entered had many of the local librarians green with envy. Paintings, photographs, and shelves of books covered the walls, all the way from the thick pile carpeting up to the high, open beam ceiling. Both men had been here before—many times—and often enjoyed the privilege of wandering among the many volumes, admiring the artwork and pictures, as well as the displays, filled with memorabilia and artifacts from all over Texas.

Amelia Wills, who sat waiting for them, knew the pair well. In their youth, she had been the mother neither of them had ever known.

Hanging their hats on a nearby rack—a tangled construction of horns from a number of long-dead pronghorn antelope—they greeted her in unison. "Good morning, Miss Amelia."

They acknowledged her with smiles on their faces—and tears in their hearts. She sat before them, a shrunken caricature of the once vibrant beauty of a few short years ago. The ravages of cancer, chemotherapy, and radiation treatment having aged her far beyond her actual years, not yet fifty, she, now, looked twice that.

Towering over her, Jimmy bent forward to take her pale hand in both of his. He gave it an affectionate, light squeeze.

In contrast, James, even though he stretched himself to his fullest and wore boots with high riding heels, still stood no more than a few inches taller than she in her power chair. He spoke first. "You're looking well this morning, Miss Amelia—"

"I'm not paying you to stand there and tell lies. You're both as bad as all my doctors. They never listen to me either—but they're still willing to take my money. Sit down there, and talk to me.

"James, you pour us some iced tea. I feel like having a glass myself, and I know it's already hot out there for this time of year. I do hope the drought breaks soon." She gestured toward two chairs and a small table already set with a large pitcher of cold tea, several glasses, and an ice bucket.

Each man obeyed her commands with a polite, "Yes, ma'am."

Next to the tea pitcher, sat a platter piled with soft, chewy, chocolate chip cookies for which her Chinese cooks, the Singh brothers, were duly famous. Still warm from the oven, their aroma destroyed all of Big Jim's resistance. He moved his chair to a point within arm's reach and grabbed a handful as he sat down—he had very large hands.

"I knew you were coming." She watched him with a smile that temporarily erased many of the wrinkles around her face.

James moved over to the tea trolley, filled the glasses with ice, and began pouring the tea. "Ahh." Tea sloshed onto the tray. He stiffened and glanced around the room, his eyes

The Ghost of Grandpa Wills

open wide. He bit his tongue to avoid saying anything more colorful.

Amelia turned to him. "What? James, were you saying something?"

"Did something frighten my little brother?" Jimmy asked with a smirk.

"Cold air," James replied, glaring back at his brother. "Just a blast of cold air from one of the AC ducts, I guess."

"Maybe it was the ghost," Jimmy grinned down at his brother. "Oh, I forgot, you don't believe in ghosts. They're just a figment of everyone's imagination, aren't they?"

"You two, quit your arguing. I swear, I don't believe either of you will ever grow up. You should be thankful you have each other.

"Now, talk to me, and tell me what you've found." Pain was stealing away her normal good nature and patience. "Time is growing short as you well know."

"Yes ma'am, we, now know-" Jimmy said.

James returned with the iced tea. "We have confirmed what we first suspected, Miss Amelia," He passed the glasses around. "We feel certain that the man in question is most definitely the correct one. The DNA report is 99% conclusive." He passed a glass to his brother, frowning at the depleted pile of cookies.

"But the DNA report will not stand up in court?" she asked.

"No, ma'am; it was not obtained in a legally recognized manner," Jimmy replied. "Chewing gum retrieved from a trashcan, most probably, would not hold up in court, if contested."

"You know what to do. You must get him here. I want to meet him. We'll have the test done properly, once he arrives."

She hesitated a second and glanced over at a far corner before adding. "There will be one more test."

Turning back to her guests, she continued. "Now, you have your instructions. Don't tell him any more than necessary. Tell him that we may be long lost relatives—but, only, if you have to. If he's who we think he is—I want to be the one to break the news."

She added in a softer voice, "Please, don't fail me; time is short."

The two sat with her and talked for a time—small talk about this and that. They knew she was lonely, that confinement to a wheelchair was very difficult for someone such as she, who had once been so active. James looked at his watch. "We have a plane to catch, Miss Amelia. We want to be in Dallas tonight so we can see him tomorrow. We hope to have him here by the middle of next week."

"You said he has a family?"

"Yes, ma'am. He does—a wife and two children," James answered.

"I surely hope so," she said with a smile and a sparkle in her eyes. "That means I have grandchildren. All of a sudden—after all these lonely years—I'm a grandmother. I want to meet them all. I want to know my daughter-in-law as well."

Both men stood, excused themselves, and stepped toward the door. "Don't bother calling anyone." Jimmy reached out to grab another handful of cookies. "We know our way out. And tell Mr. Singh we enjoyed the cookies."

"We'll keep you informed," James opened the door and reached for his hat.

Outside, as they crossed the driveway, James looked up at his brother, "That's the first time I've seen her smile in a long time."

The Ghost of Grandpa Wills

Amelia sat for a few minutes, staring at the library door. Her eyes turned back to the same faraway corner.

"Well," she demanded. "Speak up; what do you think?"

A pale light shimmered and the form of a man appeared out of the air. Dressed in old-fashioned clothes, battered, dirty, sweat-stained, and threadbare, he looked out of place in a room where everything else was spotless and unsoiled. He wore an old shirt, leather vest, brown pants made of some timeworn, heavy cloth, held up by grimy suspenders, along with boots that gave the impression of having walked all over West Texas. A beat-up, sweat-stained hat sat on his head, and the butt end of a large, antique revolver peeked out of his waistband.

Amelia looked up at him, the smile still on her face, "Well, Franklin, we should know something for sure in a few days."

In a quiet voice, almost a whisper, the apparition answered, "Maybe so, Amelia, maybe so. I do hope so." His eyes shifted away from her, as though he saw something in the far distance. He spoke again, "There is still something I have to do, something I must get done, but I just don't know what. It's been so long—such a very long time."

Chapter Three
Midland, Texas

Lawrence Larue Larson, hands clasped behind him and his back to the interior of his office stood staring out the large plate glass window. From his lavishly furnished law office high up in the Larue Building, he could see all the way across Midland, Texas, and on west, to the city of Odessa. Sometimes, he enjoyed the panoramic view, but, at this moment, he stood lost in another world, another time, and another place.

The sounds of Hank Williams, Sr. washed over him, immersed him—filled him to the very brim of his being. At times such as these, L. L. Larson became Hank Williams, Sr. He was the entertainer reincarnated. Lawrence had long ago memorized the lyrics of his idol's songs—every word of every song, but his favorite was *Lonesome Whippoorwill*.

The Ghost of Grandpa Wills

On the wall directly behind him hung a video screen, the largest Lawrence could find, accompanied by the very best digital sound system. At this moment, Hank Williams, Sr. stood on stage, dressed in his characteristic western style white suit and Stetson. He stroked his guitar and crooned out the sad words:

"Hear that lonesome whippoorwill; He sounds too blue to fly..."

Lawrence Larue Larson sang along with him, regretting that he had been born decades too late, wishing he could have heard him live, seen him perform, known him personally—and maybe even saved his life. *Oh, what a loss it was when that great man died so early—so tragically early. Life was very unfair.* Lawrence deeply mourned his hero's untimely passing even though it had happened years before his own birth.

The cell phone in Lawrence's shirt pocket vibrated. Yanking it from his pocket, he flipped it open as he rushed back to his desk. There, he slammed a hand down on the video mute button.

"Yeah," he answered, letting his anger show through his voice. Lawrence was an impatient man, and he had been expecting this call for some time. Besides that, any type of interruption when he was listening to his hero always turned his mood very dark.

His scowl changed to a mirthless sneer. He concluded the conversation with, "Be sure you keep me well informed." He closed the phone and returned it to his pocket. The two words, "Thank You," were not a part of Lawrence Larue Larson's vocabulary—especially to those he deemed to be his underlings.

He glanced up at the video screen where Hank Williams,

Sr. stood frozen in the midst of a downward stroke on his guitar, mouth open, and the pain of loneliness written over his face. Lawrence, once more, gushed his adoration. "What a man. What a singer. What a performer."

However, Mr. Larson had a couple of other items to attend to before he could return to his idol. Sitting at his desk, he pulled an electronic tablet from a bottom drawer and pressed the power button. While it booted up, he retrieved the phone from his pocket and punched in a number. While waiting for the other person to answer, he opened the email app on the tablet

He heard a gruff voice growl, "Yeah."

"Ferrell, I have the information. You'll be getting it within minutes. You know what to do." That last comment was a statement—not a question.

"Yeah," came the brusque reply. "Consider it done."

"It had better be," Lawrence mumbled. He returned the phone to his pocket. confident the man would do whatever it took. He, also, knew that such little niceties, as the law, would not get in Ralph Ferrell's way. He had done business with the man before.

Chapter Four
R. G. Hawks Insurance Agency

William Wordsworth Watson (A.K.A. Will or Willie Boy) was doing what he did best—leaning his chair back on two legs with his feet on his desk, jaws working a piece of bubble gum, eyes closed, and hands clasped over his belly—daydreaming, yet again:

Sergeant Watson stared at the remains of his battered M-16, studying it. Hesitating for only a moment, he threw down the useless firearm and drew his knife from its sheath. Evil looking, the weapon carried an eighteen-inch blade, honed to a razor's edge with deep serrations along its spine.

"It will have to do," he decided.

"There is no other way." He knew from hard experience.

"No other choice." His mind was set as he returned the blade to its sheath.

Sergeant Watson crept out into the darkness. There would be blood spilled this night—of that, he was quite certain.

If anyone had asked, Will would have stated that he was planning his day, cogitating on his next sales call, or, maybe, if he trusted the questioner—he might explain that he was laying out the plot for a book he was writing. Moreover, he actually was writing a book—several to be exact. He possessed numerous notebooks and file folders full of disconnected scrawling about half-formed stories and musings; a page or two here, a chapter there, a scribble regarding this, and a few words concerning that—all stuffed into the drawers of a file cabinet in his garage.

Today was already a disaster, and lunchtime still an hour away.

The morning appointment had never shown up. Then, the *jerk* even refused to talk to him on the phone.

The afternoon appointment had been nice enough to call—only to give some *lame* excuse about a prior commitment.

Upon checking the Payment Office records, he discovered that two of his recent sales had canceled; policy lapses meant a loss in commissions and a big cut in his next paycheck.

On top of it all—he hated selling insurance. Period. Full stop. End of story.

However, at this moment, the hero of his current imagining (who just happened to bear a striking resemblance to himself—black hair and eyes along with a dark complexion) was within minutes of saving the life of a fair damsel-in-distress when his heroics were interrupted by the irritating shrill of a telephone.

Will thumped his chair to a level position, knocked a bottle of sodium-free, natural spring water onto the carpeted floor, and grabbed his desk phone, answering with the required company spiel— "Good morning. R. G. Hawks Life Insurance and Financial Planning, William Watson speaking. How may I be of service?"

Dial tone.

Another shrill.

He dropped the receiver into its cradle and grabbed his cell phone from his shirt pocket, "Yeah."

"Heads up, Willie. Hawk's on the prowl." It was friend and co-worker, Jake, whose cubicle sat in a more advantageous position, and who, also, knew that "Willie" had been caught with his feet up before.

"Thanks, man. I owe you one."

"You owe me a dozen—with cream on top," A click ended the conversation.

Will pocketed the cell phone and picked up his desk phone. He dialed the number of the *First State Bank Time and Weather Service.* With his free hand, he took a pencil and began scribbling meaningless notes about dates and times on a yellow legal pad. The bank's computer finished its spiel about the services offered. Will heard the "Hawk", along with his entourage, approaching. They were making their way through the maze of cubicles, most of whose owners were out on sales calls.

He heard voices, raised in sycophantic greeting:

"Good morning, Mister Hawks."

"Have a good day, Mister Hawks."

"Yes, sir, Mister Hawks."

No one ever said "No" to Mister Rutherford G. Hawks.

The procession rounded the nearest corner. Will's nose detected the parade before it came into view—essence of cigar, sweat, cheap aftershave, garlic, and onion.

Keeping the receiver pressed against his ear and raising his voice enough to ensure that he could be overheard, he began making an appointment to meet the bank's computer at the computer's office later that same afternoon. "Yes, sir, and what time would be best for you this afternoon, sir? Three o'clock or four, sir?"

The convoy barged into the cubicle and halted next to his desk, the bank's computer responded to Will's query with the current temperature of ninety-four degrees Fahrenheit, the humidity rating of ninety-five percent, and a forecast for continual thunderstorms over the next five days—typical late spring weather for North Texas.

A blue gray cloud surrounded the group, and tendrils of the foulness drifted into Will's airspace. He tried to hold his breath but started coughing and dropped his pencil. It rolled off the desk and landed next to the water bottle.

"I'm sorry, sir," he apologized to the bank's computer. "Someone has just come in. I'll see you at four this afternoon."

The Hawk's appearance fitted his name. His eyes were large and protruding—black pupils surrounded by jaundiced yellow—eyes that moved without ceasing, always on the prowl, searching for prey, and looking for victims. His nose, a large protuberance that stuck out from a bony, wrinkled face, resembled the beak of a large, predatory bird, and his suit looked as though it came from sometime back early in the previous century.

Like a hunting bird eyeing its prey from high above the

The Ghost of Grandpa Wills

forest, Rutherford G. Hawks towered over Will, glaring down at him with predatory eyes. He ignored the *"Thank You for Not Smoking"* sign, raised an enormous cigar to his mouth, sucked in a lungful—and without waiting for Will to put down the telephone receiver—admonished him in a loud, coarse voice. "Persistence, Mr. Watson, per-sist-tence."

He gestured, using the hand that held the cigar. Gray ash floated down, to rest on Will's notepad. "Per-sist-tence is what succeeds." He continued, biting off the individual syllables, "Nev-ver-quit." His motions jabbing the glowing coals ever closer to Will's face.

Will, forgetting to breathe, shrank back into his chair, wishing he could crawl beneath it.

Bending from the waist, the Hawk glared deep into his prey's eyes, "When I was your age, young man, I never used the telephone—wore out a pair of shoes every week, walking door to door. Had calluses on my knuckles from knocking on those same doors. I-nev-ver-gave-up." At last, he straightened up.

Desperate for breath, Will sucked in some of the pollution.

Ignoring his employee's discomfort, The Hawk continued spitting out his admonishments. "Grab hold. Hang on. NEV-VER-LET-GO." His voice lowered to a growling snarl, "You have to be a shark in this business." Every breath expelled more of the blue-gray foulness as more cigar residue descended to the desktop.

With his brows knit together in a deep frown, the Hawk's voice changed to an angry high pitch as he sneered, "You have not met your production quotas for the last two weeks, young man. You will not find any sales sitting here on your backside." Scraggly eyebrows rose as his eyes widened, and spittle sprayed, "Persistence is what counts. Do you hear me? PER—SIST—TENCE."

Wicked, sneering grins spread across the faces of the sycophants standing behind the old man. Abruptly, the Hawk stood straight and, entourage in tow, turned about-face, marched out of the cubicle, and disappeared around the corner.

To torment some other poor soul, Will was certain. He reached down to retrieve the pencil and water bottle. A cockroach lay feet up on the floor, legs waving feebly.

A shadow fell across the floor. A familiar voice asked, "A casualty of his foul presence?"

Will straightened in his chair to see his friend, Jake, standing at the cubicle's entrance. Almost as wide as he was tall and with an even larger, effervescent personality, Jake's presence could never be ignored.

"I have heard stories of flies falling out of the air as he walked by." Jake's black face creased in a huge grin that exposed his white teeth. "Now, I can truthfully say I have seen a cockroach felled by the mere nearness of his foul presence." With an aerosol can in each hand, he slid his bulk through the entrance and filled the air with a flowery air freshener from one and a disinfectant spray from the other. That done, he moved to the chair in front of Will's desk. The ancient piece of furniture groaned as he eased himself into it.

"I'm quite positive the rumor is true."

"Which rumor?" Will asked in a sour tone; he was not in a good mood.

"That he killed and ate all his own children."

"What woman would ever have him to father her children?"

"One that lives in a little gingerbread house—deep in the

The Ghost of Grandpa Wills

dark, dark woods."

"He has the foulest breath of any man alive."

"No doubt," Jake agreed. "However, all vampires exude the same foul essence."

Will came back with, "It is said that bad breath is better than no breath at all."

"I will gladly make an exception in his case."

"He claimed he never used a telephone when he was my age."

"Telephones had not yet been invented when he was your age. I'm not sure electricity had been discovered either."

This verbal exchange would have continued well into the afternoon except that Will's desk phone rang. Grabbing the receiver, he answered, "Yeah, Watson speaking."

It was Cathy, the receptionist. "You have visitors. I sent them on back." The dial tone filled his ear before he could ask any questions. He hung up. Distracted by Jake, he had forgotten about the fallen pencil and water bottle. He bent to retrieve them.

Will's fingers closed around the two objects. A pair of boots—western style cowboy boots—came into his view. With the exception of the size 70 boots worn by "Big Tex" at the State Fair of Texas, these were the largest examples of footwear he had ever seen or imagined. His eyes moved upwards, and the pencil and the bottle fell from his fingers. The legs, to which the boots came attached, were a little smaller than telephone poles, or so it seemed.

Will continued looking upward, his eyes came upon a belt buckle, one of those fancy silver things worn by all the "wanna-be" cowboys ("goat-ropers," Jake called them). However, this shiny buckle appeared to be the size of a dinner plate, with a replica of the head of a bull or a cow, he did not know which, mounted on it.

Will stumbled to his feet. Rising to his full height, his eyes continued upward. He measured out at a little less than six feet, but, even so, he barely came level with the man's shoulders.

"I, uh, I'm Will Watson. I…"

The giant smiled, exposing a huge amount of gold. A hand stretched out toward him, a hand that would have dwarfed a catcher's mitt.

Will realized that his own mouth was wide open, and his chin somewhere down near his desk. Jake, sitting across the cubicle, was also, for once in his life, speechless. He timidly responded to the proffered hand, barely. The giant extended an oversized paw. Will responded, managing to get a grip on two fingers.

"We're attorneys from the law firm of *Smithson, Smith, Murchison, Ferguson, Braselton, Sampson, and Schmidt* with offices in Midland, Odessa, Alpine, Fort Davis, and several other cities throughout West Texas."

Puzzled, Will paused with his hand still in the other's grasp. The voice carried a much higher pitch than he had expected. The giant's face still wore a broad smile; his lips had not otherwise moved. Finally, he realized that the voice he was hearing came from below his own eye level. Releasing the giant's fingers, he looked down to see another, much shorter man, of stocky build, who could have walked under Will's outstretched arm. While this second person was small in stature, he, nevertheless, exuded nervous energy, power, and authority—immediately taking command of the conversation.

"Mr. William Wordsworth Watson? We have some very important confidential business to discuss—with you, Mister

The Ghost of Grandpa Wills

Watson. In private, if you please—Mister Watson." The little guy stared up at Jake.

Jake found his voice, "I believe I have an appointment." Rising, he moved to exit the cubicle. It was a matter of some moments before he and the giant could make room for each other through the narrow entranceway.

Once Jake was gone, the shorter man spoke again, "My name is James Randolph Smithson, and this is my brother, James Alfred Smith."

"Your brother?" questioned Will, his eyebrows going up.

"My twin brother to be exact," James replied. "I'm the eldest," he added as though it were of some importance.

"You're twins?"

"Yes."

"But you're the oldest?"

"Yes, I am a day older than Jimmy."

Will said nothing, although his imagination was having a field day, wondering how their poor mother had endured.

Jimmy spoke, and when he did, his deep voice rumbled as though there was a restless volcano deep inside. "James was born one minute before midnight. I was born four and one half minutes after midnight."

"Ahh, I see. You're Mr. Smithson, and you're Mr. Smith—and you're brothers? Twins?"

"Call me Jimmy," a smile creasing his rugged features. Will was sure that he had never before seen so much gold in one place.

The shorter brother frowned, as if disapproving of such a show of familiarity.

"People are often surprised to hear that we are related," the giant continued.

An understatement, to be sure, Will thought.

Jimmy moved to the chair Jake had vacated and eased himself into it. Will winced. It was like watching a gorilla sit down on a child's chair. *Oh, well, if it will hold Jake-*

Mr. James Randolph Smithson interrupted Will's thoughts, "We were separated at birth and put up for adoption right after our mother died…"

"It's a long story," Jimmy interjected.

"Separated, you say," were the only words Will could think of. He was having visions of these two, as babies, conjoined at their heads. "I'm sorry about your mother. How may I help you?"

"You sell insurance?" Jimmy asked.

"I am a financial advisor," Will attempted to begin his memorized spiel. "I…"

"We are not here to buy insurance," James interjected.

"I need some," Jimmy frowned at his brother. He turned back to Will with a smile, and explained, "I'm getting married."

"Congratulations," Will responded.

"Thank you. I have her picture here. She's a real sweet little thing." The big smile returned. He pulled the photo out of his inside coat pocket and thrust it toward Will. The three-by-five color print looked the size of a postage stamp in the giant's hand.

Will took it and studied it. The "sweet little thing" was very attractive with a dusky complexion and coal black hair hanging down her front in two long braids that ended well below her breasts. "Sweet" she may have been, but Will had his doubts about the "little" part.

Leaning against a large, black and white Hummer, the top of her head was level with its roof. The vehicle carried a bar of red and blue emergency lights on its top and an official looking emblem on the door. With her eyes hidden behind a pair of large, dark aviator style sunglasses, she stood dressed in a law officer's uniform. A gun hung in a black holster on her left hip, and a large white Stetson rested on her head.

Altogether, she had "Law Enforcement" and "Don't Mess with Texas" or "Me" written all over her.

Will decided that "little" was a relative concept, and anything less than King Kong would seem small to the giant sitting across from him. Moreover, even a stern-looking, gun-toting, law-woman must have her "sweet" moments—sometime or other.

"She's lovely," he said, wanting to be polite. He returned the photo. "Now, how may I help you?"

"Are you Mr. William Wordsworth Watson?" James asked.

"Yes, why-?"

"Do you have identification?"

"Yes—wait a minute. What is this? Who are you? What do you want? Why should I have to prove who I am? What business is it of yours anyway?" He did not like lawyers in general, and he was beginning to get very suspicious of these two. *"Maybe they were not wanting to buy insurance after all?"*

"We represent…" James began.

"You told me who you work for," Will insisted. "What do you want?"

"We represent Miss Amelia Priscilla Annette Wills of Presidio County, Texas. Near the city of Marfa," Jimmy explained.

"Do you know her, or have you ever heard of her?" James asked.

The question caught Will off guard. "Yes. No. I don't

think so. No, never heard of her. Why? Where is this Pre-, Pre—whatever the place is—anyway?"

He racked his brain trying to remember if he had ever sold this Miss Priscilla Annette—anything. *Maybe she wants to sue me? Maybe these two weirdoes are here to serve me with a summons.*

"Presidio County is approximately 500 miles southwest of Dallas, about 200 miles west of San Antonio," James offered, before asking in a tone of condescension. "You do know where San Antonio is, don't you?"

"I do believe I might have heard of it, yes," Will replied, his voice carrying an edge of sarcasm.

James continued, "Miss Wills has reason to believe that you may be a long lost relative of hers, and she would like very much to meet you."

"I don't have any relatives," Will replied. "I'm an orphan—no parents. I don't know where—or exactly when—I was born. However, if this Miss Wills is here in Dallas, I'll be glad to meet her—just to be friendly. I doubt she's a relative." *Maybe she just might need some life insurance.*

"Miss Wills is not in good health," Jimmy said.

No chance for life insurance here, maybe some kind of investment.

"She is, therefore, unable to travel," James spoke in a sharp tone that Will found irritating.

"We have been asked to extend an invitation to you," Jimmy straightened his tie.

Will sat back, giving them his full attention.

"Miss Wills is requesting that you visit her, at her home on the Wills Ranch," James broke in.

Will raised his eyebrows at this revelation. "We've never met; I've never heard of this, Miss Wills, but you expect me to drop everything and go all the way out to Martha?"

"It's *Marfa*," Jimmy's deep voice filled the cubicle.

"Whatever," Will retorted.

"We are prepared to cover your expenses as well and make it worth your while as well. Your presence is requested within a week, by this coming Friday, if possible," James continued. "And, the invitation includes your wife and children."

He opened his briefcase and removed a large manila envelope. He also extracted a pair of black, horn-rimmed glasses from his coat pocket. After putting them on, he opened the envelope, pulled out the contents, and arranged some papers on Will's desk.

Worth my while? Will pondered the possible meaning of the words.

"We need to establish your legal identity. May we see your driver's license and your social security card?" Jimmy requested in a matter of fact manner.

Will reached for his billfold, took out the desired items, and handed them to James, who made some notations on a note pad and returned them.

"There are certain provisions…" Jimmy said.

"Provisions, to which you must agree," James broke in. "Realizing that committing yourself to traveling all the way to Presidio County on such short notice may…"

"May be a real hassle," Jimmy broke in. "therefore, Miss Wills is, and I repeat, willing to make it worth your while."

"All expenses will be paid…" James added.

Jimmy interjected. "We can arrange for you and your family to fly out if you wish."

Will squeezed in a quick comment. "School's not out for another two weeks. Both kids are in school, and my wife's a teacher."

Frowning, James spoke in an authoritative tone. "You come to Presidio now…"

Jimmy interrupted again, earning another scowl from his brother. "We'll arrange to bring the family out as soon as possible."

Will, feeling like an observer at a tennis match as the two lawyers threw comments at him, managed to insert a few words. "I have to talk to my wife and ask for time off as well. I could lose my job."

The two attorneys glanced at each other.

Looking hard at Will, James put some more papers on the desk in front of Will. "Read and sign these." His tone of voice, together with the expression on his face, made this an order. "You will agree to travel to the Wills Ranch in Presidio County, State of Texas forthwith, arriving within the next seven days or sooner."

Jimmy leaned forward in the chair. "We have a bank draft made out to you for the amount of $25,000. Will that be enough to cover expenses for you and your family?"

Will blinked. Intimidated by James' aggressive words and incredulous at the dollar amount offered, he mumbled in reply, "I believe it might." This was more money than he had earned during the previous twelve months of selling life insurance.

James continued, "By signing these documents, you will agree to travel to the Wills Ranch, method of travel to be your choice, arriving forthwith, within seven days or less, from midnight tonight. Should it be duly shown that you are not her relative, you may keep the full amount of the monies received. However, should you sign these papers, take the money, and not travel to the Wills Ranch as agreed, you will be required to repay the full amount within thirty days."

"In full, to the penny, plus any and all legal costs that might be incurred," Jimmy added.

"Where did you say this ranch is located?" Will asked without caring. He was willing to drive to Outer Mongolia for that kind of money—after all, money was money!

"County of Presidio, near the Davis Mountains, State of Texas, north of Marfa, west of Alpine, south of Fort Davis, two hundred miles west of San Antonio," Jimmy explained.

Davis Mountains. Real mountains!

Will, who could not remember ever having been further west than the city of Fort Worth, found himself lost in his own little world, having often dreamed of living in the mountains—any mountains—anywhere. *Tall trees, endless forests, clear skies, bubbling brooks, snowcapped peaks, winter skiing, summer hiking, autumn colors, clear skies. Any city with a name like "Alpine" has to be a mountain lover's paradise.*

As for Marfa—he had never heard of the place. *Maybe someone with a lisp named it. Maybe it was named for Marfa Stewart*, he mused, inwardly laughing at his own little joke. *Fort Davis—Ummmm—probably some army base.*

He signed the document without any further thought.

"Please initial here, here, and here," James pointed out as he handed the check over. He looked Will in the eye and concluded in a somber tone. "I repeat, you have seven days from midnight tonight to appear at the Wills ranch. Failure to do so will result in the forfeiture of all monies you have received to that date—including all legal fees and court costs involved."

"Yeah, sure," Will replied, never taking his eyes off the slip of paper in his hand. Never had he seen so many zeroes on a check—at least, not one with his name on the line reading, "Pay to the order of."

"One last question, please, Mr. Watson," Jimmy he pushed himself up from the chair. Without waiting for a response, he asked, "Do you believe in ghosts?"

"Ghosts?" Will looked up in surprise. "Never met a ghost I didn't like."

The big lawyer smiled as a low chuckle rumbled up from within. His shorter brother glared up at him. They both turned and walked away.

Will watched them disappear through his cubicle opening. Weirdoes was the word that came to his mind as his eyes found their way back to the check in his hand. He snatched up his copy of the signed agreement along with all the other papers. Reaching into a drawer of his file cabinet, he extracted a large manila envelope and stuffed everything inside—except for the check. He folded it with care, put it in his shirt pocket; there was a branch of his bank at ground level, twenty floors below.

Vacation time—he had two weeks due. And some sick leave. Of course, he had promised Tracie and the kids a trip to the beach—Galveston Island to be exact, but they would just have to understand. *Twenty-five thousand big smackers. How could anyone say "No" to that?*

He made a mental checklist.

First thing, request vacation time—effective immediately, either that or I suddenly get sick—very sick. Next, tell Jake. Wonder what he'll say? Will he believe me? I can't believe it myself. And don't forget to deposit the check. Last of all, get home and tell Tracie and the kids. What will she say? More importantly, what will she do? Well, she will just have to understand.

The Ghost of Grandpa Wills

Thinking about Tracie's reaction stopped him in his tracks for a few moments. The family had planned, scrimped, and saved for a trip to Galveston for more than a year. The kids were excited about seeing the ocean—or, at least the Gulf of Mexico—for the first time in their lives.

Well, they will just have to settle for a trip to the mountains instead.

From his desk, he sorted out some personal items to take. Photos and a few other things went into his briefcase; not everyone in the office could be trusted. He also found several bags of corn chips and chocolate chip cookies, forgotten behind some old files in the bottom drawer.

At that moment, Jake bounced into the cubicle. "Hey—ho, Daddy O'. Whar ya gonna go-ee oh?"

"Hey, Big Jake, sorry, but I can't make lunch with you." He tried to gesture but dropped the bags of cookies and chips instead. "Big changes." He explained, bending to retrieve everything. "I'm out'a here. Gone. It's vacation time for me. I'm taking a trip out'a this here place."

"Hey. Easy Willie, I know ol' Buzzard Breath is hard to take at the best of times, but a man's gotta eat, ya know. And your landlord'll be wantin' his rent money som'time reeeal soon. So cool your jets, man, rev down your engines ta idle speed. Take some friendly, free advice from Big Brother Jake. Let me buy ya lunch, and let's talk this over, reeeeeal slooooow and eeeeaaaaasy like."

"No, Jake, you don't understand. Here, take these chips and cookies."

"What happened?" Jake asked, eyes wide in surprise. He grabbed the offered goodies. "Was it something those two escapees from the circus said?"

"They're lawyers."

"Lawyers, I shoulda recognized their type right away. Thought maybe the little runt was part of the mob, the big'un might be an undertaker, and they had come here to put the squeeze on ya."

Jake paused for a second, opened a bag of cookies, and inspected the contents. "You been playin' the cards?" He brought his head up to look at Will. "Have ya? I told ya, don't ever go up there, north, on the wrong side of the river." He snatched a couple of cookies, gesturing at Will with them. "Those casinos up there are big-time bad news. An' besides, I hear those Choctaw up there are still a takin' scalps."

"Listen, you big dummy, you know I've never been near any casino. Never even been to Oklahoma neither."

"Okay, if you say so. Anyway, I think I could handle the little shrimp by sittin' on 'im. But, that Goliath might be a bit of a problem. Unfortunately, my name ain't David, and I'm outa practice on using slings with little rocks in them." He bit into a cookie. "However, I do have some friends that might be willin' to assist. They got a real beef against lawyers."

"No, Jake, it's not what you think," Will said, excitement in his voice. "They're on my side." He waved his arms. "They brought some real good news; I have a long lost relative who's dying."

"That sounds like real good news; it sure does. Just remind me to not ask for sympathy next time I get a cold."

"No, you don't understand. What I mean is, she wants me to come see her, real soon. She has cancer, and we've never met and all that." He leaned back against his desk. Jake moved over to his usual chair and made himself comfortable.

"You? What long lost relative? You're an orphan. You don't even know where you were born."

"Don't you think I know that? They pulled me out of a

car wreck somewhere alongside the road down south of here. That's all I know. Anyway, I'm going to meet her. And she's paying all my travel expenses, plus making it worth my while."

"Where?" Jake inquired with suspicion written over his face. "Where're you a goin' to—to meet this looooong lost relative?" He contorted his face into an exaggerated expression of doubtful suspicion.

"A big ranch, out near Martha—or someplace like that, way out west, up in the mountains, and there's an army base of some kind nearby…" Will ran out words as he attempted to explain.

"A ranch," Jake's eyebrows went up. "You never sat on a horse. You don't even know which end the bridle goes on. Furthermore, you don't know the difference between a steer and a bull."

"Of course I do. A steer has longer horns. Besides, that's not important; I have seven days, or they'll want all the money back."

"Seven days ta what?"

"Seven days to get there, that's what."

"And, where, exactly is 'there' might I ask?"

"I told you; it's close to Martha. Up in the mountains with lots of clean, fresh air, snow, and trees, and all that stuff."

"Martha? What state is that in? Or maybe, I should ask what country?"

"Texas, of course, and that's in the United States." Will screwed up his face in concentration. "Must be out west somewhere. There aren't any mountains close around here.

"I think I saw a map once that showed some mountains somewhere out west of here. The lawyers said it was about five hundred miles. And there's a Mount David, or something similar close to it."

Jake inspected the next cookie before biting into it. "How long you had these things, anyway?"

"Can't remember. They were in the bottom drawer, and I had forgotten about them. Couple of months, I guess."

"Well, look, Sonny Boy," Jake tossed the remaining cookies into a trash can. "I went out to Midland, back when I was a kid. I've even been all the way out west to El Paso." He waved a hand in the general direction of West Texas. "I'm here to tell you that there's nothin' even close to a snow capped mountain out there, especially compared to the real stuff in Colorado."

He leaned forward, aiming a finger at his friend. "So, when it comes to snow-capped peaks in Texas, they're nothing more than a figment of your over-active imagination." Standing straight, he placed his hands on his hips. "What's more, the only place in Texas I know of that's called Martha is a lot closer to Houston than to any mountains."

"Maybe they named it after Martha Stewart," Will responded in a weak tone.

"Nah, she lives up north somewhere; she's a Yankee."

"Here's the paperwork." Will pulled out the contents of the envelope. He searched through it until, "Here it is. The ranch is near a place called Marfa. I thought he was mispronouncing Martha."

"Marfa," Jake responded in a tone of disbelief. "You best check your maps. That place is out in the middle of no-wheres-ville. But I did read something once about space aliens and ghost lights showing up near there."

"Maybe that's what he meant by his last question?"

"What was that?" Jake asked.

The Ghost of Grandpa Wills

"He asked if I believed in ghosts."

Jake started laughing, "And you answered?"

"I said I've never seen a ghost I didn't like, but it doesn't matter because I've never seen a ghost; don't want to see one, and I don't believe in'm anyway. Besides, you're about as alien as anything I can imagine." Will glared at his friend and nodded his head to add emphasis to his comment.

"And, by the way, I did sit on a horse. Once, when I was a kid. They put me on one of those little ponies where you get your picture made." An expression of chagrin crossed his features. "But, the flash must've scared it. The thing ran away. I had my arm in a cast for almost six weeks."

"A pony," Jake burst out laughing, slapping his ample thighs. "You fell off one of those little Shetland ponies, broke your arm, an' now you're a gonna go out west to be a cowboy."

Jake turned serious. "You really gonna do this?" he added, adopting an expression of deep sorrow, "You for real goin' to leave me, your onliest, truest, ol' buddy here—all alone to face ol' buzzard-breath all by hisself? And here, I thought we were friends an' all." He slapped his knee with an open palm.

"Only for a week or so. I'm taking some vacation time. Besides, for this much dough, what would you do?" He pulled the check from his pocket and waved it at Jake.

Jake snatched the piece of paper it and stared at it, "Little Bruthur, if it was me, I'd already be gone, halfway there. Not sittin' around talkin' to some old fat guy like you're a doin'."

Jake paused to take a breath. A serious tone came into his voice. All humor disappeared from his face. "By the way, an' I don't mean to be nosy, but have you, by any chance, told your lovely wife that she and the kids are about to take a trip out yonder to the middle of nowhere—instead of to the beach?"

"Not yet," Will answered in a flippant tone. "I'm going to surprise them all. But I know they'll love it." He snatched the envelope and papers, grabbed the check from Jake, and disappeared through the cubicle's doorway.

On his way down to the parking garage, Will stopped at the HR department and applied for his vacation time. "It's an emergency, illness in the family," he claimed. *She is my long lost relative, and she is quite sick.*

He made two more stops on his way out of the building. Keeping a handful of cash, he deposited the remainder of the check in his bank account. Next, he dropped by the fast-food, greasy spoon next door—Jake's favorite palace of culinary delights, where he ordered two triple-decker cheeseburgers along with a double order of French fries and two extra thick chocolate malts with added chocolate syrup. All of which he sent up to Jake.

Chapter Five
Conspiracy

Case Anthony, tall and wiry, with thinning brown hair and wearing a dirt smeared uniform with the words "Wallace Express Cleaning" stitched into his shirt, carried a bored expression on his unshaven face. He lazily pushed a long-handled, dry mop along the hallway floor, never getting far from his grimy janitor's cart. Passersby saw a janitor—nondescript, worn-out, and bored with his job. Someone they would neither remember nor identify—just what Case wanted.

His eyes, however, were neither tired nor bored. They shone bright and alert, sweeping over each person that entered the hallway—with a special interest in those passing through the glass doors opposite the elevators. The sign on the glass doors read "R. G. Hawks Insurance Agency—Sales Personnel

Only."

Fidgeting with the ear buds he wore, Case adjusted and readjusted them, removing and replacing one or the other amid muffled grunts and curses. As soon as Will entered the hallway, he casually pushed his dry mop over to the cart. Still mumbling under his breath while pretending to work, he watched Will waiting for the elevator.

As soon as Will stepped into the elevator, and the door hissed to a close, Case extracted a cell phone from his shirt pocket, punched in a number, and began talking. After a short conversation, he returned the phone to his pocket. Glancing around and seeing no one, he pushed the cart through the double doors into the sales area.

Once within the warren of cubicles, Case moved, seemingly without purpose, but always closer to Will's area. Entering, he took a cloth and started wiping the top of the desk. Working around the cubicle, he felt underneath the protruding edge at the desk front. He paused long enough to remove an object and place it in his pocket. He repeated the action at the rear of the desk, reaching underneath the middle drawer. Next, he moved over to the chair that had previously groaned beneath Jimmy's weight where he removed a third, small item. That done, while whistling a nondescript tune, he wandered through the double doors, into the hallway, and over to the elevator.

Case stepped out of the elevator in the basement parking area, dressed in a pair of brown denim trousers and a nondescript blue shirt, the janitor's uniform having been stuffed deep into the now abandoned trash cart.

Ralph Ferrell, heavy set and beefy, with an unruly mop of red hair on his head, appeared out of a shadowy corner and gave a low whistle. Case responded by turning and walking over to him.

"Got'm?" Ralph muttered, in a low tone.

"My pocket. No-one saw me." He tapped his right side as he spoke.

"Good. It's best we don't leave traces behind."

"Yeah, agreed. But I don't think this Bozo would know what they were even if he found'm." Case leaned against an old pick-up truck and looked around the parking garage. "Where's his car?"

"You're leaning on it."

Surprised, Case turned to survey the vehicle. "You're kiddin' me. This heap is a wreck waitin' to happen. It's gotta be older than both of us put together."

Ferrell gave a rough chuckle that came out sounding more like a series of grunts. "Older than you, at least—and, if this piece of junk breaks down somewhere out in the middle of nowhere, that just makes our job easier."

Case nodded in agreement, smirking as he commented, "There's a whole lot of nowhere between here and where he's headed."

Chapter Six
You What?

Will found the northbound traffic much lighter than usual. With the MP3 player switched on and Vangelis thundering in his ears, his imagination transported him to a time and place— far, far away:

"Hey, Boss," the tall cowboy hollered. "Storm's a gettin' worse. Drift's a gonna be up to the horses' bellies by mornin'." He clapped his gloved hands together and flexed his fingers as he struggled forward, wading through knee-deep snow.

"Get both of the Hummers out of the barn," Boss Watson ordered. "There's a bunch o' greenhorns lost out thar." He pointed toward the now invisible mountain. "They need a rescuin' an' thar ain't nobody else kin do it." He concluded the order by forcefully ejecting a dark stream of tobacco juice

into the icy wind.

He growled into the blizzard, "Ain't nobody's agonna freeze to death on the Watson Ranch—not if Boss Watson has anything to say about it."

The angry discharge of a truck's klaxon interrupted Boss Watson's rescue attempt. Returning to the real world, Will found himself staring into the spinning hub of an eighteen-wheeler's front wheel, mere inches from his pickup window. In a panic, he swerved back into his lane where he was greeted by an irate blast from a Cadillac's horn—accompanied by an obscene gesture from the driver.

His cell phone shrilled, and he grabbed it from his pocket.

"Yeah, Watson here."

"When ya leavin' Littl' Bruthur?" Jake asked in a cheery tone

"Two days, maybe three. Why?"

"Have some vacation time comin'. I'd kinda like to see that part of the world again before I die."

"What?"

"Look' Willie Boy," Jake's voice turned serious. "You never been further west than the middle of Fort Worth. I'll come along, enjoy the fresh air, and give you comfort and guidance. Then, in a couple of weeks, we'll be back home, safe and sound, here in civilization. I might even fly back."

"Fly? Do they have airports out there? Have they ever heard of airplanes out there?" Will asked.

"Sur' man. Doan't ya know all those big Texas ranchers fly their own jets. I betcha there's a big runway out back of the house where you be a goin'—with a two jet garage right next to it."

Chapter Seven
A Little Excited!

"YOU WHAT?" Tracie's deep blue eyes, which usually held him entranced, now burned with fury. She was excited—just not the way Will had hoped.

"You quit your job." Waving her arms, she advanced on him.

"I didn't say I quit."

Retreating from her fury, he whined, "I said, 'I'm taking my vacation.'"

Small and petite, Tracie stood just over five feet tall in her bare feet, however, at this moment, every inch and every ounce spat fire and rage. "How about 'OUR' vacation? You, me, and the kids! You remember them—don't you? Or, have you forgotten that we were taking them to the beach—to Galveston. First trip to the ocean and all that."

The Ghost of Grandpa Wills

"My first time too," Will confessed, with his back against the wall.

She glared up at him, declaring in an icy tone, "Who cares?" With both hands balled into fists, she spoke through gritted teeth. "So, now, you suddenly decide to run off to all-the-way-out-beyond-nowhere, to some place none of us ever even heard of." She raised her fists. "You don't even tell me about it; much less ask how I feel about it. You just do it."

She dropped her arms, stepped back, and lowered her voice. "We are part of the family, aren't we?"

He stammered, trying to find his tongue. "W-we can go to the beach afterwards. You know, stop by the ranch on the way. See some mountains and the ocean all in one trip."

She replied in a low monotone, her eyes boring into him. "School. Summer school, to be exact. Remember that? I signed up to teach this summer in order to pay for our trip to the beach." She paused long enough to take a deep breath. "And it's called the Gulf of Mexico. We won't be anywhere an ocean."

He gestured in a helpless manner. "I guess I forgot."

"What did you call this place, anyway?" she asked, with a sudden change of subject. "Martha, Marpa…"

"Marfa."

"Whatever," she screamed, before lowering her voice again. Her eyes bored into him. "Who is this long-lost-relative anyway?"

"S-She's a long lost relative." Palms up, he shrugged.

"WHO is she?" she asked, her voice rising again.

"I don't know?" he replied with a sheepish grin on his face. "If I knew who she was, then she wouldn't be 'long lost,' would she?"

Tracie cast her eyes up for another long look at the

ceiling before shifting her voice back to the low-tone Will, long ago, had learned to fear. She continued speaking, fists on her hips, her eyes boring into the depths of his soul. "So some stranger invites you out for a visit, and you just decide to run off to the middle of nowhere without even knowing who she is?"

She took a deep breath. "Furthermore—so what if she lives on a ranch!"

Her hand moved, she wagged a finger perilously close to his nose. "What kind of ranch? A big ranch? Little ranch? Sheep ranch? Goat ranch? How do you know it's not some five-acre hellhole way out where there's no air conditioning, no electricity, and the bathroom's a hundred yards off in some cow pasture somewhere?"

Then, as if to settle the question, she asked, with a look of triumph on her face, "What do you know about ranching, anyway?" Tossing her head in a way that sent her golden curls flying about, she twirled around and stormed away, leaving a parting shot. "You don't even know which end of a cow milk comes from."

"Milk comes from dairies, not ranches," he squeaked.

"Whatever!"

He winced and retreated a step.

The screaming ceased, replaced by the much dreaded low-tone. From across the room, Tracie turned to face him. "Ranches, dairies, cows, bulls—whatever. You don't know the difference between them anyway."

Her eyes locked onto his. "So, you simply take off from work, come home, and tell us all to pack our bags to go running off to some place none of us ever heard of."

She advanced on him. "Did it occur to you that the kids are in school for another week? And, so am I. I can't just call up the school and tell them I'm not showing up next week—the very last week of school. They'd tell me to go away, stay away, and never come back. Then, where would we be? Huh, smart guy, where would we be then?"

She was back in his face when she asked, "And, Mister Watson-Wiseguy, while we're at it, just how are you planning to pay for this little trip out into the-back-of-beyond—anyway?"

The tears started; fast and furious, they streamed down her pretty face. She swiped her golden tresses from her eyes. Her voice rose in both volume and pitch. "You may like playing cowboys and Indians and going on trail drives—but not me. Moreover, West Texas is just crawling with bugs and spiders, ants and scorpions, mosquitoes and snakes." She stomped a foot on the floor. "Rattlesnakes!"

A fire blazed in her eyes. "Did you ever think about that? People die when they get bit by rattlesnakes. And, we'll be a million miles from the nearest doctor. Do they even have doctors out there? I'm so mad I could scream…" And she did.

"We have plenty of money. See?" He snatched the deposit receipt from his pocket and held it up with a faint smile on his lips.

"Com' on, Hon,'" he begged. "You've always wanted to vacation in the mountains—clean air, lots of trees, and stuff. Snow in the winter and all that."

Silence.

Tracy stared at the deposit slip for a moment before snatching it away. "That's a lot of money," she replied in a stunned whisper. "Twenty-five thousand dollars just to drive out there for a few days."

"Yeah," he answered, the little smile grew to a big one. "And she's invited the whole family to come meet her."

Looking down at he, he clasped her shoulders. "There's enough here for all of you to buy tickets and fly out there; you don't have to drive. And the kids can ride some horses and milk a cow or two."

"How do you know she has horses?" She turned away as though leaving the room.

"She's got to; every ranch has cows and horses." He lifted his shoulders with an expression that implied superior knowledge. "Everybody knows that."

"I'll help you pack," she interjected with a wave of surrender. "But, the first thing tomorrow morning, you use some of that money to get that old truck tuned up along with some new tires. And, buy some decent new clothes for yourself."

The fire came back to her eyes. She wheeled back to face him.

"And, I still don't know how the kids are going to take it, buster. You're not out of the hot water yet." The dark look in her expression gave strength to her words.

"It's a deal," he said, and before she could stop him, sealed it by planting a big kiss on the frown that creased her forehead.

Chapter Eight
Cowboy

Katie stood with her fists on her hips and shouted. "I don't want Daddy to go away," She stamped her foot and shook her head, tossing blond curls to and fro.

"Katie, Daddy has to go away for a few days. Later, we'll all get on an airplane and fly out there to meet him. You and Robby will fly with me. You have to go; you cannot stay here by yourself, even if it is only for a few days."

"Why not?" the nine-year-old asked in a defiant tone. "You can't make me go. I'll run away. I hate out there."

"How do you know? You've never been out there. Besides, you don't even know where 'out there' is."

"Can I ride a horsie?" a small voice asked.

Tracie's attention moved to her six-year-old son who sat at the table with a spoonful of cereal halfway to his mouth, milk dripping onto his lap. "Who said anything about horses?"

"Las' nite, Daddy said there were cowboys and Indians with horses and cows eberwhere. I wanna be a cowboy and shoot bows and arrows."

"Indians shoot bows and arrows, you dummy," Katie threw back, in a superior tone.

"Stop it, both of you—now," their mother ordered. "It is a ranch. If they have cows, then I guess they have cowboys." Looking back at her daughter, she added, "They may even have some cowgirls," she conceded. "Horses too, so you can both go riding, but I don't know about any Indians. Now, hurry up and get ready, or you'll miss the school bus."

That afternoon, Tracie heard the roar as the school bus pulled away from the curb. Minutes later, six-year old Robby tore through the front door like a hurricane hitting the Gulf Coast. "They do have Indians, and they're 'Paches like G'romeo, and they have ghosty lights from space." He wrapped his arms around his mother in a tight hug, but the words kept spilling, unrestrained, from his lips. "And Kat'y said they all have a million horses, and I can shoot bows and arrows like a real 'Pache. Will I hafta go to school, Mom? Huh? Cowboys doan hafta go ta school, do they, Mom?"

Before Tracie could answer, a second storm burst through the front door. "Mom, Mom—I looked it all up on the internet. My science teacher, Mr. Barnes, helped me. There's an old fort where there were Buffalo Soldiers, an observatory with a telescope, weird lights from outer space, and the Apaches say they come from the stars."

She stopped long enough to take in a breath. "And, it sounds like a neat place. I'll go if you promise I can ride a horse. And, Mr. Duncan, my history teacher, used to live there, and he says that there's lots of lost treasures, old mines, and everything like that all around there."

A look of deep concern replaced the excitement on her face.

"Can Rosa and Amy and Julie come with us? I told them they could all come out and spend the whole summer. Is that okay, Mom? When do we go, Mom? I have to tell Rosa and them so they can tell their Moms and Dads. I told them we would probably go tomorrow."

"Whoa. Stop. Hold it. Slow down." Tracie was laughing as she tried to corral her two wild broncos. "One question at a time."

Her tone changed as she turned to her son. "Robby! Spit it out now! I told you—no candy after school. Trash can, now." She spat out the order in a voice that left no room for discussion.

She turned back to her daughter, and in a softer tone, with her hands on her hips, continued, "Now, young lady, which question do I answer first? I don't know how many horses there are on the ranch, but I believe that a million might be a few too many. And, you and Robby may ride one each—maybe.

"We are not going out there to live. We won't be there more than a few days.

"Your father is leaving tomorrow—after he gets some things done to the truck today.

"However, you, Robby, and I have to finish this school term."

Moans, groans, and other sounds of protest interrupted this unpleasant announcement.

"Quiet. Listen up. Daddy's going first. We'll follow after

school is out. We'll fly out on an airplane.

"Furthermore, Miss Katie Dear, your friends—Rosa, Amy, and Julie—will all have to wait until you get back. Then, you can tell them about it. I'm afraid they cannot go with us."

Twisting around, she explained to her son. "And, yes, Robby, cowboys do have to go to school. However, school will be out when we get there, so you won't have to worry about homework."

With her face screwed up into a big pout, Katie whined, "Why? I promised them?"

"Well, that's too bad," her mother answered in a firm voice. "Next time, you should ask me first."

"Is Daddy going by hisself?" Katie asked.

"Himself," Tracie corrected. "And no, Uncle Jake is going with him."

"Does Daddy know how to get there? He got lost at the State Fair last year, remember? And then, he couldn't find the zoo, and he took me to the wrong school for the play, and…"

"He'll get a map, and Uncle Jake will be along," Tracie answered. She knew—all too well—her husband's proclivity for getting lost.

"He'll lose the map," was Katie's frowning response. "I'll make him one on the Internet. I'll make it tonight. Mom, how do you spell that place where we're going with all the ghost lights and all? I forgot."

"Your Daddy will not get lost. He'll be all right," Mom said. "*I hope*," she added, under her breath. "Now get your clothes changed, both of you." She clapped her hands and barked out the order, "Move."

They heard the familiar noise of the old pickup clattering into the driveway. Shortly afterward, they saw Will through the glass of the front door.

"Daddy. Daddy," Robby squealed in childish delight.

The door opened, and *Cowboy* Watson entered the room. Robby rushed to get the first hug. Tracie stood and stared. Katie took a few steps forward, then looked back at her mother for an explanation.

Will picked up his son, held him close, and, beaming with pride, asked, "What do you think? Am I a cowboy, or am I a cowboy?"

"Daddy's a cowboy," Robby cried, wriggling to get down.

Tracie stared, open-mouthed. Katie broke out in raucous laughter. Neither had ever before seen such a *cowboy*—or rather what was trying to pass for one. Perched high on Will's head was a large, white, ten-gallon hat with a broad brim molded to a sharp 'V' in the front. He also wore a long-sleeved, western-style shirt that bore white snaps instead of buttons, bright red shoulders, and a deep blue body with intricate patterns embroidered on it. A red bandanna encircled the cowboy's neck. He, also, sported a brand new pair of tight fitting western-cut jeans supported by a wide leather belt—tooled with a fancy design and buckled by a large, ornate silver buckle.

On his feet, he sported a pair of Western boots with high riding-heels and tooled tops that reached almost to his knees. The main body of the fancy footwear was dyed bright red with elaborate designs sewn in. His pant legs were tucked into the boot tops.

"I have never…you look…" Tracie tried to find a polite way to express herself. Katie made no such effort; she stood, staring with her mouth open.

"Picked it all out by myself," Will declared, beaming

with pride. He lowered Robby to the floor. The youngster disappeared in the direction of his bedroom. Will strode into the room, and, with an exaggerated swagger, bent to get a welcome-home kiss from his loving wife.

She stopped a few inches from his face.

Her face contorted into a frown. "What do you have in your mouth?" She stepped back. "What are you chewing? You stink." Her voice rose in both pitch and volume. Her hands on her hips, she faced him, her entire body radiating angry defiance.

Katie joined in, "Ewweeee Yuuuckk... Dadddddyeeee..."

"If I'm goin' to be a rancher, I need to at least look like one," he answered with pure innocence written across his face.

Tracie switched to her low, threatening tone. "Whatever that is in your mouth—and I know what it smells like—you will not come into my house with that in your mouth. You will sleep in your truck tonight. You will go to West..."

She was interrupted by shouts of, "Giddy up, giddy up, yahoooo." Robby, running at a full gallop, tore around the corner with his stick horse between his legs.

Rushing between his mother and sister, his head connected with his father's body taking them both down to the floor in a tangled heap, accompanied by screams of surprise and agony.

Fortunately, for Robby, his head missed his father's oversized belt buckle and hit a much softer spot—a short distance below it.

Unfortunately, for *Cowboy* Watson, his son's head missed the oversized belt buckle and hit a much more tender area—just beneath it.

The Ghost of Grandpa Wills

Katie screamed.

Tracie gasped and grabbed Robby. In one swift move, she pulled him off Will and onto the sofa. Seeing that the youngster had suffered no visible harm, other than surprise and fright, she turned back to her husband.

Cowboy Watson lay on his side in a fetal position, hands between his legs. However, at this point, Katie was making more noise than her father.

She screamed, with tears welling in her eyes. "Daddy, Daddy, are you okay? Does it hurt? Daddy, please be okay!"

Daddy lay doubled-up, coughing and moaning—making incoherent gurgling sounds. Brown saliva dribbled from between his clenched teeth.

Tracie's concern turned back to anger. "Will Watson, if even a drop of that filth lands on my carpet—or anywhere else in this house—you are dead. Do you hear me? DEAD!"

With both hands balled into fists at her sides, her voice rose in volume. "Spit it out, now," she demanded, before changing her mind. "No, no, not here. Get in the bathroom, and spit it where it belongs." With a stony glare and an outstretched arm, she pointed and ordered, "Flush that filth down the sewer."

The would-be cowboy made no immediate effort to obey his wife's commands. Moans and gurgles continued for a few more moments until all became deathly quiet and still.

"Mommy, why's Daddy turning green?" Katie asked, her eyes growing wide. Robbie watched from the couch, one hand to his mouth, the other wiping tears away.

Will struggled to his hands and knees and began to crawl with one hand holding his lower body. Tracie started laughing. Despite all of his misery and discomfort, she could not restrain herself.

"You swallowed it, didn't you, *Cowboy*?" She put bitter emphasis on the word '*cowboy*.' "Well, serves you right for putting that filth in your mouth and then bringing it into my house."

She waved at Katie. "Out of the way, Dearie, and let this fancy pants, would-be *cowboy*, get to the bathroom."

Will crawled into the bathroom and shut the door.

"Turn on the exhaust fan," Tracie yelled. "We don't want that stuff stinking up the house any more than it already has."

The only response was the sound of gurgling, coughing, gasping, and wheezing—the sounds of someone wishing he could die but knowing he was much too miserable for such a merciful thing to happen.

Later that night as Tracie tucked her daughter into bed and prepared to switch off the light, Katie asked, "Is Daddy going to be okay?"

"Oh, he'll be a little green around the edges for a day or two, but he'll live through it. He just better not do it again; that's all."

Not if he wants to stay alive.

"Is he really going tomorrow?"

"Yes, he is, and we'll be joining him real soon. Don't you worry your pretty little head. Okay?"

"What if he gets lost? He gets lost just going to eat somewheres. And then, he went to White Rock when he was supposed to go to White Lake. How's he supposed to find some little place like Marfa that's way out in the country where nobody ever heard of it?"

"We've talked about this already, Sweetie." Tracie tried to reassure her daughter. "He'll have your maps, and lots of people know about Marfa. You said yourself that you looked

The Ghost of Grandpa Wills

it up on the internet, so stop worrying, and go to sleep. Besides, I've already told you that Uncle Jake will be with him, and Uncle Jake always knows where he is going."

"Okay, I guess," came the doubtful reply. "Good night, Mommy. I love you. I think I'll say my prayers for both Daddy and Uncle Jake."

"That's wonderful. Good night, Sweetie—and, say your prayers for all of us."

"Mommy, why doesn't Daddy ever say his prayers?"

"I...I don't know. Maybe, someday he will. Now, please, you say your prayers, and close your eyes. Daddy will be all right." *I hope*. She switched off the light and softly closed the door.

Chapter Nine
Departure

The day of departure broke with glowering thunderheads, sheets of lightning, and pouring rain. The radio poured forth a continual stream of storm warnings, flash flood alerts, and tornado watches, with more expected to be coming in from the west—the very direction Will would be traveling.

Both children had said their good-byes and were on the school bus, but Will and Tracie sat around the breakfast table, having a last cup of coffee. She had called the school and would be going in late. He was dressed but not looking too enthusiastic about his planned trip, not having had much sleep; there had been several trips to the bathroom during the deepest hours of the night. Tracie thought she could still see tinges of green on him, and he carried the air of someone having recently passed through the gates of hell itself. Even so, she felt no sympathy for him.

Last evening, once they were out of hearing range of the children, she warned him in a voice of cold steel, "If you ever do that again, you won't have to worry about the tobacco killing you, because I'll do it myself." He had never used tobacco in any form, and she was determined that he never would—not while she was married to him.

This morning, she was still not in a forgiving mood. "You didn't get the new tires. Nor did you get the engine tuned up, or the oil changed, but you did find the time to buy those ridiculous clothes you wore home."

He sat in silent acquiescence, knowing of no defense that would stand before her scathing judgment.

Will insisted on wearing his new jeans and boots, Tracie won out over the shirt, convincing him to put on something less colorful, but more comfortable with short sleeves. Now, dressed for the road, he sipped his coffee in silence. The breakfast—two eggs, sunny-side-up, with sausage and biscuits, were more than he could stomach. Two huge yellow eyes staring up from the plate, together with the smell of Jimmy Dean's favorite, which under normal circumstances would have had his mouth watering—this morning sent him back to the bathroom to kneel before the throne of misery. He settled for a couple of tablespoons of antacid along with the coffee.

Suddenly, his thoughts of self-pity were interrupted. Tracie held an object out in front of him, and before he could stop her, thrust it up under his nose. "Wanna' try another plug of 'baccy, Cowboy?" she asked with a wicked grin on her face.

It was the un-chewed remains of his plug of tobacco, which he thought were in the trash. Where she found it, he did not know and did not wait to ask. His stomach churned, and poor 'Cowboy Watson' made another agonizing dash to the bathroom.

Tracie watched him as he disappeared down the hallway. She had no intention of forgetting, or forgiving—at least, not anytime in the foreseeable future.

"Where are Katie's maps?" Tracie asked. they stood together, rain splattering through the open door.

"In my briefcase; I won't get lost," he answered. "Besides, all I have to do is just what the man said."

"What man said what?" Her brows came together.

"Herschel Gearly—that's who. He talked about all those young men going west to get their fortune—that's what. So, I'm going west to claim mine." He pointed east. "Martha, here I come."

Tracie sighed and she looked up at the ceiling. "Greeley was his name—Horace Greeley—and he, at least, knew which direction west was. I'm not so sure about you."

She stood with arms folded and watched the rain drip from his hair down his forehead.

"Just be careful, please," she pleaded. "You're going to Marfa. The city of Martha is east of Houston, a few hundred miles in the wrong direction. And you're just going to see some sick old lady—not seek your fortune."

"Have no fear, Tracie dear," A grin broke across his face. "We shall soon be reunited together as a loving family—the long days and lonely nights will pass swiftly—of that I am most certain."

He swiped at the rainwater with his free hand.

"Besides, I have my trusty cell phone; I'll keep in touch. Nothing—absolutely nothing shall happen—that Brother

Jake and I cannot take care of."

Tracie looked up at the top of the doorframe and shook her head in doubt.

Speaking in a very dramatic tone, he turned to the door. "I must be off. My destiny awaits me."

As if to contradict his bravado, lightning struck nearby. The flash filled the house, and thunder shook it to its foundations. Tracie jumped, crying out in surprise, "I hate these storms. They make me want to go hide in a closet somewhere."

She found herself talking to an empty doorway—her last sight of her hero was him running across the lawn, through the pouring rain, his briefcase held over his head.

Chapter Ten
Heading West

Will pulled up next to Jake's apartment building. The big man was waiting beneath the cover of a carport, sitting on a large steel footlocker. He wore a pair of jeans along with a well-worn pair of leather loafers for his feet. He wore his favorite sports coat—old and comfortable corduroy, with leather patches on the elbows.

"You staying for two weeks or two years?" Will asked as they manhandled the footlocker into the back of the truck.

"Supplies, Bruthur. Be prepared is my motto."

"I didn't know you were a Boy Scout."

"I was, and I still like their motto." Jake stood and surveyed the old Chevy that was going to carry them to West Texas. "Littl' Bruthur, I don't want to hurt your feelin's any, but are you sure this ol' crate'll make it all the way out to the

The Ghost of Grandpa Wills

Big Bend country and back again?"

"Jake, my best, and my onliest buddy—you wound me deeply." Will placed one hand over his heart in mock pain.

Jake shook his head in slow motion, "I have no desire to wound you, or any other person for that matter—but I don't like the idea of walking half-way across Texas either."

The fearless duo pulled out of the apartment's parking lot. Weather alert kept coming—dire warnings about the present severe weather conditions with more of the same expected from the west. In addition, two major freeways were closed because of wrecks.

Jake stuffed a pillow behind his head and fished an engraved silver flask out of his coat pocket. "Want a swallow of Brother Daniel's cough medicine?"

"Not while I'm driving, Jake. That stuff's going to kill you someday."

"Nobody 'scept you would know I'm gone. Maybe Tracy and the kids—do ya think so? You're my only friend, Littl' Buddy. You know that? You got two sweet kids, Bruthur Willie. You don't know how lucky you are."

Will had no answer for his friend. He never knew what to say when Jake went into one of his dark moods. They had occurred less frequent of late but still popped up unexpectedly. Jake seldom spoke about his past.

Will understood that he was ex-military. He also knew that a few years ago, Jake had lost his wife and both children in a single moment—an eternal instant of squealing tires, breaking glass, and grinding metal. And, his friend had not been a drinker before then either nor had he been so heavy.

"Sorry, Littl' Bruthur, I'm just missin' them is all—guess I always will. Turn off all the bad news on that radio, an' I'll shut both my mouth an' my eyes—an' let you drive."

He took another swig from the flask, returned it to his pocket, and settled into his seat, closing his eyes.

Will did as requested and switched on his MP3, stuffed the ear buds into place, and selected his favorite music piece. Turning the volume up, he was soon lost in his own private world.

Minutes later, he found the LBJ Freeway, and following Mr. Greeley's advice, turned west.

The rain continued unabated—as did Will's imagination:

Trucker Watson, driver extra-ordinaire, drove on, into the dark night—the rain pelting against the glass of the big windshield. The downpour turned into a flood. Roads were closing behind him, and bridges were washed out down south. Even so, there would be no detour for him tonight.

The supplies must get through.

People were sick.

People were dying.

Trucker Watson had to reach them in time…

Time passed; Jake's snores filled the truck cab. Will drove on. Lost in his own faraway, imaginary world, he almost missed the exit to I-35E that would take him south to I-30. Amid the sound of squealing tires and blaring horns, he crossed two lanes of traffic onto his intended route.

Chapter Eleven
Don't Worry Your Ugly Head!

A black Ford Excursion followed, staying several cars behind. "Ferrell, are you sure that's the target?" Case squinted through the rain-smeared windshield and dodged a small compact that swerved too close. "If he keeps driving like that we won't have to stop him. He'll do our job for us."

"Yeah, I'm sure," Ferrell answered. "Double checked the plate number. I remember seeing the black guy back there where our bozo works. Maybe they're meetin' somebody. Don't know. Don't care."

"Yeah, well, I don't like it," Casey replied. "The more people there are—things just get more complicated."

"Don't worry your ugly head about it. We're being paid—well paid—to do a job. We stop him, no matter what. Somebody gets in the way—like his fat friend up there—we'll deal with'm. Whatever it takes."

He added, with a sneer and a low chuckle, "Now, don't forget that exit just the other side of Fort Worth where we'll go pick-up a couple pets for our two friends up there."

"I ain't gonna forget them pets, as you call'm. They give me the creeps just thinkin' about'm, much less having'm in the car with me."

Chapter Twelve
The Giant Triple, Triple, Triple

The overhead clouds were gone by the time Will and Jake approached the town of Sweetwater. The sun was past its midpoint in the Texas sky and would soon be low enough to shine into Will's eyes. His stomach sent signals it was empty—very empty. The rigors and pain of the previous night were now but a dim memory. He felt as if he were starving.

A sign displaying a giant triple-patty hamburger advertised the *Amazing Extra Special, Special, Special Triple-Decker Cheeseburger with a Giant Triple-Thick, 64 oz. Killer Malt (48 flavors to Choose From!!!) PLUS The Giant Triple Bucket of Sweet Potato Fries—the Giant Triple-Triple-Triple Killer.* Will swerved onto the exit, ignoring the horns blaring behind him. It was a truck stop complete with restaurant, garage, and gas station. The entire operation sat encircled by acres of graveled parking area and a multitude of vehicles—cars, eighteen-wheelers, pickups, SUV's, buses, horse trailers, motorcycles—and three saddled horses tethered to a wooden hitching rail near the restaurant's front door.

The pickup's tires crunched across the parking lot. Will nudged Jake awake and pointed toward another big sign. The big guy rubbed his eyes and exclaimed, "Tell me I ain't died and gone to heaven. I'll take three of everything—'cept that snake burger. You can order it if you want, but you'll hafta sit at a differ'nt table." He frowned as he looked around, "Where in Texas are we?"

"Ever been to Sweetwater? Know where it is?"

"Yes, to both questions, and I don't recollect having left anything here that I needed to come back for."

"Well, welcome back anyway," Will quipped. "and I stopped here because I'm hungry."

The pickup rolled to a stop. Jake spoke up. "Littl' Bruthur, bring the map in with you. Let's take a look at it while we eat." He yanked at the door handle. There was an accompanying screech as he shouldered it open. "Their food must be good 'cause it looks like half of Texas is here."

Chapter Thirteen
A Rattlin' Bad Time

Later, after finishing their orders of Triple-Burgers and Triple-Fries, they sat nursing the remains of their Triple-Size, Triple-Thick Shakes when Jake asked for the map. Together, they spread it across the table.

"Stay here on I-20. Keep going west through Abilene," Jake said, "and let me drive awhile if you start feeling tired." He jabbed at a spot on the map southwest of Odessa, "Over here, just a little off the Interstate, is a wide spot in the road called *Sandlot*."

He sat back in his chair, causing it to squeak in protest. "I used to know a fellow that I think moved there. Bought a motel or some kinda business. Maybe he's still there; perhaps, we can get a good deal on a place to sleep. After that, it'll still be several more hours on to the ranch of this long-lost relative of yours."

He scratched his chin. "I expect we'll probably need to stop and ask directions to wherever she lives. We'd best be doing all that in the daylight. Those written directions your lawyer friends left are kinda vague."

"Howdy."

Will looked up to see a scruffy, bearded man dressed in grimy blue denim coveralls standing next to him. The stranger offered a grease-stained hand but withdrew it quickly. "I'd shake your hands, but what with y'all still eatin' and all..."

Seeing the mangled nails, ingrained with black, accompanied by a strong whiff of diesel, Will wrinkled his nose but said nothing.

"That your ol' Chevy pickup out there?"

"It's mine," Will answered, trying to measure the stranger, wondering how much money he might be about to ask for. Jake sat, eyeing the man with open suspicion.

"Al Richards," the newcomer drawled. "Like to find trucks like that, fix'm up, resell'm. A real market for'm once they get restored, ya know. Old trucks like that, they were made outa real metal, real steel. Not the aluminum and plastic junk like they do today. That's one reason so many people like'm."

"Well, that one's not for sale," Will hastened to reply, wanting to end the discussion.

"Yeah, well you change your mind, le'me know, but ain't why I'm botherin' ya. You got anyone's mad at ya? Maybe, got a weird sense of humor for playin' nasty tricks?"

"I don't think so," Will glanced at Jake.

"Neither of us knows anyone around here," Jake added. "Why?"

"Well, noticed when ya came up, 'cause I'm always

watching out for a truck like that, somebody might be wantin' to get rid of. So, anyhow, I was a standin' in the shade 'side my garage and a lookin' at yourn, from a distance. Then, this big black SUV, 4X4, one with those big cowcatcher bull-bars on the front. It drives up, real slow like."

He paused, thinking about what to say next. "One of those big un's, ya know, like all you city boys buy when you want ta look like a real man."

Will and Jake glanced at each other. Al continued, "Anyway, it sits there a while 'fore anyone gets out, and when he does, acts real suspicious like."

Al took a breath, looked straight at Will. "Then, he sorta snook around to your truck while carryin' a burlap bag in his hand. That's when I saw him open the driver's door and put somethin' in."

He now, had their full attention. They leaned forward in their chairs.

"You surely oughta lock your truck when you leave it, ya know," Al admonished them.

"The lock's broken," Will snapped back in a defensive tone.

Al drawled on, "Now, I'm the curious sort, even about things that ain't none o' my business."

A twisted grin split his face, exposing several tobacco stained, and very crooked, teeth. "So, after he sorta of slunk back to his big truck and drove on outa here, I just moved on over to yourn to see what he left ya. Just kinda meandered by, pertendin' I was mindin' my own bisness, like."

He paused again, but neither of them said a word nor took their eyes off him until Jake broke the silence with impatience in his voice, "Well?"

The smile disappeared, replaced by a frown. "Took a

peek in your window, didn't open the door. You mighta thought I was snoopin'. Maybe thought I'd put it in there."

"What?" Will broke his silence. A sudden chill shot up his spine. "Who put what in where?"

"Snake, of course," Al answered with a laugh, enjoying the attention. "And in your truck, driver's side, what's more. Actually, snakes might be closer ta being more truthful. I think there mightn' be more'n one. Anyway, that feller dropped least one in your truck, a big diamondback. A real beauty it looks, too. Saw it through your driver's window."

With his mouth open, Will looked across the table at his friend. Jake sat without moving, studying Al with doubt in his expression.

With a gleam of pride in his eyes, along a with a low chuckle, Al added, "Know snakes, that I do—'specially rattlers, ya know. Go snake huntin' regular. Tellin' ya, it's a big'un out there."

The wood creaked as Jake stirred in his chair. He looked hard at his friend and asked, "Willie, ol' buddy—you have any customers upset enough to want to kill you, or at least make you real sick?"

Shaking his head, Will could think of no answer. This was a situation completely foreign to him. Imaginary heroes, facing imaginary dangers, was one thing, but this was real life.

Jake poked him in the arm, "Let's go take a look."

Coming up to the truck, Will grabbed the driver's door handle and pulled.

"Don't..." Al yelled, but it was too late; with hinges screaming, the door swung open. A loud, threatening, angry BRRRR reverberated from the interior, filling the air around them.

Will stood frozen, unable to move, afraid even to

breathe. Never before in his life could he remember being face to face with death. Now, here it was—coiled in the truck seat, hideous, and ready to strike—mouth open, fangs glistening, forked, red tongue flicking about, and the tail standing erect—vibrating its threatening alarm.

In one quick motion, Al shouldered Will out of harm's way, sending him sprawling on the gravel while slamming the door.

As Will struggled to his feet, Al warned him. "You stay back, ya' know—less'n you know to work with rattlers. If you ain't careful, find yerself in the hospital real quick like. Didn't mean ta hurt ya none, but the feller in there'll be havin' a nasty bite if he were to git ya. There might'n be more'n one of'm, too." With those words, he pulled out his cell phone, punched in some numbers, spoke a few words, closed it, and returned the device to his pocket.

"Help's on the way," he said. "Me and my Bobby, as I done said, we been huntin' and collectin' these critters for years."

"What in the world do you do with them?" Will picked himself up and brushed the dust off his clothes. "Eat them?" he asked with a chuckle, laughing at his own joke.

"Yeah, matter o' fact we do," Al answered. "Fact is, I'll stretch this fella out and skin'm." He paused and lifted his eyebrows. "Ahh, if you don't mind?" He shrugged his shoulders. "Less, of course, you might be a wantin' to keep him. I guess he's yourn seeing as how he's been left in your truck and all."

"Oh, no," Will grimaced, shaking his head. "Feel free—you can have the thing—skin and all. Just get it out of my truck."

"First we milk'm, so's can sell the poison. I tan the hide,

sometimes make belts out'm. If'n I get enough, sell'm to ol' Howie Jones across the way. Makes boots out of m, is what he does."

He jerked his thumb back toward the diner. "Thelda, m' wife, takes the meat 'n we put it on the menu here in the diner most ever' Saturday—when we have enough. Our 'Bar-B-Q Rattler Burgers' sell real good."

He coughed and spit into the gravel before saying, "Ahh, here's my Bobby."

A tall, lanky teenager ran up carrying a burlap bag and two long poles. An uncombed mop of red hair exploding from beneath a Texas Rangers baseball cap, turned backwards, sat on the youngster's head. The kid was dressed almost identical to Al and every bit as greasy. One of the poles had a set of pincers activated by a trigger device on the opposite end. The other pole ended with a large "U" shaped hook.

The teenager glanced at Will and Jake in a shy manner, before offering a quiet, "Howdy."

Will raised his eyebrows in surprise, Bobby was a Bobbie.

"These are my snake catch'n tools. M' Bobbie here made'm fer me fer Father's Day last year," he said. "Smartest kid in these parts." Another huge smile broke across Al's face. "She could do a tune-up on this old truck o'yourn, have her runnin' like new in no time."

"Very nice," Will replied shaking his head. "Thanks for the offer, but as soon as you get those snakes out of there, we'll get some gas and move on down the road."

"Have it your way, son. Now, you two stand back an' all." Al waved them aside with one hand, reaching for the door handle with the other. He paused, staring at the door for a minute. "Oh yeah, I was meaning to ask ya, what's ya got

The Ghost of Grandpa Wills

stuck on these doors? It looks like some kinda steel plate or somethin'?"

"Oh, that's boiler plating," Will answered. "The old truck used to belong to a company that made boilers and other stuff. That was part of their advertising."

"Yeah, well that'll all have to come off if ya ever do restore this ol' heap. Maybe have ta replace the whole door." Al repeated his order again, "Now, y'all stand back."

Will and Jake backed away; neither needed to be warned twice. Bobbie moved in closer.

Al stood eying the interior for several minutes. He grunted and spat into the gravel, narrowly missing Will's boot. He grabbed the door handle and pulled. The rusty hinges protested with a loud squeal. An angry BRRRR exploded from of the cab.

Will retreated a few more feet. He had never heard such a sound, except on TV, and he didn't like it—not even a little bit. He glanced over at Jake, who stood watching, showing no sign of fear.

"I'll be," Al exclaimed, "in luck, Bobbie gal; they be two of'm. Maybe more, an' these here are a pair of big'uns. Ol' Howie'll get a set of boots outa these two alone."

Chapter Fourteen
Back on the Road

It was mid-afternoon when Will drove back to I-20 and pointed the old truck west. He sat behind the steering wheel, both hands on the wheel, saying nothing, staring straight ahead, his music player on the seat beside him.

Jake was reading through the paperwork left by the two lawyers. He put it down and looked over at his friend. "What's up, Littl' Bruthur? You're awful quiet—not going to sleep on me are you?"

Will's responded with hesitation, "No, I'm awake. Jake, do you think someone was trying to kill me—or you—or both of us?"

Jake's reply was slow in coming. "I don't know. I really don't know." He shook his head in slow motion, "But if they were just playing tricks, making some kind of sick joke..."

The Ghost of Grandpa Wills

"Then it wasn't very funny, and I'm not laughing," Will interjected, biting his words off in an angry tone. "Jake, you were in the Army, weren't you?"

"**Navy**, Littl' Bruthur. The United States **Navy**!"

"You never told me, but did you ever get shot at?" Will asked in a subdued voice.

His friend sucked in a lungful of air before he answered. "Bruthur Willie, sometimes there's things a man doesn't talk about." He paused again. "But—yes—I was shot at—lots of times. A whole lot of times."

Jake sat, looking out the truck window, but not seeing the passing scenery. He took another breath before continuing. "They brought my chopper down more than once. I lost some close friends, buddies that didn't get to come home…"

Will, without taking his eyes from the road ahead asked, "Were you ever scared?"

Jake turned to study Will for a few seconds. "Every time, Bruthur Willie—Every-Single-Time," he answered with a hard emphasis on each word.

"But you kept doing it, didn't you? Did you ever run away, or even think about it?"

Jake turned back to stare out the windshield. "Once things started happening, didn't have time to think—just did what I'd been trained to do. There was a job had to be done, and men's lives dependin' on me to do it."

He hesitated for a few seconds before continuing, "Usually, it wasn't until after it was over that I had time to think about being afraid; then it was too late. It was all over and done."

Will exhaled, puffing his cheeks. "I've never been shot at. Don't remember ever being in danger—at least with my life threatened—not until now that is." He took his eyes off the road long enough to glance over at his friend.

"Jake, that snake scared me silly. I've never seen anything so ugly looking. And I can't figure out why someone would do it."

Jake replied in a soothing tone. "First time's always the worst, but you never actually get used to it. You just do what you have to do. You do your job."

The truck coughed, jerked, and rattled as Will pressed the accelerator and swerved into the left lane to pass a slow moving truck. "I daydream about being brave. I make up stories about rescuing people, saving their lives, and all that stuff; but back there, back there, I didn't know what to do. I was just plain scared silly." He slapped the palm of one hand down hard against the steering wheel.

"Listen, Littl' Bruthur, being brave doesn't mean not being afraid." Jake reached across to put a hand on Will's shoulder. "I can't remember who said it, but courage is doing what you gotta do—even when you're afraid—no matter how bad you're afraid."

"Back there, I was scared so bad; I couldn't move." He glanced over, feeling overwhelmed with shame. "I didn't do anything. I'm just a coward, Jake. A day dreaming coward. Petrified." Turning back to stare at the road, he added, "I just fell down and rolled around in the dirt while…"

"You were knocked down, Ol' Buddy—you didn't just fall down."

"And what if Tracie—or one of the kids—had opened that door?"

"Well, they weren't there, and I'm sure you would've acted differently if they had been."

Will glanced over at Jake.

The Ghost of Grandpa Wills

Jake had shifted in his seat and sat looking at him with his eyebrows raised.

Anticipating a question, Will asked, "What?"

Jake indicated the papers he had been reading. "Changing the subject a bit. Did you ever read all this stuff about where we're going? Katie certainly did her homework about the area before she printed it off for you."

"No, I guess not," Will answered with hesitation. "I didn't have time, and I wasn't feeling too well last night—a bit of upset stomach."

Jake laughed. "Oh, really. And what would upset that cast iron stomach of yours, you're always braggin' about?"

Will's answer came with reluctance, "Just something I ate—I guess..."

Chapter Fifteen
A Long, Lonely Road

Will's pickup moved out of the parking lot and turned toward the I-20 entrance ramp. A black SUV followed from a distance.

Inside the vehicle, Ralph Ferrell banged on the dashboard with his fist and cursed. Case Anthony responded with a sneer. "Told you it wouldn't work."

Ferrell threw an angry glare at his cohort and snarled. "Shut up."

He beat against the side window in frustration. "We'll just do it the hard way. Going to be dark soon. Looks like a nice big storm ahead an' lots of people have accidents when it's raining."

He pointed a thin finger, "There's a whole lot of lonely road where they're goin', too." He turned to scowl at Case. "So shut up and drive. You're being paid to do as you're told—not mouth off."

Chapter Sixteen
Storm's A Comin'

An hour later, they were still driving under a clear sky, but straight ahead, another bank of angry dark thunderheads towered high into the sky with the sun soon to be disappearing behind it. There was the promise of a glorious sunset to precede the coming storm; Will saw none of it. With his music player on high volume, he was deep into the plot for another book:

Clad in armor that once had shone like silver in the sunlight, Sir William the Courageous, Knight of the Round table, tired but still proud, sat straight and tall upon his sweat-drenched charger. The once glorious suit of armor now dented and grime covered, weighed heavy upon his weary body.

The Ghost of Grandpa Wills

All about him, the countryside lay ruined in smoldering waste. The stench of death heavy upon the land and the smoke of many fires rose high into a cloudless sky.

The dragon had vented its terrible wrath; devastation was all about.

Now, save for the dead and dying, Sir William, weary warrior that he was, stood alone—deserted by all, every companion gone. He would face the dreadful, fiery foe unaided..."

With the music of Vangelis blaring in his ears, Sir William sped into the growing sunset, oblivious of all around him—the small matter of a pair of ugly rattlers having vanished from his mind.

As the reddening sun disappeared behind the gathering clouds, the increasing darkness made it impossible for Jake to focus on his book. "Where are we?" he asked putting it down. Getting no response, he nudged Will on the arm.

"What?" Will removed the ear buds and, with reluctance, returned to reality. Sir William the Courageous, valiant warrior, having slain the mighty dragon, had been in the process of making his deepest desires known to a certain fair young maiden, lately rescued from assured death. The glorious warrior definitely did not welcome such a rude interruption.

Jake repeated his question as he studied the passing countryside. "Where are we? We should be near Big Spring by now."

"Is there any water in the big spring?" was Will's pert response. "And, Dearest Cuzin, we actually passed the Big Water several miles back."

"Bruthur Will, where's your maps? Have you even

looked at them since Sweetwater? Have you done gone and got this poor Mississippi boy lost somewhere out in the middle of West Texas?" Looking ahead, he added, "An' that sur' looks like one bodacious big storm up ahead."

"I believe you're sitting on the map, Cuzin Jake," Will responded in a flippant tone. "So no, I haven't looked at it. But, I assure you, we are still going west on Interstate 20."

Jake shifted to retrieve the map. "Okay, just a few miles—fifteen or so—past Odessa, look for an exit off to that little place I mentioned earlier, called Sandlot."

"Sandlot—weird name for a town."

"Well, they've got a lot of sand—not much else."

Then, the storm was upon them—big drops, windblown, falling fast, and furious—attacking them in great sweeps. Along with the waves of rain, came hail that clattered and pounded on the old truck. From that moment, Will's attention was taken up trying to stay on the road.

Jake pulled out his silver flask and swallowed deep before commenting, "Good thing this old jalopy's made of old fashioned steel just like Al said."

"Jalopy," Will exclaimed in mock anger. "You will hurt the lady's tender feelings. Then, we'll both be walking across Texas."

Within minutes, however, the deluge of hail passed, and a torrent of rain eased into a more manageable heavy shower. But all sunlight was gone, blocked by the clouds.

Will relaxed, picked out another music selection, and stuffed the ear buds back into place. He was soon back to the important business of rescuing—not just fair damsels-in-distress—but entire communities:

The engine's powerful headlight threw out a beam of bright

light, cutting into the darkness ahead, although much of its brilliance was reflected back by the pouring rain. Engine Driver Watson sat alone in the cab; no one would accompany him on this suicidal mission.

"Suicide, is it?" the courageous engineer spoke aloud as if challenging the elements. "Well, maybe it is. Then again, maybe it ain't. These supplies a gotta git through; lives be dependin' on it."

With those words, he pushed the throttle-handle forward and felt the surge of power vibrate up through the floor plates.

This train would get through; Engine Driver Watson would not fail.

The heroic run by Engine Driver Watson was rudely interrupted as a large, dark vehicle approached from behind at a very high rate of speed. It came to within mere inches from their rear bumper and hung there, tailgating them with its headlights on bright. Then, the mysterious driver switched on a set of halogen spots. The pickup's interior was flooded with an intense, dazzling light, followed immediately by a jarring crash.

"What the..."

Another jarring crash.

"Speed up, Bruthur," Jake screamed. He banged a fist on the dashboard. "Try to outrun'm. I think someone's got it in for us. It may be your friends that like to play with snakes back there."

Will might have been a carefree speed demon in his daydreams, but in real life, high speed scared him. Now, it was dark and rain was pelting down. He hesitated.

"Move it, Willie," Jake demanded. "Put your foot to the floor; do it now."

Before Will could respond, the mysterious vehicle accelerated and swerved into the left passing lane. Moving fast, it sped alongside holding position for a moment, it edged closer. With the rain obscuring his view, all Will could discern was a dark form. The storm drowned out any sound that might have come from the truck, or van, or whatever it was.

Without warning, the vehicle crashed into them, pushing them to the edge of the pavement. Their outside mirror disintegrated, disappearing into the stormy darkness.

Will gave way for a few seconds, and the old truck edged toward the shoulder and the rainy darkness beyond.

Jake leaned forward straining against his seatbelt. With hands braced against the dashboard, he stared at Will with the whites of his eyes showing against his dark features. He screamed, "Push'm back, Willie, push'm hard."

Will responded, giving the steering wheel a hard twist to his left. He was rewarded with a hard jolt and the sound of metal ripping and tearing. Both vehicles veered to the left, closer to the median.

With the rain almost blinding him, Will pulled back into the right lane and floored the accelerator. The old truck coughed, sputtered, and hesitated a fraction of a second before surging ahead. All eight cylinders finally came to life. Their attackers faded from sight.

Within seconds, the dark shadow reappeared beside his window, pushing in closer until the shock of collision and sound of bending steel told him they had been hit again. He gave way once more.

"Drive, Willie, drive hard and fast," Jake screamed. Will's side window exploded inward, showering him with pieces of broken glass and needle-like drops of icy, wind-driven rain. A jagged hole appeared in the side window next to Jake, accompanied by a metallic thud it. Another ragged cavity appeared in the doorpost just above his outstretched arms.

Jake bellowed a warning. He threw himself against the seat back. "Incomin' Bruthur, we're taking fire. They're a shootin' at us." He spat out orders, "Hit'm Will, turn into'm. Hit'm hard. Don't try to out run'm, attack'm. Knock'm off the road. Do it! Now, now, now!"

Will gripped the steering wheel with both hands, twisting it hard to the left. The two vehicles came together with a jarring crash and the sound of grinding, screeching metal.

"Keep pushing, Willie. Drive'm off the road. Push'm all the way."

Will kept up the pressure against the other vehicle. Realizing their attackers had moved into the left lane, he decided to take the offensive. He yanked the wheel to the right, momentarily separating the two vehicles. Metal, ripped and torn, screamed. The two vehicles came apart.

Flooring the accelerator, Will turned back into his attacker with a bone jarring crash. It was a lethal dance. The vehicles strove together—surging left, then right—a mortal fight to the finish.

Jake screamed again, panic sounding in his voice, "Look out—ahead, in the road."

A large object, black in the rain filled light, lay across the road, a dark shadow in the headlights. It lay stretched across the road like a huge black serpent. Will held the steering wheel with an iron grip. He felt the truck buck and twist as if it was a living creature. The front-end rose and crashed back down, the old truck shuddering and booming as they rolled over the object. The truck's interior immediately reverberated with a deep, rumbling roar. From the corner of his eye, Will saw their shadowy assailant lurch up into the air as it tore away from them.

Fighting a hard shimmy coming from the front wheels of his own truck, Will fought to regain control before swerving across the freeway into the far right lane. Sucking in a deep breath, he shouted, "Can't believe we're still alive."

Jake answered with a bellow, "Hurry, Willie; don't let up. Take the next exit. That'll go off to Sandlot."

Will squinted his eyes against the pelting rain and took a quick glance through the hole where his window had been.

"Where'd they disappear to? And, what was that thing we ran over?"

"Don't know, don't care—turn now!" Jake ordered.

Chapter Seventeen
Welcome to Sandlot

"Our visitors appear to be gone," Will shouted over the roar. "Maybe they realized how unwelcome they were? You see what happened to them?"

"Last I saw of'm was the glow of their taillights, dancin' up and down. Looked like they were hightailing it across the median. Hope they're lying upside down in a muddy ditch somewhere," Jake responded, anger in his voice. "But don't slow down, they might still be back there and comin' after us."

The storm moved eastward, stars appeared in the sky ahead of them. "I thought it would never quit raining," Will shouted. "Does it always rain like this out here?"

"Only when it rains. And it only rains around here about once every twenty years or so." He pulled the silver flask from his coat pocket and took another deep swallow.

Distances in the high plains of West Texas can be very deceiving. The glow of lights on the western horizon had, at first, not seemed so far away—no more than a few miles, but Will and Jake drove for another thirty minutes before they could distinguish individual lights amidst the glare.

Street lamps and neon lights for the few businesses provided the only signs of life in the place. A small desert town—it sat silent and asleep as they roared into its center.

Everything was closed.

Everyone had gone home.

Everyone had gone to bed.

Well—not quite everyone.

The somber duo roared into the town, speeding through its one and only traffic light. Jake shouted, and motioned with his thumb. "See those flashing blue lights behind us, Littl' Bruthur? We be in some big trouble now, and the longer you take to pull over—the bigger the trouble we gonna be in."

Flashing blue lights immersed their truck, reflecting off the glass in the storefronts. Will sighed and pulled over. It was only when he killed the truck engine that he heard the siren. He started reaching for his wallet in his back pocket. Jake stuffed the engraved silver flask inside his coat.

As the officer exited the patrol car, Jake sat motionless, staring straight ahead. His voice was almost a whisper. "Will, O' Buddy, Lil' Bruthur, ol' friend, my only true friend, please keep your brain in gear, and please, please, please—keep a brake on your mouth."

Will turned to lean out the window and look back. He watched the officer approach, framed by the bright lights of the patrol car, augmented by a powerful spotlight. Silhouetted against the glare the officer appeared to be small in body, with a uniform hanging loose on a sparse frame.

The officer approached with a swagger and a great show of authority, carrying an enormous gun, holstered on the right hip and, clasped in the left hand was one of those extra-large, extra-long, extra-heavy, extra-bright, extra-black flashlights.

Why is he wearing sunglasses this time of the night? Will wondered.

The law arrived at Will's side. The beam of the extra-extra-extra-extra-extra flashlight burned into his eyes. He felt as though the inside of his head had been illuminated all the way through the back of his skull.

"Welcome to Sandlot, Texas. I'm Deputy-Sheriff Bernese Josephine Firth. Driver's license, please," Her words spilled out in a high-soprano voice.

Will gave her the piece of plastic.

"Speed limit is thirty miles per hour and posted at the city limits."

"Sorry, I didn't see it."

"You also drove through that red light without stopping."

"Sorry, I didn't see it, either."

"Had much to drink?" the Deputy asked.

"Some coffee, back up the road apiece," Will answered.

"Dallas, eh," the officer sneered as she studied the license. "You big city guys always think we're just a bunch of peyote-eating, country bumpkin, redskins out here, don't ya?"

"No Sir—er, ma'am. Not at all, ma'am. Never thought much about Indians eating coyotes. I always thought you ate buffalo meat and rattlesnake."

The officer exploded, in her high-soprano voice. "Okay, wise guys, out, out, out. Out of the truck, now! Both of you!" The light flashed over to Jake, "You too, fat boy."

She stepped back and un-holstered her revolver. Will's eyes opened into wide circles of fear; the weapon looked like a cannon. Still barking out an endless stream of commands, she strutted over to the front of the truck.

"Ever'body out—now!" Her orders poured out of her in rapid fire fashion. "Front of the truck—now! Face the vehicle—now! Hands on the vehicle—now! Assume the position—now! Spread arms and legs—now! And zip your lip, now—Mr. Big City Funny Man! You're on MY huntin' grounds now!"

Jake's size, the truck's height above the ground, and his liquid relationship with "Uncle Jack," combined with fatigue, did not make for a graceful exit. He stumbled and fell full on his belly.

"Freeze—now!" The cannon's muzzle swept from Will to Jake and back again. "Nobody move! Get up, Fat Guy—now! 'Round here—now! Don't move—City boy!"

From her mouth, the term 'City Boy' came out sounding as if she were describing something she had stepped in—in a cow pasture.

"Assume the position—now!"

As Jake struggled to his feet, the silver flask fell from his coat pocket, hitting the pavement with a clatter.

"Boozin' it up weren't ya—City boys. We country bumpkins got just the place for big city drunks like you. Move it! NOW!"

Will could not take his eyes from the cannon clutched in her fist. He sat mesmerized by fear as the barrel swung back and forth.

Chapter Eighteen
Cross Bar Hotel

Jake wrinkled his nose with disgust as the deputy led them into the jail's holding area.

"Don't like our accommodations, City Boy. Prefer the Sandlot Hilton, maybe? Well, this is the best you can expect when you come speeding through town on my watch."

The cell was ugly, filthy with dust and debris from previous occupants—uninviting, and smelled worse than it looked.

Jake threw his coat on the bottom bunk and, then, sat down with his head in his hands. Will struggled to the top and stretched out full length on the lumpy mattress.

Minutes passed, before Jake, with a deep sigh, rose to walk over to the cell door where he uttered a deep sigh. He turned and pace restlessly, to and fro, as if he were a caged tiger.

"Jail," he fumed. "Caged like an animal. No, it's worse. I'm locked up like a criminal. Momma told me to stay away from all you white boys. She said you was always a pack of trouble." Waving his arms about in frustration he paused, looked up at the ceiling, and then turned to face his friend. "Now look at me, Willie, my friend. My good friend. My only friend. My dearest ol' buddy."

He pivoted, and resumed his pacing. "Twenty years in the Navy. Years during which I sailed around the world twice."

He stopped, grabbed the cold steel bars with both hands and glared out at the bare concrete wall opposite. "I've been in twenty-three countries on six continents. An' I've been in forty-three of these fifty states plus Puerto Rico, Guam, and the Virgin Islands, and I have never—NEVER—been in jail—until now!" He raised his arms to the ceiling, his voice rising to a crescendo, "Never!"

He wheeled about and stomped toward the rear wall. "I've been all over New York, Paris, London, Singapore, and Hong Kong and never have I ever seen the inside of such a place as this—anywhere, anytime, anyhow, anyway!"

He stopped, to once more face his friend. "Until I go on a trip with you." He crossed his arms and, chin up, he took a defiant stance. "One trip with you and look at me, now. What do you have to say? Huh? What **do** you have to say about this?"

His only answer was a loud rasping snore from the top bunk.

Sir Will O' the Lake, courageous Knight of the Table Round, fair and bright, bursting with honor and bravery, stood alone facing the dreadful dragon. The bodies of his slain

companions lay about him, twisted and torn, broken and mutilated, scorched and burned, brought down by the dragon's wicked, slashing claws and foul, fiery breath.

Holding his enchanted shield before him and raising his magic sword high above his head, the valiant warrior strode forth to meet his destiny.

The fearsome dragon roared, belching forth flame, fire, and death.

Sir Will held his ground. He would not retreat.

Roars!

Explosions!

Noise of battle!

Shouts of anger!

The dragon's voice broke through the raucous din.

Strangely, it was a familiar—but most unwelcome—voice.

A high pitched woman's voice.

He knew that voice from somewhere in his recent past.

"Up and at'm, City Boys. Butts outa bed. Feet on the floor." The Deputy shrieked as she strutted along the outside of their cell, crashing a large steel bar against the iron bars.

"Judge'll be in her courtroom—thirty minutes. You got half an hour from now to look pretty for her." She was obviously enjoying their misery. "Move it! Move it! Move it!" Her orders spewed forth in a high-pitched stream.

The prisoners responded with unintelligible groans, but she did not stay to listen; she turned and marched out before either could get his feet on the floor.

Will looked at his watch through blurry, sleep-filled eyes. "Five o'clock," he complained. He looked down at Jake, "The woman's insane. She's a sadist."

Chapter Nineteen
Order in the Court

The two prisoners, handcuffed and prodded by the deputy's nightstick, stumbled into a courtroom shrouded in darkness.

There was nothing either bold or brave about Will's appearance. Sir Will O' the Lake had died with the rude awakening. Jake looked no better.

Neither had shaved, and both had slept in their clothes. The full extent of their toiletry supplies had been cold water and paper towels. No breakfast. No coffee.

Without warning, the Deputy hit the switches. Bright lights stabbed their eyes. Her shriek cut through the tomb-like silence. "Be polite, keep your noses clean, and maybe she'll let you off with less'n twenty years—jus' maybe."

She led them to seats in the front row and pointed with her nightstick, "Front row, City Boys. Sit down, shut up!

The Ghost of Grandpa Wills

Judge'll be here shortly."

"Any chance of our seeing a lawyer?" Jake asked tentatively.

"Nearest one's in Odessa," she sneered. A smirk creased her thin face. "Probably be three or four weeks before he can get here. Tell your problems to the Judge, City Boy. But keep it short and sweet. She's goin' out of town this mornin'."

Suddenly, a door slammed open behind the Judge's bench.

"ALL RISE." the Deputy squeaked in her most authoritative tone. "Court is now in session. Judge Sharon Abigail Red Wolf presiding."

The Judge swept into the room with an expression that bode ill for all that crossed her way. She thrust her arms into a black robe as she took her place behind the bench and glared out across the courtroom. "Bernie, what in heaven's name are we doing here at this ungodly hour of the morning? Why is my robe still here in the courtroom? Thought I took it home yesterday afternoon."

Her glare settled on Will and Jake. "What crimes have this nefarious pair committed that could not have waited until later?" Not waiting for an answer, her eyes searched the courtroom. "Where is my bailiff? RAYMOND!

"And, someone bring me some aspirin and a coke. I should never have stayed at that party last night."

She turned her attention back to the nefarious pair. "What are you two standing there for? Sit down."

They sat.

Jake leaned over to whisper in Will's ear, "Littl' Bruthur." He took a quick glance up at the bench where the judge sat scowling down. "We ain't never gonna git outa this here place. You can say goodbye to your long lost relative an' your kids an' your luvly wife 'cause we're gonna be bustin' rocks for the rest of our ..."

"Quiet," the Judge ordered. "Silence in the courtroom." Her gavel crashed down onto the bench in front of her.

The nefarious criminals cowered before her wrathful visage.

In a more honeyed voice, she looked over at Bernie, "Now, Deputy, Darlin', would you kindly fetch me some coffee?" Using her gavel as a pointer, she waved it at the deputy. "Since you thought it necessary to interrupt my beauty sleep for this court session and you thoughtfully allowed the bailiff to continue in his repose, you will make the coffee. And, no, you will not be getting off early to go see your friends in Odessa either."

She looked back at the prisoners. "And what about you two? You both look like you're a little short on beauty sleep yourselves. Were the facilities lacking a little bit? Not quite up to your standards maybe?"

"He snores," Will pointed at Jake. "And I've seen better beds in Motel Six." Jake looked upward as if pleading for mercy.

The Judge laughed. "Motel Six, hey. You have high standards. Didn't the Deputy leave the light on for you, Darlin'?" She turned back to the deputy. "You go get the coffee, please, Deputy, Dear. I think I'll be safe alone with these two hardened criminals."

She reached down under the bench and pulled out the biggest nickel-plated revolver Will had ever imagined—larger even than the deputy's. The Judge made a show of laying it out in plain sight. "Colt, Navy model 1851 cap and ball, black powder revolver, .36 caliber, single action—a replica of the one favored by Marshal Wild Bill Hickok.

The Ghost of Grandpa Wills

Anniversary present from my dearly beloved." A big smile creased her round, dark face. "He's the romantic type."

She showed teeth that gleamed white against her black skin. "Been giving me lessons, too, he has. Says I'm real good, a natural. I can hit a jackrabbit with one shot, and him goin' at full clip." The smile left her face. "Never tried my luck with a man, though."

The two desperadoes sat still—very still.

The Judge picked up some papers and shuffled through them for a few minutes before looking back at her prisoners.

"Which one of you is Ralph Waldo Jacobson?" she asked.

Will's eyes popped wide open. "Waldo? That's your middle name? You never mentioned that before—Wally."

Jake glared down at his companion as he rose from his seat. He turned to face the Judge, trying to put on a friendlier look for her benefit. His middle name had always been one of his most closely guarded secrets.

"That's me, your Honor."

"Have we ever met before?"

"Not that I know of, ma'am, ah, Your Honor."

"You've never been in my courtroom before?"

"No ma'am, I've never been in Sandlot before."

"I never forget a name." She paused for a moment while she opened a sealed plastic bag.

She held up a silver flask and asked, "Which one of you claims this?"

"It looks like mine," Jake confessed.

She unscrewed the top and sniffed the opening. Her eyebrows went up as she smiled. "Jack Daniels—I approve of your taste in whiskey anyway. Where did you get it?"

"At a liquor store in Dallas, ma'am."

"Not the whiskey—the flask." She waved it at him. "Where did you get it?" She asked again as she studied it. "Did you pick it up in some pawn shop?"

"No, ma'am," Jake answered firmly. "I bought it and had it engraved in Naples, Italy."

The Judge looked him straight in the eye, before rising from her chair. She barked out a command. "Chief Petty Officer Ralph Waldo Jacobson, you will stand at attention when being addressed by a senior officer." The gavel crashed down onto her bench. "Do you understand?"

Jake jumped to attention and found himself saluting before he realized what he was doing.

Judge Sharon Abigail Red Wolf burst into a gale of laughter.

"Stand at ease, sailor. We're both civilians now." She moved from behind the bench to step down toward him.

"Chief Petty Officer Ralph Waldo Jacobson, I told you I never forget a name—especially yours. You certainly got me into a lot of trouble. I don't know if I should hug your neck or sentence you to life imprisonment."

Jake stood there with a puzzled look on his face, "Do I know you?"

Will sat with his mouth open and his eyes wide.

The Judge walked down among the chairs, pushing them aside when they were in her way. Closing in on Jake, she reached out her arms and wrapped them around him.

"I think you deserve a great big hug," She squeezed with all her might.

At that moment, the door opened, and Sheriff Richard Red Wolf stormed into the courtroom, with his revolver drawn.

Chapter Twenty
At the Red Wolf Grill

"Red Wolf Grill?" Will held a well-worn menu in his hand. "You own this place?"

The Judge had insisted that the court recess and immediately reconvene at "The Grill." Once there, she passed sentence on Will, finding him guilty of running the only traffic light in town, creating excessive noise, and operating an unsafe motor vehicle.

According to the deputy's sworn testimony, one headlight was smashed, the left turn signal was not working, and the muffler was missing.

Will's sentence was to have his truck repaired at the local garage (owned by the sheriff's brother and opened especially for that purpose) and to buy breakfast for everyone. All charges of drunken and disorderly conduct, for both of the alleged nefarious criminals, were dismissed and forgotten.

Following the others into "The Grill," Will felt as though he had stepped back to a time before he had been born.

Furnished with antique wood tables and matching straight-backed chairs, the dining room spoke of an era long passed. The odor of past decades hung in the air. The table covers were red and white checked oilcloth, cracked with age and long usage. The tired old wood floor sagged, complaining with creaks and groans as they walked across it. Will wondered whether it would collapse under Jake's weight.

"My brother's place, the classiest place in Sandlot—also, the only place." The Sheriff motioned to a table and pulled a chair back for his wife. "Try the venison steak with your eggs. Shot the deer myself, last season. Oh, and the soda fountain still works just like it did back in the forties."

"I'll order for you," the Judge said. When the waitress arrived, Will and Jake stared up at her in surprise. It was Deputy Firth, still in uniform, but with the addition of an apron around her waist, and looking very bleary eyed.

"She's been temporarily demoted down to doing waitress duty until she learns how to better conduct herself as an officer of the law," the judge explained. "Besides, she woke me up out of deep sleep just because she wanted to get off early."

Bernie took the orders and disappeared back into the kitchen.

"If you could shoot well enough to hit a deer, how could you fail to hit something as large as Jake here?" Will asked.

"Thanks, littl' Bruthur, you sound like you're sorry he missed," Jake interjected.

"He lost his contacts, and he's too vain to wear glasses," the Judge answered.

The Ghost of Grandpa Wills

"This is the second time I've been shot at in the last twelve hours, and I don't like it," Will continued.

"I was shootin' at the big guy here, not you," the sheriff explained

"It was me you almost killed," Will returned.

"I got a little carried away when I saw him attackin' my wife—in her own courtroom," the Sheriff clarified.

"I thought she was attacking me until I realized I was being hugged," Jake replied, with a big grin.

"I couldn't believe it when she said you're the very same guy that pulled me outa the water that night," the Sheriff responded.

"What water? When?" Will asked, feeling left out of the circle.

"Back in the Gulf War," the Sheriff explained. "My jet picked up some flak from one of Sadam's AA guns, and I went down before I could make it back to the ship. I thought I was shark bait for sure until this guy came along." The Sheriff reached over and punched Jake on the shoulder.

Waitress/Deputy Bernice Firth arrived with a tray of coffee mugs and a large thermos of coffee. The conversation continued while she served everyone and returned to the kitchen.

"Your friend here picked several of my fellow pilots out of the water and also helped get some others back that went down on land," the Judge continued.

"You did all that, and you never told me about any of it," Will said with respect in his voice. "An' I don't even know how to swim."

"Just doin' my job like everybody else," Jake answered. "Nuthin' worth braggin' about."

"Maybe not," the Judge interrupted. "But if you hadn't

fished his backside out the water when you did." She wagged a finger at Jake. "Then, you got him back on board ship, where he asked me out for a date. Right in the middle of while I'm helping him with some legal stuff," she exclaimed, gesturing with both hands. "Never mind all the rules and regulations, flyboy here just ups and says, 'How about we have dinner together when we get shore side again?' Such nerve!"

"And you said?" Will asked, his coffee mug halfway to his lips.

"I said 'Yes,' of course." Her eyes rolled up at the ceiling. "How else do you think I ended up living in this place and being the mother of his six children as well?"

The venison and fried eggs arrived so they all turned their full attention to the food until the Sheriff put down his knife and fork, looked hard at Will and asked, "What did you mean, a few minutes ago, when you said that was the 'second time' you had been shot at?" He waved his steak knife in Will's direction. "Did I hear you right, or were you just wisecracking again?"

"Dead serious, Rick," Jake answered, all humor disappearing from his eyes. "That's why the truck's in such a mess and why we came in so fast last night. We didn't know if the bad guys were still after us or not. And your Deputy wouldn't give us a chance to explain either, so we ended up spendin' the night in your jail."

"Well," Will broke in, "You said we might get a good deal on a place to stay the night."

Jake glared at him.

Ignoring Will, the sheriff continued, "Explain, from the beginning—who was shootin' and why. All the details, please."

The Ghost of Grandpa Wills

After they'd finished their story, the Sheriff asked, "So you have no idea who or why?"

"No," Will answered. "Except, maybe it was the same guys that put the rattlesnakes in the truck."

"Whoa. Wait just a minute," the sheriff exclaimed. Hi eyebrows rose and he shifted in his chair. "Did I hear you right? Rattlesnakes, inside your truck, yesterday, before the shootin' started?"

"Sweetwater." Jake leaned back in his chair, holding his coffee mug in both hands. "Snakes came on board back in Sweetwater. Shootin' started later as we came around Big Spring."

"Okay." The sheriff slapped both hands down and pushed himself away from the table. "We're going back to the courthouse. My office. We'll rehash all this. You'll tell both stories, the snakes and the shooting. In detail. In front of a video camera. Now."

He picked up his cell phone and punched in some numbers. Outside the café, he motioned them to wait out on the sidewalk. "This is how we're going to do this. My brother down at the garage is comin' to take your truck over and treat it as a crime scene. He'll go over it an' look for evidence. Paint scrapin's and such. Also, I want to know if there were any witnesses back in Sweetwater. This matter's goin' to the State Troopers. Shoot'm-ups on the Interstate is their jurisdiction."

"Sheriff," Will broke in. "I have a deadline to keep. I need to get to the Will's Ranch before Friday."

"You'll get there, Mr. Watson, you'll get there," the Sheriff replied, hitching up his gun belt. "And I'm calling my sister down in Presidio County."

"Your sister?" Jake asked. "I didn't know you had a

sister."

"She's the Sheriff of Presidio County—where you're headed. I want to fill her in on all of it. My gut feelin' says there's someone doesn't want you to get to where you're going. I think Sis'll want to know all about it."

With one thumb hooked into his belt, he worked a toothpick between his teeth. "She talks a lot about the Will's ranch and Miss Amelia, who runs the place. I've met her, and she's quite a lady. Everyone in this part of Texas knows about her. The ranch has been in her family for more'n a hundred years."

He shook his head slowly. "It's really too bad how the cancer has taken hold of her."

He looked from Will to Jake, "Anyway, you both'll stay over here in Sandlot again tonight. I promise you a good deal on a real motel room with a definite upgrade from where you spent last night."

He turned to Will, "Your truck'll be ready sometime in the morning—late. I suggest a set of four new tires. The left front is ripped up, and I'm surprised you made it into Sandlot on it. All the others are nearly bald—can't believe you left Dallas on tires like that."

He pointed across the street and stepped off the curb. "I'll have my brother, Joseph, put in another headlight and get the taillight fixed. He'll straighten that left front fender enough so that it won't ruin the new tire, and you need a new exhaust system, muffler, catalytic converter, and such."

Will walked at his side, listening. "As for the windows that got shot out, Howie has a couple of doors from an old scrapper out back he'll give you, but there's no time for him to take care of that stuff here. He'll put'm in the back of your truck."

The Ghost of Grandpa Wills

He stopped in the middle of the street. "In the morning, I'll show you another route south to where you're going; stay off the interstate. There're a couple of counties between here and Presidio. I'll escort you to the end of my jurisdiction. I'll also talk to the other sheriffs about you. They'll be watchin' out for you."

He turned toward the east end of town. "There's a phone in my office down in the basement of the courthouse. Feel free to call whomever you wish. Then, take the rest of the day to see the sights of historic downtown Sandlot."

Chapter Twenty-One
There's A Whole Lot of Texas

"This ol' truck is sure a truckin' right along," Will commented as they sped south. "Joseph did a good job on it." He surveyed the passing landscape—an endless vista of flat prairie stretching to a far horizon where the purple of distant hills met the blue of the sky. He spoke in a thoughtful tone, "I didn't know there was so much of Texas."

"You ain't seen the half of it yet, Littl' Bruthur. You've still never seen the piney woods of East Texas."

"I can't wait to see those snow-topped mountains," Will added in a wishful tone. He switched on the MP3 and stuffed the buds back in his ear:

"Mr. Watson, sir. They's a real norther a comin'. The

The Ghost of Grandpa Wills

temperature's a gonna be lower than a snake's belly, and snow's a gonna be higher than a horse's eye." Hank, the Ranch Foreman, stood holding his hat in his hand. "Hit's a gonna be extra mean, up thar in the high country."

"You say all our stock's down off the high pastures?" Boss Watson leaned back, deep into his overstuffed chair listening to the ranch supervisor.

"Shore nuff, Boss. I took care of it all."

"How about the Widow Franklin?"

"Wal now, she's shore in a bad pinch, what with her husband dead and two of her hands gone and left her." Hank twisted his hat in his hands while he studied a crack in the floor at his feet. "Half her herd done be up thar, still."

The Boss sat up and declared, "You and the rest of the boys take all the Hummer's an' get over to her place real quick like." He stood so fast, his legs slammed his chair against the wall behind him.

With his thumbs in his belt and a determined look on his face, Boss Watson declared, "I'm firin' up the trusty ol' whirlybird. I'll scoot on up thar ahead of y'all an' run'm down from the air."

Hank looked up, genuine fear in his eyes, "Boss, if that norther catches ya up thar, you'll be a gonner for sure."

Boss Watson stretched himself to his fullest height and reached for his Stetson. "Hank, ain't no widder woman gonna lose her herd while I'm around and kin do som'thin' about it." Still talking, he stomped across the wood floor. "That's what neighbors are fer. We help each other out. That's the Watson tradition." With his hat anchored to his head, he strode out of the door.

Jake's voice cut into Boss Watson's rescue plans. "Bruthur

Willie, how much of this stuff have you read?" He held Will's folder with all the paperwork open on his lap.

"I sorta scanned it real quick like. Go ahead. Fill me in on the details."

"Strange ol' lady, this long lost relative of yours." He paused for a few minutes before continuing. "Will, my dear ol' friend and buddy, do you believe in ghosts?"

"You asked before. Ghosts are a figment of foolish people's fevered imaginations."

Glancing at his companion, he turned his attention back to the road. "No, I do not hold to the belief that such apparitions now exist, nor have they ever existed. What's more, once we're dead, we're all dead, dead all over—dead just like dear ol' Rover."

"You don't have a dog named Rover."

"Never had a dog, any dog, by any name and mores the shame. None of my foster parents would ever let me have a dog or a cat. I had a goldfish once but had to leave it when I was moved to a new home."

"Was moved ever few months or so." Will's voice carried a tone of sorrow. "I did stay at a couple of places for a year or two. Some of the memories still haunt me." He paused for a moment.

Jake sat, without comment, and listened to his friend's unexpected revelations.

"Memories may haunt me," Will continued in a flippant tone. "Never a ghost 'cause they don't exist." He turned to look at Jake with a mischievous smirk. "However, if they did exist and, if I ever saw one—I would stand firm, look it in the eye, and order it to go back to wherever it came from." He burst into an off-key ditty, "Who's afraid of the big, bad ghost, the big bad ghost..."

"Look out," Jake bellowed. He stared ahead, dropped his book, and threw his hands hard against the dashboard in alarm.

Out of the corner of his eye, Will saw a dark form in the road ahead, and, without thinking, swerved to his right. He hit the brakes in a panic, and the truck went into a skid, swinging around until coming to a halt, crossways in the middle of the road.

The odor of burnt rubber wafted into the cab. Both men sat looking straight out the windshield.

Jake spoke first, slow and in a soft voice, almost a whisper. "Momma said there'd be days like this. I just don't remember her saying there'd be so many all in a row."

He turned his eyes to stare at Will. "Littl' Burthur, are you trying, on purpose, to make ghosts outa both of us?"

Will sat, unmoving, with his hands still tight on the steering wheel. "What was that?"

"I believe it might have been a steer. Or, maybe a bull. I was somewhat distracted and failed to notice such minor details."

Jake turned his head, looking to his right and studied the arrow-straight ribbon of road that ran southward. "Don't see anyone coming our way, Willie Boy, but I still don't think this is a good place to sit and pass the time of day."

Will took his foot off the brake pedal, eased down on the accelerator, and maneuvered the truck back into the southbound lane.

"What was that cow doing in the middle of the road anyway? Do the farmers just let'm run loose around here?"

Jake settled back into his seat before answering. "Point number one, as I mentioned earlier, it was most likely a steer."

He counted off on his fingers. "Point number two, if you

value your life, never call a rancher a farmer."

He held up three fingers. "Point number three is that the fence is there, but I saw several broken strands just before you decided to demonstrate your superior driving skills."

Will drove in silence for several more miles. "Why are you asking anyway?"

Jake put the papers down and looked at Will. "Asking what? I don't believe I've said anything since you tried doing circles in the roadway back there."

"Ghosts, dear ol' Friend. You asked me about my belief in dearly departed spirits and all that."

"Because, Littl' Bruthur, according to what it says here, there's one where we be a goin'. You and me are going to be spendin' a few days with a real live ghost."

Will's eyes widened. "A real live one, you say? Does it say who this ghost is—or was?"

"According to this article, the ghost is your long lost relative's Grandfather, her great-great-great-great-great grandfather."

"How many "greats" did you say?"

"Five."

"What's the ol' boy's name?" Will asked, a smirk on his face.

"Franklin Percival Wills."

"A real live ghost, huh. And just how long has this real live ghost been dead?"

"Died in 1849."

"So, we have a real live ghost that's been dead for over a hundred and sixty years." Will grinned at his friend. "That, ol' buddy, is a contradiction in terms, doncha see? Cause if he's been dead for 160 years, how can he be a real live anything?" He chuckled at his own witticism.

The Ghost of Grandpa Wills

Staring straight ahead, Jake asked, "You keep your eyes pointed straight ahead, please, while I continue. If I may?"

"Pray, continue. O wise one." Will replied, still chuckling at his own joke.

"For someone who doesn't believe, you're sure getting' picky all of a sudden."

"If he, being the ghost, is related to her, being my supposed long lost relative, then he, being the ghost, must also be related to me. Cool. Never had a real live ghost in the family before." Will hesitated for a second before adding, "But—then I never had a real family either…"

As if to hide his true feelings, he gave a forced laugh and blurted out, "Hah, I know what we'll do; we'll exercise him. That'll get rid of him." Pleased with himself, he turned to Jake, flashed a wild grin and said, "We'll find someone, like in that movie, 'The Ghost Bashers' where they chased that big one up to the top of the Empire State Building, and he turned into the giant marshmallow man. He became the world's biggest toasted marshmallow."

Jake shook his head and sighed, "'Ghostbusters', Bruthur Willie, the movie was 'Ghostbusters', and you don't exercise ghosts; you exorcise them."

"That's okay, Cuzin' Jake. Nothin' to worry 'bout cause ther ain't no such thing anyway." He went back to singing, "Who's afraid of the big bad ghost, the big bad ghost, the big bad…"

Jake rolled his eyes upward as he responded, "Shut up, Willie. I'd rather hear the ghastly moans of your old family phantom than listen to what you pass off as singing."

"That twas a mighty cruel thing to say, Cuzin' Jake, mighty cruel."

Jake went back to his reading.

Will went back to his imagining:

Will Watson, owner, manager, CEO, and Chief Ghost Hunter of Ghost-Hunters International approached the house with calm determination. The haunting within the walls of this once fine residence was of a particularly malevolent type.

One person was known to be dead; the death certificate stated "Death by unknown causes." The police investigation has turned up nothing but the expression of sheer terror on the victim's face.

Ample evidence, Chief Ghost-hunter Watson decided that the victim had not died from 'natural causes'..."

Chapter Twenty-Two
Presidio County

"The county line is just ahead," Jake looked up from the map.

"I see mountains over there." Will offered.

"Mountains without snow, Willie. I keep telling you, snow-capped peaks in Texas are a figment of your overactive, and much fevered imagination."

"Does look like desert; I have to admit."

"You learn fast, littl' Bruthur, real fast," Jake replied. "I'm sorry to have to disappoint you about the snow, though."

About a quarter mile past the county line, they passed a large white Hummer sitting on the side of the road. Equipped with police emergency lights, it also bore the emblem of the Presidio County Sheriff's Department emblazoned on its door. The lights flashed on, the siren whooped, and the Hummer pulled out into the road behind them.

"I hope he's just here as an escort," Will said, looking doubtful. "I don't want another night in one of your discount motels." He pulled onto the side of the road and slowed to a stop. He watched in his new rear-view mirror as the Hummer's door opened and the "Law" exited the Hummer. "Oh, oh," he exclaimed. "It's the 'sweet little thing.'"

"Willie, what are you…?"

The "Law" was there, hat in hand, bending down to peer through the driver's window—where the glass had once been.

"William Wordsworth Watson?" she asked in a voice, low and mellow.

"Yes, ma'am," Will squeaked in a voice, high and nervous.

Jake said nothing; he sat staring straight ahead.

"I'm Sheriff Sara Red Wolf. Welcome to Presidio County." Her teeth shone white through her smile. The sparkle in her eyes belied the authoritative uniform she wore. Will wondered whether she might be enjoying his discomfort.

She stood up, took a step back, and studied the truck, turning her head as she did. "Well, it's every bit as bad as Ricky made it out it to be. Appears somebody's really got the devil in for you.

"Now, here's the plan," she continued, without waiting for a response, and returning to his window. "I will escort you from here to the Wills Ranch. I lead; you follow.

"Ricky sent you in by the back door—no straight way in from here. Lots of twists and turns. No cell phone towers—try not to get lost. Once we reach the ranch house, you'll take your things out, and, then, we'll take a closer look at the truck. We'll see if my big brother missed anything."

Now, she spoke with a tone that brokered no disagreement. Her size, together with the uniform and the

The Ghost of Grandpa Wills

weapon on her hip, just added to the aura of "Don't Mess With Me" that enveloped her.

Will recalled Jimmy's words as he had shown her photograph, *Sweet little thing*, the big guy said. *Wonder Woman in a sheriff's uniform* is what passed through his mind. This time, however, he kept his mouth shut.

Chapter Twenty-Three
Way, Way Out West

"Littl' Bruthur do you have your rememberin' cap on?" Jake asked. He was watching the scenery as it flew past—trees, cacti, flat-topped mesas in the distance, and craggy mountains with rocky faces further out. "'Cause we've made more twists and turns than a chef in a pretzel factory. Is there any way you could find our way back outa here?"

"No, sir, Cuzin Jake, I'm as lost as you. She's the sheriff, so I guess she knows where we're going."

The summer sun was nearing the end of the day's journey, almost touching the mountain peaks on their right when the sheriff's Hummer rolled to a stop. Will pulled up, got out, and went to meet her halfway. They met in front of a large, weathered rural mailbox with the words "Wills Ranch" printed on its side in large letters.

She looked down at him, hands on her hips, western hat on her head, black braids down her front, and a six-gun at her side. He looked up to see his own face staring back from the reflection in her sunglasses. He waited for her to speak.

"That's your turnoff to the main house." She said, pointing to a narrow gravel road that disappeared among a forest of mesquite trees off to his left. "Through that gate."

The 'gate' consisted of twin granite pillars surmounted by ornamental cast iron posts connected by a large banner, of the same material, arching high over the entranceway.

Looking up, Will read the words "WILLS RANCH" cut into the metal curving over the entranceway. A matching pair of formidable looking gates, each decorated with a large silhouette of the state of Texas, barred his entry. He eyed the edifice with awe and a sense of intimidation.

"The property starts right here, but it's about two miles to the house," she explained. "You'll cross Wills Creek—dry right now, though it carried water before the drought. You'll cross it just before you get to the Castle. And, be sure to close any gates behind you when you go through.

"They're expecting you. Miss Amelia's real excited about meeting you."

She leaned forward, and the sunglasses bore into the depths of his being. She lowered her voice to an authoritative tone. "All of us around here think she's something special, a real lady, so you be nice to her. You hear?"

She paused, staring him down as if daring him to do otherwise.

Will mumbled, "Sure. Ahh, yes, Ma'am."

"Now, I was intending to escort you in and say hello to Miss Amelia myself, but I got a call from dispatch. I'll be back out, hopefully, tomorrow. I still want to take a closer look at your truck." She stepped back, rose to her full height and put her hat back on. "Did all that damage come from what happened when whoever-it-was shot at you?"

"Yes, ma'am. There were a few scratches but no dents and certainly, no bullet holes."

"At least five shots. What's this steel plating on the outside of the door?"

He told her.

"That stuff probably saved your life, you know," she commented. "How many shots went through the window?"

"Three—I think."

"I'll be asking both you and Mr. Jacobson more questions when I return. I'm very curious as to why anyone would want to keep you from getting here."

The sunglasses bore down on him once more. "And I don't take kindly to trouble happening in my county—especially here, around Miss Amelia. She's the same as family—to all of us."

Keep you from getting here—the words caught Will by surprise. The idea that someone might want to prevent his arrival did not sit well in his mind, but he had never been shot at before either. He stared at her for a minute without replying.

She asked, "Do you have any ideas?"

"No, none at all."

"Well, think about it—sleep on it. I'll be back." With those words, she turned about and strode back to her truck. He watched her drive off, then returned to his pickup.

"Well?" Jake was turned, looking back through the rear glass as Will climbed inside.

"She wanted to know why someone would try to keep us from getting here."

"I keep asking myself the same question, Littl' Bruthur,

and I haven't come up with an answer—unless you're keeping secrets."

"Jake, I'm serious; I'm not hiding anything, and I don't know why anyone would be shooting at us." He put the truck in gear and rolled toward the turnoff. "This is the driveway. She said it's two miles from here to the house."

Activated by an unseen sensor, the gates swung open, then closed behind them.

Several yards past the gate, the drive split into two lanes and curved around another massive granite pillar. Will allowed the pickup to roll to a stop. He craned his neck to view the bronze beast glaring down from its pedestal. "That's some hunk of cow up there."

Jake sighed. "Littl' Bruthur, I keep a tellin' you that you best be learnin' some basics about ranchin'. They's a big difference 'tween cows, bulls, and steers. And you best learn about it or else keep your mouth shut, lest you'll be laughed all the way back to Dallas." He pointed with a finger. "You're a lookin' at a life-sized Texas longhorn steer."

Will grimaced at the mild reprimand. Still eyeing the creature, with its tail raised and head held high, he said, "Glad it's bronze and not real." Turning to Jake, he added, "Looks mean."

"Only when they're angry, Littl' Bruthur, only when they're angry."

Swinging around the monument, they followed the road as it twisted and turned amongst the trees and underbrush. Will negotiated the curves with care, expecting to meet a herd of longhorns around each bend in the road.

"Cuzin, do you think they ever have any mesquite-smoked barbeque around here? It looks like there might be a plentiful supply of firewood."

"My mouth's a watering just a thinkin' about the possibilities, Littl' Bruthur."

"This must be the creek she was talking about," Will slowed the pickup to a stop. "She said it used to have water in it."

"When? Last century sometime?" Jake asked. "It looks a bit dry. I guess they didn't get any rain from our little storm the other night."

Chapter Twenty-Four
Little House on the Prairie

Will started the truck moving again, and they drove around another dense thicket of trees. Passing into a clear area, he braked to a stop. They both sat staring for several moments without speaking.

Jake broke the silence, speaking in a quiet voice, "Not exactly the *Little House on the Prairie*, is it?"

The lowering sun, sinking behind them, cast long shadows from the trees. To their right, the darkness stretched across a lawn of trimmed, well-watered grass. In front, lay an expanse of crushed white gravel. Golden sunlight splashed across a wall of white limestone standing three stories high, punctuated by windows that reflected the sunset, the whole of which stood crested by crenelated battlements, resembling nothing less than a medieval fortress.

"Not exactly what I expected either." Will looked at Jake. "Is it a house or a castle? The Sheriff called it that you know; she called it 'The Castle.'"

"Probably the bunkhouse for the ranch hands," Jake responded. "No doubt we'll find the main house on down the road another mile or so." He pointed up toward the roofline, "Cast your eyes up that way, Littl' Bruthur."

Will bent his neck to look up through the windshield. A cold shiver crawled up his spine. He spoke in a subdued voice. "What are they?"

Perched along the battlements, sinister, dark shapes sat outlined against the fading sky. As Will watched, the sun moved from behind a cloud to bring them out of the shadow. "Are they real or are they carved statues?"

At that moment, the closest one spread its wings, flapped a few times and, to Will's horror, dove toward them before climbing high into the sky. Thereafter, the entire flock followed suit. In a moment, they were all gone.

The sun sank behind the distant mountain ridges, and they found themselves in the twilight.

"They're real, Bruthur Willie, very real. Buzzards is what they be. Now, do you possibly think you might've took a wrong turn somewhere back there?" Jake asked, his eyes still fixed on the roof line.

"Why? You know there weren't any turnoffs."

"We didn't accidentally end up at the Munster's old house did we?"

"Monster house?"

"Munster's," Jake corrected him. "The old TV show. Now don't tell me you never saw the reruns on cable TV."

"Yeah, I watched them with the kids a few times…"

"Now, if Herman Munster opens the door, don't be a

gettin' in my way. I may be leavin' real quick-like."

"I have the truck keys, so it'll be a long walk if you don't wait for me. But, I guess we best move closer, get out, and ring the doorbell."

The tires crunched as they rolled forward over the stones of the driveway before stopping just short of the flagstone paving. The white of the limestone faded to grey seconds before the twilight gloom was shattered by the glare of security lights.

Will hesitated before reaching for the door-handle. Although he would never have admitted it, butterflies were flitting around in his stomach. The possibility that he might be meeting family that he never knew existed was more than a little daunting. In addition, the spooky reception committee upon the battlements did nothing to bolster his courage.

Muttering under his breath, he opened the truck door and stepped down. "How could I be related to anyone who lived here?" The big wooden doors of the castle swung open, and two men stepped out.

"Looks like your lawyer friends," Jake commented.

"James and Jimmy."

"Someone will bring your luggage in shortly." Jimmy strode forward holding out his hand. "Come on inside."

They followed the lawyers into the main entranceway. Stepping over the threshold, Will came to a full stop, awed and speechless, for a few short moments. He remembered Tracie's explosive questions about it being some "hellhole with an outhouse somewhere out back."

His mind strained to take it all in from the now darkened skylight high above, down to the large curved "$\mathcal{W}$" that lay encircled in the middle of the polished red granite floor.

"That's the brand," Jimmy explained.

"Brand?" Will muttered.

"Yeah, like when you stick a red hot iron to a steer's rear-end, so's everyone'll know who it belongs to," James added in a sarcastic tone. "This is a cattle ranch, you know."

"So I've been told," Will responded in awe.

"Miss Amelia awaits you in the library." James led them toward another set of large double doors. He paused and turned to look straight at Will. He spoke in a quiet, authoritative tone. "Her illness has left her very weak, and she tires easily. Remember that." He opened the doors and motioned them inside.

Chapter Twenty-Five
I Pay for Results

Larue Larson paced the length of his office, yelling into the cell phone he held against his ear. Wild-eyed, he kicked out at pieces of furniture as he stormed past. Spittle flew from his lips as he vented his rage at the person on the other end of the call. So far, there were two overturned chairs, a side table, and a smashed table lamp scattered across his office floor. A portrait of his father hung askew, the glass splintered by a flying paperweight.

He bit off the words of his next sentence, one syllable at a time. "Fer-rell, you-failed-me. You-let-me-down! I-said-STOP-him!"

Storming over to the west side where the large sliding patio doors stood open, he ignored the multihued sunset and the evening breeze. Taking a deep breath, he collected himself and continued the conversation in the most scathing tone he could muster. "What part of 'Do-what-ever-it-takes' is too complicated for your feeble mind to understand?"

He listened for a few minutes before cutting the other party off. "Ferrell, I don't care how dead your friend is; his demise is of no concern to me. Your failure to do your job is what concerns me."

Pausing again, he chewed on his lower lip, listening for a few seconds before exploding again, in a hard, bitter tone. "Owe you money? I owe you nothing, Ferrell. I pay for results—not excuses."

He paused again, before responding in a cold voice. "Was that a threat, Mister Ferrell? No one threatens me, Ralph Ferrell—least of all you."

Screaming out a flurry of invective curses, Larue drew back his arm and threw. He watched the cell phone fly through the open doorway. It curved high in a graceful arc before plummeting to the street more than thirty floors below.

Chapter Twenty-Six
The First Meeting

Will held back, lagging behind Jake and the lawyers, and so he was the last one to pass through the doorway, a strange reluctance building up inside him. Doubt filled his mind—*This can't be happening, can't be true*. After a childhood of false assurances with hopes shattered, promises of families and homes never fulfilled—always dissolving, falling apart. Expectations built up, only to be destroyed, as he was shifted from one place to the next. *This cannot be real* kept echoing through his mind.

Bright light illuminated the cavernous room. Will cast his eyes around the many tables and desks, shelves upon shelves, books as well as photos and paintings—were everywhere. He observed it all—while seeing none of it.

She sat amidst stately grandeur, surrounded by

antiques—tables, lamps, and upholstered chairs. Wrapped in blankets, pale and shrunken, she leaned forward in an electric power chair.

"Miss Amelia," Jimmy said in a respectful manner.

"Mister Will Watson," James interrupted. "And, his associate, Mister Ralph Jacobson." With a flourish, he motioned to each in turn.

"Everyone calls me Jake, ma'am."

"Welcome to the Wills Ranch," she said with a gentle smile and extended a trembling hand.

Will remembered hearing about her cancer, but he never expected this—so shrunken and frail looking—he was looking at a pale, thin ghost of a woman. Inwardly, he shrunk away for he had never been near a seriously ill person. He found himself both horrified and saddened—at a loss for words. He had seen cancer portrayed in movies, but this was real; this was life.

Jake stepped forward and gently took the offered hand. "I'm very pleased to meet you, ma'am. I want to apologize for arriving unannounced and uninvited. It is my intention to find a motel in town. I don't want to inconvenience you."

"Nonsense, young man," she replied, speaking in a stern voice, in spite of her frail appearance. "You will do no such thing. I was told of your 'unexpected' arrival. There are more than a dozen available guest rooms in this old barn of a house, and one has already been made ready for you. Do you hear me?"

"The sheriff has impounded the pickup so you can't drive it until she releases it." Jimmy said.

"Besides, it's at least thirty miles to the nearest motel," James piped in.

Jimmy finished off with a smile on his face and a twinkle

in his eyes. "In these parts, no one ever says 'No' to Miss Amelia."

Jake smiled while bowing slightly at the waist, "I know when to surrender, ma'am."

A smile spread across her face. "It's nice to see we finally have someone around who has good manners." Her eyes fell on Will. "Now, if the rest of you don't mind, I have something private to discuss with Mr. Watson."

She looked around the room. "Please, if you will excuse us, I will call when we are ready to join you for supper. And, Jimmy, please see that someone takes their luggage up to their rooms—thank you."

She dismissed them with a wave of her thin hand.

Will stood silent and nervous, not knowing how to respond and wondering what he would say when she did speak to him.

As soon as they were alone, Amelia turned to him. "Please, pull one of those chairs up close and sit down." She coughed lightly, cleared her throat, and said, "My voice is not as strong as it once was; then, none of me is what it once was."

She looked up at him. Will felt as though he was being evaluated for something; he did not know what.

"I have a story to share with you—my story." She waved him to sit down.

Will grabbed the nearest chair, an antique made of dark wood, and pulled it closer.

She paused for a moment as if to gather her strength. "I was born here, in this house. My people have ranched this land for more than a century and a half. Many of my ancestors lie buried in the family graveyard not too far from here. I never married but…" Her eyes never wavered from his.

Will listened with mixed emotions, hope mixed with

doubts. He wondered how it all applied to him. Without warning, she paused and held up a piece of newspaper, protected within a sleeve of clear plastic. She placed it in his hands. "Read this—please."

He accepted the fragment and read the headline: **"Three Die in Flaming Car Wreck; Infant is Sole Survivor."**

A chill ran down his spine. He read the article, slowly and expectantly, knowing that somehow, this was important—to him, but he dared not think in what way.

He finished the article and turned his eyes back to Amelia. She continued with her story. "Jimmy and James found this, this scrap of newspaper, a few months ago in an old office safe. They were clearing out a building that once belonged to their grandfather."

She leaned back into her chair, casting her eyes about the room for a moment as if remembering—something. He sat watching, without moving.

"Their mother died when they were born, so they were adopted out. Later their father reclaimed them, took them back. They really are twins though some people refuse to believe it."

She brought her eyes back to him. "Anyway, they found that." She indicated the article. "It was stashed along with a bunch of other papers and old journals of their grandfather's." She reached out for the paper. He passed it over to her. Her fingers brushed his as she took it. Will saw moisture collecting in the corners of her eyes.

She held the article up and pointed to the photo. She spoke in a soft voice, but Will heard the emotion behind her words. "Mister Watson, that is my baby, my child, in the photo you see there. The very same baby that my father me told me was deformed—and stillborn."

The Ghost of Grandpa Wills

Her voice dropped lower. Will leaned closer to catch her words. She continued, almost in a whisper. "My own—my own father lied to me. My own father stole my baby away." Tears ran down her cheeks.

"Why," Will asked, astonished. "Why lie to you? And steal your baby?" Feelings rose inside him, an unfamiliar mix of emotions broiled within. Questions sprung to his mind: *What if? What if that happened to me? What if someone stole my child? My children? Or Tracie? What if?* Unanswerable questions. His family was safe. He forced his thoughts back to what she was saying.

"Why? You might well ask. You didn't know my father." Her voice rose again, with a sharp edge of bitterness in it. "He was proud, arrogant, and hard."

Anger shone within her dark eyes, fiery anger mixed with deep sorrow. "Hard to the very core of his heart." She twisted her frail hands together, her thin fingers interlacing, then unlacing, over and over again. "I wasn't married, you see, and, to add to the shame of it all, the baby's father, my lover—he was a full blood Apache. That meant my son—his grandson—was not only illegitimate but also, in his opinion—a lowly half-breed."

She straightened herself in the chair. "So, he stole him away. Secretly gave his own grandson away—to the young woman you see in that photo."

She paused for a minute to catch her breath, more tears running down her cheeks. She tried reaching for a nearby box of tissues. Will grabbed it and handed it to her.

"We had a funeral, you know. For my dead baby." Her voice was hoarse, cracking with emotion. "It was a private family affair, closed casket. Just father, mother, and me—no one else at all. Not even a preacher." She twisted the tissue into pieces. Will handed her another one. "Couldn't have anyone knowing about the shame I had brought down on the family—his family, his honor." She bit off the last part of her sentence, one word at a time.

Taking a deep breath, she recovered her poise and held the article up before him.

"After finding this, though, I had the grave opened."

With her eyes downcast, her feeling overwhelmed her, and her voice returned to a whisper. "Will, the casket was empty. Empty, I tell you—no bones, no body, no remains—just dry earth."

Will slid his chair closer to hear her next words. "My father, my own father—stood beside me and watched me weep over—over a casket—a casket full of dirt, my own father."

Tears streamed down her cheeks. "All these long years I have mourned over an empty grave. How many times have I taken flowers up there?" She pointed up in a vague direction. "How often have I tended it with my own hands—pulling the weeds with these very fingers—and wept—over—an empty grave?"

Wiping the tears away, she paused for a moment, took another deep breath, gathered herself, and sat up in the chair. "Will, take a very close look at that photo."

With a dry mouth and pounding heart, Will obeyed. She looked him straight in the eye. "Will, the baby in that photo is my son."

He held his breath, afraid to think what she might be about to say.

"Will, the baby in that picture is you. You are the baby stolen away from me so many years ago. You are my son."

Chapter Twenty-Seven
Discovery

Will sat speechless, stunned into silence. He realized he was holding his breath. As a youngster, he dreamed of someday hearing someone say those very words, "*You are my son.*" As an adult, he gave up thinking that such could ever happen. Now, that it was actually happening, it seemed as though it was a dream—one of his imaginary stories. It sounded wonderful but could not be real. He had wondered why she had summoned him, why she was willing to spend so much money—just on the chance that he might be a "long lost relative."

"You're my mother," he replied in a whisper, locking his eyes with hers. "I have a mother?" He turned his hands palm upwards, a gesture of supplication, fearing that it might turn out to be untrue, imaginary. "You're not dead? You're real?

You didn't just—just throw me away?" The words spilled out without thought; he regretted them as soon as they passed his lips.

She rolled her chair closer as she leaned forward. She pleaded through flowing tears. "Throw away my own child? Oh, no, no. Never." Her voice cracked with sobs. "They told me you were dead, my own parents. I told you there was a funeral…"

Lost in sorrow, she could say no more. After a pause to catch her breath, she held her arms out, "Please, I want to hold my son—please?"

Tears streamed down Will's cheeks as he fell forward on his knees, opened his arms, and collapsed into hers. "Momma," he sobbed. "I have a mother."

"I have a son. My son is real. My son is alive."

Their words intermingled, along with their tears.

They held each other for long minutes until Will released her and squatted back on his heels, still holding her hands. He looked at her and asked, "How do you know?" He shook his head slowly while studying her face. He wondered what she had looked like as a young woman. When she gave birth to him…before the cancer ravaged her body.

"What makes you think I'm your son?" He wanted to know, had to be sure. "I mean, we've never met before today. I'd never even heard of you before a week ago. How do you know, for certain, that the baby in the picture is me?"

"DNA," she answered. A smile broke across her face, and a new light sprang into her eyes. She relaxed back into her cushions with her hands still in his. "James and Jimmy did all the detective work. We compared your DNA with mine, and it was a perfect match, or almost perfect, but close enough to convince everyone. The sheriff'll be back here in the morning to take an official sample from you."

"Official?" Will asked, with a puzzled expression.

"I'll let Jimmy explain it," she whispered.

Will released her hands and stood up. "This is a lot to…I mean, this is…"

"This is…what?" she asked. "I hope you were going to say 'wonderful'."

"It is—I mean—yes, it's great, ma'am. I, I just, I just don't know what to say. I mean all my life I…"

She reached out and took one of his hands in both of hers, "You can begin by saying one word."

"One word?" he asked, puzzled. "Which? I mean, what?"

She smiled up at him, and still holding his hand, said, "Mother."

"What?"

"I am your mother—after all."

"Yes, I know, I mean, sure. Okay." He broke into a big smile and finally said it, "Mother."

She laughed; he laughed; they both laughed together. He knelt down, took her in his arms again and hugged her. "Mother," he said in a voice, both soft and tender.

"My son," she answered through flowing tears, "My son. My son."

They held each other for several minutes before he released her and stood up.

"Are you hungry?" she asked. "There's some supper waiting in the dining room. Later, when my new family is all together here, we'll have a big barbeque out back. I want to introduce my new found family to the whole world."

Will stood up. "Okay, yeah, ah, Mom, er, Mother."

In silence, she watched him for a minute. "Will, don't you think there is something else we should do first—before going to eat. I know you must be hungry, but…?"

He stopped, waited, and asked, "What?"

"The telephone is right over there," she replied, pointing.

Will frowned in confusion, "Telephone?"

"Isn't there someone you would like to tell before we announce it to the world?"

Standing with a blank expression on his face, he said nothing.

"Your wife, Will. Tracie's her name, I believe. Right? Shouldn't you tell her? Besides, I want to talk to my daughter-in-law—and my grandchildren as well."

With excitement building in her voice, "Will, I have two grandchildren I've never seen or even spoken to." Laughing aloud she declared, "After all these years, I'm not only a mother—I'm a grandmother and a mother-in-law. Now, you get yourself over there and call them this minute." She pointed. "And, remember, I want to talk to them all."

"Yes. ma'am, ah, Mother." He looked at his watch. "They'll be home now. Probably having supper. She's a teacher, you know."

"The phone's right over there." She pointed again, with urgency in her voice. It was a cordless model mounted in its charging cradle, sitting on an antique side table. She backed away across the room to give him some privacy, while giving one more order. "Tell her we'll fly them out here. It's too far for her to drive out here alone, with two children, besides it would take too long, and I—I don't have much time left."

Will grabbed the phone and punched in the numbers. Suddenly, he realized that he missed Tracie and the children. This was the first time they had been apart—for even a single night. Now, he wanted to hear her voice, but what would he say? He had given no thought to that. How he would break

The Ghost of Grandpa Wills

the news? It was all so new; he still did not know how to explain it to himself.

He heard it ring a few times before there was a click. Then he heard her voice. "Hello."

At first, he was tongue-tied, and then he blurted out, "Trace, hi—it's me, your sweet Will."

"Will," There was concern in her voice or was it anger? He could not be sure. "Where in the world have you been? Why haven't you called? We've been so worried. Why haven't you called?" She repeated herself, and this time, he heard her anger.

"Trace, cell phones don't work well out here in this part of Texas. And I just got here to the ranch, where there's a regular phone, And, Tracie, I've—I have a mother. I found my mother."

Words tumbled out of him, rapid-fire, spilling over one another. "Trace, I found my mother. I mean, actually, she found me. I have a mother. She thought I was dead, but I'm not. She was my long-lost relative, and, now, she's my mom. And, oh, she wants to talk to you and the kids. They have a grandmother. And you have a mother-in-law."

"I have a mother-in-law?" Tracie responded with doubt in her voice.

"She wants all of you to come out to meet her, as soon as possible."

"What? Now? Right away?" Her voice rose.

His voice dropped to a whisper. "Trace, please, she's sick and can't take long trips."

"It's a long way to drive—just me and the kids."

"By air, Trace. You're not driving any further than the airport. Mom—my mother—she's going to fly all of you out here; so get your bags packed."

"Will, there's the small matter of a little item which you seem to have overlooked; the kids are still in school—and my job. One of us has to worry about paying the…"

"She's waiting to talk to you right now. Her name's Amelia. I'm giving the phone to her now. Everything's going to be all right. So talk to her, and call the kids."

"Will..." He never heard her final words.

He walked over and placed the handset in his mother's hand. As she took it, he saw the smile on her face, but the tears remained.

Tears of joy? Maybe? He wondered.

Amelia put the phone to her ear. Will turned and gave his attention back to the room. Amelia's revelation had held his attention. Now, he could study the room and its contents.

But his mind still whirled—

A mother.

The ranch.

This house.

Getting shot at.

He walked around, wandering slowly amongst the bookcases, moving away from where Amelia sat near the empty fireplace.

His mind spun, filled with the new revelations. He ran his fingers along the spines of the volumes stored there, seeing them—but not seeing them. "Books," he whispered to himself. "Shelves and more shelves, floor to ceiling. Never seen so many before, except in a library. Awesome."

Many of the books were old—very old; some were new. Absent-mindedly, Will scanned the titles and subjects—Texas, West Texas, Indians, Apaches, the Comanche, lost treasure, Texas History...

His wanderings took him along the west wall—opposite

from where his mother sat, still talking on the phone. In the northwest corner, he came upon the life-sized portrait of an old-fashioned cowboy. A lamp mounted above the frame threw a beam of light down on it.

The oil painting held Will's attention. It looked old, but he was no expert so could not be sure. The man portrayed was an old cowboy, or, perhaps, a prospector. Everything about him was timeworn, grimy, dirty, tattered, and threadbare. A hat, battered and sweat stained, sat lopsided on his head; a shirt, leather vest, trousers, and boots that looked as if they had walked all over West Texas, made up the remainder of his attire.

The cowboy's face and hands were rough, work worn, weather-beaten, wrinkled, and scarred. However, it was the eyes that captivated Will. Looking straight at him, they caught him and held him. He felt as though the old cowboy was about to step out of the frame and speak to him. In addition, the man held a gun in his right hand, pointed straight ahead. Will had the uncomfortable feeling that the weapon was aimed straight at him.

For reasons he could not explain, Will reached out to caress the painting. He felt the ridges and valleys left in the oils as the artist had moved his brush across the canvas. He started to touch the face but held back. Again, it was the eyes—they stopped him. He stood there with his hand outstretched, less than an inch from the sun burnt, weather-beaten face.

The right eye winked at him. With an exclamation, Will stumbled back a step. He could not believe what he had just witnessed.

"He's your ancestor," Amelia said from behind him. Will jumped again. He had not heard the quiet hum of her power chair. "He's your great-great-great-great-great-great-grandfather to be exact. His name was Franklin Percival Wills. And, that portrait was painted by your great-great-grandfather.

"Murdered in 1849, by Apaches it has been claimed. His body was never found. However, that's another story—for another time."

She paused for a moment, and then, thrusting the phone at him, continued, "Your wife, Tracie, sounds like a very lovely person. I'm anxious to meet her. For now, though, let's see what Singh has waiting for us in the dining room. I'm hungry."

Supper was a quiet affair, attended only by Amelia and Maria, Will and Jake, and served by the Singh brothers and wives. His mother threw dozens of questions to both of them, always including Jake in the conversation. It was very apparent that she already knew a lot about both of them—James and Jimmy had been quite thorough in their investigations, but she asked anyway.

The food kept pace with the questions, arriving in a never-ending supply. The expected simple supper turned into a feast, lasting well into the evening. Will found himself putting away more chili than he had ever dreamed possible, accompanied by copious amounts of homemade bread and many large glasses of iced tea. All of which had been followed by liberal amounts of apple pie and ice cream. Everything was homemade.

Chapter Twenty-Eight
Straight Through the Heart

Amelia said her "Good nights" and asked Maria to take her up to bed. Will and Jake said goodnight. The Singhs cleared the table.

Will followed Jake up the northernmost of the staircases. With fatigue and his gluttony overtaking him, he stumbled forward, clutching onto the carved rails for support. Following Jake's directions, he found his bedroom.

Opening the massive door, it occurred to him that this was his first visit, and he had no idea where anything was. Reaching the end of the short entranceway, he halted to survey the room. As with every other part of the house he had seen, this room was large, high ceilinged, and furnished with antiques.

Close to his right sat an enormous dresser, made of

polished wood decorated with an intricate carved design. He estimated it to be six feet wide and almost waist high. Above it, mounted on engraved wooden supporting posts, hung an antique mirror as wide as the dresser, and framed with a matching pattern.

Across from the dresser sat an old-fashioned four-poster bed, with its headboard against the far wall. Constructed of thick, well-polished solid wood planks, its carved designs matched the dresser.

He also saw an overstuffed chair, a large rocking chair, and side tables with lamps on either side of the bed. In addition, a number of tanned cowhides lay stretched out on the floor, or maybe they were steer hides; he could not tell which and, at this moment, did not care. The chili and jalapeños were already fighting with him.

A groan escaped from his lips when he saw his luggage lying, unopened, on the bed. He would deal with that problem in a few minutes. At this moment, another issue demanded his urgent attention. Seeing a door off to his right, he rushed over and yanked it open. It was just what he needed. He hurried in, closing it behind him.

Will emerged several minutes later, knowing that the battle was not over; the jalapeños would surely make their presence felt again before morning—probably well before sunrise.

Just to the left of the dresser he spied another door. He opened it. A deep cold engulfed him, chilling him to the marrow of his bones. He felt as if he were freezing from the inside out; the hairs on his arms and the back of his neck stood up. He shivered and backed away from the closet. The cold disappeared. He glanced up to look for the air conditioning vent and saw one in the ceiling, almost directly overhead.

The Ghost of Grandpa Wills

Shrugging his shoulders, he pushed the matter from his mind and stepped inside. The walk-in closet was empty, but for several wire coat hangers.

He returned to his suitcase, and unpacked his things, stuffing most of them into the drawers of the old dresser. He took the time to hang some items in the closet. Finished, he picked up the empty suitcase and carried it into the closet.

There was a shelf up above the clothes rod. Rather than get a chair to stand on, he simply lifted the suitcase over his head and gave it a toss. There was a loud thump as the suitcase hit something and bounced back, off his head, and down to the floor.

Muttering under his breath, Will kicked the suitcase out of his way, looked around the room, and spied a wooden chair that looked as though it might support his weight. Bringing it into the closet, he placed it on the floor, and climbed up. On the dust-covered shelf, he discovered a cloth wrapped object lying against the wall. His curiosity piqued; he grabbed it and found it to be heavy and solid beneath the covering.

Jumping down, he carried it to the far side of the bed next to one of the lamps. Within the cloth, he found an ornate wooden box. Releasing the simple latch, he opened it and discovered a handgun—a nickel-plated revolver.

Will had never owned a gun. He held one—once—when he was ten years old, having found it hidden away much as he found this one. He had been caught by its owner, his foster father. His reward for being curious was several harsh cuffs on his head. Afterward, he had spent the night locked inside a closet—with neither light nor supper. He had not touched a real gun since; only daydreamed about imaginary heroes who used them. But always in the right way and always for the right reason.

Lifting the weapon from the box, he felt the cold, smooth steel in his hands and admired the intricate, but worn, engravings that covered the weapon. He raised it up and sighted down the barrel as though aiming at something—or someone. He squeezed the trigger, but nothing happened; it refused to move. Remembering a scene from an old movie, he thumbed back the hammer until he heard, and felt, it click into firing position. Raising the gun, he took aim at a photograph high up on the wall. Suddenly, the terrible cold returned. He shivered but chose to ignore it.

"Has the cowboy found himself a new toy?" A strange voice spoke from behind him, the words carried a cold, hollow tone. Shivers danced up and down Will's spine. Hairs on his neck and arms came erect. Goose bumps traveled over his body. A terrible sense of fear flooded over him. He froze, unable to move a muscle.

"You best be careful, son, lest you hurt someone with that thing. It might even be loaded."

A rush of adrenalin brought life back into his limbs. Rising to his feet, Will turned toward the voice, the cocked gun still in his outstretched hand. He stared, dumbfounded, at a very strange looking man. Like so many things in this museum of a house, this man looked like something that belonged to times long past. At that point, with a shudder, Will remembered the oil painting down in the library.

The person now standing in front of him, gripping a handgun—exactly as in the painting—was an exact reproduction of that image. Except, the man in the painting was dead and had been for a very long time.

"You know how to use that toy, cowboy?" A hollow, disturbing laughter erupted from the unknown visitor. "Are you man enough to do it?" The stranger seemed to be delivering a fearful challenge as he shifted his gun and pointed it at Will's chest.

Several things raced through Will's mind—rattlesnakes in his truck, gunshots on the highway, and a mysterious SUV attempting to run them off the road. Now, this bizarre looking stranger stood there with a gun aimed at his heart.

In a panic, Will stumbled, caught his boot heel on the edge of one of the steer hides and fell sideways against the bed, catching himself before going all the way to the floor. As he fought to stay upright, the noise of a gunshot exploded in the room with a deafening roar that left his ears ringing. The weapon kicked in his hand. The antique mirror behind the stranger shattered into slivers and shards that clattered, crashed, and tinkled onto the dresser top and down to the floor. The room filled with smoke. The acrid smell of gunpowder stung his nose. He relaxed his fingers and dropped the gun.

Will knew he had been shot—must have been. The stranger could not have missed at this distance. But—why did it not hurt? He should be feeling pain somewhere—or everywhere. What did it feel like to be shot, to have a lead slug tear into the flesh of your body? Moreover, why was he not down on the floor? People always fell when they were shot; at least, that was how it always happened in the movies.

The stranger uttered a loud moan. Will looked up and saw him standing with his hands clasped over his heart.

"Shot me, Cowboy," the stranger moaned. He swayed as he spoke. "You shot me real good, right through the heart." He moaned again, a horrible, gurgling noise.

The moans ceased and the man's tone of voice hardened. "At least, if I had a heart you would have shot me right through it." A strange light came into his eyes. An evil smirk creased his face. "You certainly would have killed me dead—leastways if I were not already dead." He erupted with a huge bellowing laugh that exploded from deep down inside him. "You shot your own Grandfather; that you surely did, Grandson!"

Will stared, not understanding, not knowing how to respond. *If I shot him, why isn't he dead? Why didn't he fall down?*

"I am already dead, Grandson." Those words sent icy chills running through Will. "And, I have been dead for more than a hundred and sixty years." The dead man guffawed again and his appearance altered—changing from a dusty, dirty old cowboy into a rotting corpse. The air filled with the foul stench of death.

Will stood, once again frozen and speechless, eyes wide and mouth gaping until his knees gave way. He crashed to the floor, overwhelmed by darkness.

The Devil's Mouth

Part Two

Bill Tyson

Chapter One
Gunshot in the Night

The door crashed open, thrown against the wall. Jake rushed in, shouting. "Willie, Littl' Bruthur, where are you?"

Seeing his friend face down on the floor, between the bed and the wall, Jake charged over, crying out in fear. "Oh, dear God in heaven. Littl' Bruthur, what have you done to yourself this time?"

Recognizing the sound of a gunshot, Jake wasted neither time nor effort in getting to his friend's room. The odor of gun smoke told him a story he did not want to hear. Seeing his best friend prone on the floor filled him with a horror he had not felt since the aftermath of a deadly car wreck years before.

Jake's Navy Corpsman training came into instant play as he lowered his bulk next to Will's inert body. *No blood. No visible sign of a wound.* Placing his fingers on Will's neck, he checked for a pulse. Feeling the rhythm of life beating strong, he uttered a quick prayer of relief. "Yeah, he's alive. Thank you, Lord."

"Okay, Littl' Bruthur, let's roll you over so's we can see what's on your front side." Jake stretched him out, face up. "No blood," he muttered again. "No wounds, no nothin'. So why're you out like a light?"

The sounds of frantic shouting and running feet grabbed Jake's his attention. He looked up as Maria rushed in. "What?" she cried, out of breath. "What's happened? That was a gunshot, wasn't it? And what's that awful smell? Like something's dead."

She hurried over, squeezed herself in, and knelt next to Will, opposite Jake. "Oh, no, is he dead? Is he…"

"Not dead," Jake interjected quickly as he made room for her. "He's breathing with a strong, regular pulse. No blood anywhere; no sign of a wound of any kind."

"Let me see," she demanded. "I'm a nurse." She attempted to push Jake away

Jake held up his hand to block her. "Ma'am, I was a Navy corpsman, and I've seen more gunshot wounds than you can imagine. There are no wounds or injuries that I can find anywhere on his body."

"Then, why is he unconscious?"

"Can't be sure," Jake replied, making an effort to sound gentler. "But I think he's fainted." Turning back to his unconscious friend, with a single quick movement, Jake slapped him across the face. "Wake up, Willie Boy! Wake up, and tell us what happened."

Will's eyes popped open just as another voice came from the hallway. Amelia rolled her power chair through the doorway, wheels crunching over the broken shards. "Why is

The Ghost of Grandpa Wills

there glass all over the floor? Oh my, what happened to my mirror? Why did you shoot my mirror? That was my great-great-grandmother's antique mirror."

She cast her eyes around the room. "Where is Will? Where is my son? What has happened? Is he okay? Who's been shot?" The questions poured out of her, rapid fire, tumbling over one another. "Oh, my, what is that dreadful odor?" She glanced about the room, wrinkling her thin nose. Finding nothing, she turned her attention back to Jake and Maria.

"My son, where are you? Oh, don't tell me you've gone and shot yourself?"

Will blinked and squinted, trying to get his eyes into focus. He sneezed.

"Bless you," Amelia blurted out. "Is that you, Will? Speak to me. Tell me you're alive."

Looking down, she saw his legs extending from between Jake and Maria. "Oh my, Will—my son! Speak to me! Are you hurt bad?"

Her new found son opened his eyes wide with a look of fright and asked, "Where is he? What happened? I didn't mean to shoot him. He had a gun."

Jake and Amelia spoke together, their questions piling on top of one another.

"Who are you talking about? Who was here?" Amelia asked.

"Who had a gun?" Jake questioned. "Is this the gun? The one you were lying on."

"Who'd you shoot?" Amelia shouted.

"No one here but you. Who are you talking about?" Jake continued.

"We thought you'd shot yourself. Where did you get that

old gun?" Amelia demanded. "It's been lost for ages. Where'd you find it?"

Jake, still kneeling, turned and grabbed the weapon. Holding it in one hand, barrel pointing up, he pulled the hammer back to half-cock and thumbed open the loading gate. He rotated the cylinder, one chamber at a time, allowing each of the cartridges to fall onto the bed. He counted five plus one spent shell casing. Sniffing the barrel, he looked up and announced, "It's been fired."

Pushing himself up with one hand on the bed, Jake rose to his feet, grunting as he did so. "Littl' Bruthur, I don't get down on my knees for just anybody; you owe me for this—big time."

Once up, he extended a hand down to Will, who grabbed it and allowed himself to be pulled to his feet. Amelia reached for him with open arms.

"I, I, I'm all right, M-M-Mother; at least, I, I think I am," Will stammered as he moved out from the narrow confines.

Amelia asked through tears. "What have you done, my son? You might have been killed. And where did you get that gun?" She glanced over to where Jake had dropped it. "That looks like your great-great-grandfather's old six-shooter. It was a Colt, single action just like that. It disappeared years ago. Where did you find it? How did you get it?"

"In a box, a wooden box, wrapped in an old cloth, on the shelf up in that closet," Will pointed to indicate the old dresser as he moved to sit on the edge of the bed. His eyes carried a wild look as he spoke. "He was standing right there. I was looking at the gun when he showed up. And, he had a gun in…in his hand. Then, I tripped on this old hide. And—and the gun just went off."

"Which one?" Jake asked.

The Ghost of Grandpa Wills

"One what?"

"Which gun went off?" Jake restated his question.

"My gun—that gun."

Will pointed to the weapon. "It went off. Then he, the man—he moaned. He started laughing and talking. He said I shot him—shot him through the heart, shot him dead."

Will looked around the room. Embarrassed, he dropped his voice lower and stared at the cowhide beneath his feet, wishing he could crawl under it. "I know it sounds stupid and crazy, but he said he was already dead—been dead for a long time."

Looking up at his mother, he held his arms close to his body, with arms bent at the elbow, hands extended, fingers wide and palms up, and exclaimed with a tone of desperation, "He started changing. His skin looked like it was melting off him. His bones were showing—like in some kind of horror movie. Then, I felt dizzy."

With a painful expression, Will shrugged his shoulders. "I think I fell down; I don't know."

With a sigh of resignation, head down, and shoulders slumped, Will ended with, "I just remember waking up here on the floor—all of you looking at me and all that."

"What did he look like?" Amelia demanded, her eyes locking onto her son. "Describe him, Will, I want to know what he looked like."

"It was awful. Like I said, it was just like some horror movie. With his…"

"No, no, no." Amelia broke in, leaning forward in her chair, "When you first saw him; before you shot him."

Maria looked over at Amelia with a look of surprise on her face. "Miss Amelia, please, you're overwrought and tired. Surely, you don't believe he actually saw…"

Amelia turned with a stern look at the younger woman, "Maria, you're a very smart young girl and an excellent nurse, but do not stand there and try to tell me what I believe and don't believe. There are plenty of things in this world that doctors and scientists cannot explain."

Maria obeyed.

Jake opened his mouth but decided that silence might be a better idea.

Amelia turned back to her son, speaking with authority in her voice. "Now—young man, you tell me exactly what he looked like before—before his skin began melting."

All eyes turned toward Will.

Outside in the hallway, a crescendo of voices and questions echoed through the doorway as others arrived and clamored for answers. The room filled with newcomers jostling for position. Will saw what he guessed to be the entire Singh family—from the youngest toddler to several gray-haired elders.

"Quiet!" Amelia ordered. "No one has been shot." She raised a hand and demanded, "Now, be quiet so I can hear!" She added in a tone that allowed for no discussion, "And don't anyone dare call the sheriff."

Turning back to Will, "Now, talk to me, my son."

"He..." Will hesitated, taking a deep breath. "I know you'll all think I'm crazy, but he looked just like that, that picture—the big painting down in the library. The one you said was my great-great-grandpa. He looked just like him."

"Your great-great-great-great-great-great Grand-father," she corrected him. "And that's who it was. That's one of his favorite little tricks."

"Great-great—did you say five or six 'greats'?" Jake finally spoke up. "How old is he?"

The Ghost of Grandpa Wills

"He was born, as best we can figure, in Boston back in 1798 or 99."

"What? That's impossible; no one's that old," Jake shot back.

"GHOST!" came Singh Hai's high-pitched voice from the opposite side of the bed. "I see him some time, many time. Like old time cowboy. Vely fliendly, no hurt nobody. Want to play joke, alla time play joke."

"I don't believe in ghosts," Will muttered.

"You once said you never met a ghost you didn't like," Jake replied.

"I never met a ghost, period—whether I liked him or not. They don't exist. Once you're dead, you're dead. Dead all over, just like dear old Rover. Therefore-

"We'll talk about it down stairs, in the library," Amelia interrupted.

She turned back to the crowd filling the room and issued more orders. "Everyone back to bed—except Will and Jake. You two accompany me down to the library—ASAP! Singh Hai—bring some coffee for them, hot chocolate for me."

She turned to the other Singh brother. "Loh, please, get all this glass cleaned up before someone gets cut on it." She gestured around the room.

"Now, everybody, move along. There's work to be done in the morning."

She studied the carved wooden frame that now held broken shards of antique glass. Sighing, she commented, "Such a lovely old mirror it was—once belonged to my great-great-grandmother, you know."

Looking at her new found son, she added, with a rueful smile, "You know, broken mirrors can be replaced, people can't."

Whirling her chair about, she issued another command. "Son, since you helped cause all this ruckus, you will escort me to the elevator and down into the library. Mind you, though, it really wasn't all your fault." Rolling toward the open doorway, wheels crunching on the shards of broken mirror, she added in a very firm voice, "I have a thing or two I want to say to that Grandfather of ours."

Chapter Two
Just His Sense of Humor.

"Thank you for coming along, Mr. Jacobson." She piloted her chair to the place near where Will had first met her and turned to face them.

"Some lights are kept on here at all times," Amelia commented, as Will and Jake followed close behind her. She added in a casual tone, "He is afraid of the dark, you know."

Jake's eyes opened wide in question, and he started to speak, but Amelia ignored him.

"Singh will be here shortly with the coffee and hot chocolate.

"Now, both of you find a seat and make yourselves comfortable." She gestured to some nearby chairs. Jake and Will did as ordered, moving two nearer to her.

"Now, Will, your, or rather 'our' grandfather has always

had a mischievous sense of humor, even when he was alive, I believe. He enjoys his little 'jokes' even when other folks don't." There was a stern look on her face, and she pointed her finger to emphasize her point. "What he did to you is just what he's done to others before, except that his other victims never had a loaded gun in their hands."

Her expression clouded over, and she shook her head.

"What's more, if I could take a buggy whip to his backside, I would. You know, we still have several old ones, antiques they are, out in one of the barns." She smiled. "However, you can't whip a ghost." A frown creased her forehead, "But I can unplug his computer; and I will!"

At that statement, Will glanced at Jake, with a puzzled expression. His friend sat staring at Amelia, his mouth partly open.

"His computer?" Jake asked. "A ghost with his own computer," disbelief in his voice. "And, you said, he's afraid of the dark?"

"Yes, he's learned to control computers—and his flat screen TV, as well," she said, in a matter-of-fact manner, as if everyone was supposed to know about a ghost that possessed a computer and a flat screen television. "These new 'smart' ones. He can't push buttons and such, but he can go inside someway and work the electronics, although he sometimes breaks them. I've had to ban him from all but his own because he's always messing them up so."

A light knock on the library door interrupted them.

"Come in, Singh," Amelia called out.

The cook entered, pushing a wheeled cart, laden with mugs and two insulated containers along with bowls of cream and sugar.

"Thank you, Singh. You may go now. Get some sleep.

Okay?" Amelia told him.

Singh stood, bowing and frowning. Coming fully erect, he spoke forcefully, "Ghost make bad joke this time." Anger was written on his face. "Mirror break. Very bad luck many years this house. Now, big hole in wall big time."

Jake tried to hold back a smile. Again, he was seeing humor where others did not.

Will scowled, not knowing what to think and feeling more than a little, the fool. "I'm sorry..."

Amelia waved him down.

She frowned at the cook and repeated her order, "Thank you, Singh, you may go, now."

She waited until she heard the soft click as the door closed. Sitting back against her cushions, she asked, "Would one of you mind pouring me a big mug of that chocolate, please? And, help yourselves to whichever you want. I'm sure there's more than enough. Singh never stints on anything he prepares."

While Jake served the hot cocoa and coffee, Amelia turned toward the far corner where the oil painting hung. She called out in a commanding voice, "Franklin Percival Wills! I know you're there!"

Leaning forward, she demanded, "Franklin, come out here right this minute, and show yourself so everyone can see you!" She put a strong emphasis on the word "everyone."

Both Will and Jake sat back in their chairs with surprise on their faces.

Amelia's voice deepened, adding an icy tone, "I am not in the mood for your childish games!"

Seconds passed before a chill filled the air around them. Both of the men shivered.

"Franklin," Amelia declared again. "I said, this is not the

time for your silly games. Get out here, now! Show yourself to all of us."

The chill dissipated, and a fog appeared next to Amelia. The mist slowly coalesced. A man appeared, standing upright, floating inches above the floor.

Chills crawled up Will's spine as he recognized the figure in the oil painting, the old cowboy who had faced him in his bedroom, the man he had shot—through the heart. The man who had been dead since 1849. The ghost he did not believe in. The ghost that did not exist. But—here it, or he, or whatever it was, now stood in front of him. And his mother was talking to it.

Will glanced over at Jake, who sat wide-eyed and open-mouthed, not moving.

"What do you see, Cuzin?"

"I, I think I might be seeing a real, a real live ghost," Jake whispered.

The ghost grinned, chuckled slightly, and started to speak, "Son..."

Will was angry, as angry as he had ever been in his life. Rising halfway from his seat, he cut the ghost off short. "You think it's funny, don't you?" His voice rose in pitch and volume as he shook his fist, then pointed a finger at the apparition. "You scared me half-to-death, caused me to shoot out the mirror—a shot that could've gone anywhere and even killed someone!"

He rose to his full height and stepped forward. "My family's coming out here; you going to scare them, too? My kids'll have nightmares for the rest of their lives! Anger was in his voice and fire in his eyes."

Glaring at the ghost and gesturing wildly, Will added, "What do you do in your spare time? Run off to the hospital and scare the newborn babies?" Suddenly aware of the others, he retreated back into to his seat.

The ghost faded, his image flickering. For an instant, Will saw the antique lamp shining through him.

"Don't you dare disappear on me, Franklin," Amelia ordered.

The ghost turned slowly, revolving in midair until he faced her, "I shall not be leaving just yet, Amelia, dear." With a slight smile on his face, he pivoted to look straight at Will, "The boy does have some pepper in his belly, does he not?" Turning back to Amelia, he grinned, "No one but you, Amelia, ever stood up to me like that, not in the last hundred years or so."

Facing Will again, the ghost declared, with a dark frown on his face. "Just know this, young bucko. I am not one who scares children, nor do I hurt babies." After a moment's pause, he added, "Nor women folk either for that matter." With a scowling glare, aimed straight at his grandson, he disappeared.

Both Will and Jake gasped aloud and shivered.

"What was that?" Jake asked. "Felt as if I'd been hit by a bucket of ice water—from the inside out."

"Another one of his little tricks," Amelia replied with a grimace. "When he gets too close, or even worse, when he passes through someone, he seems to suck all the warmth out of a person's insides, starting with your bones." She sighed, shrugged, and raised her hands, palms up. "He's really angry right now; doesn't like getting dressed down, but he'll get over it, always does."

She went on with a rueful expression. "He actually likes people, hates being alone. It seems that being a ghost is a very lonely business."

"He has an odd way of showing it," Will remarked, anger putting an edge in his voice.

"Even so, this house is his home. He never leaves the premises. I don't think he can. "Most of the ranch hands won't set foot inside, any further than the dining room."

"May I ask, ma'am?" Jake spoke up. "This is all new to me. I've never seen a ghost before; never wanted to see one, much less talk to it. What's his story? Is he really your grandfather? And Will's as well?"

"Pour me another cup of that cocoa, please, if you would. Have another yourself—coffee if you prefer. Drink some of it, at least." She continued with a wry smile. "The Singhs—all of them—get their noses out of joint when they think we don't appreciate what they prepare."

She relaxed back into her chair. "Now, allow me to tell you a little about how the Ghost of Grandpa Wills came to be."

She accepted a fresh mug from Jake and took a sip.

"Franklin Percival Wills—he does not like the name Percival, not at all—was born in the year 1798 or 99, as I said. Think about that for a minute; 1799 is the year George Washington died. John Adams was President of the United States.

"Born and raised in Virginia, he was in Washington when the British burned it in 1814. He later studied medicine and attended a seminary to become an ordained minister. And he…"

"You're saying," Jake interrupted, "he was alive during the War of 1812?"

"Yes," she answered, with a slight smile and a nod, "A veteran, no less. A medical doctor and a 'Reverend', as well. But he prefers being called simply Franklin or Grandfather."

The Ghost of Grandpa Wills

"How did he end up all the way out here?" Will asked, leaning forward. "This must have been way out in the middle of nowhere, back then." He gestured.

"Worse than that, it was beyond nowhere. Dry wilderness mostly. No cattle, not even any mesquite..."

"No mesquite?" Jake interjected.

"None," Amelia answered. "They came later, with the cattle driven up from Mexico."

She paused to take a breath. "Anyway, to continue, Franklin left his family back east; they had money, so they were well taken care of otherwise. I think he inherited a good bit from his father. An only child, I believe. But, he's never talked about that much. I don't think they—he and his father—got along very well."

Amelia shifted in her chair, took another sip of the hot drink, and continued. "Anyway, he came out here while Texas was a Republic—but before we became a state. No towns, just Indians all around. Comanche and Apache, usually fighting each other. Of course, neither of them liked outsiders very much either."

"Why did he leave his family?" Will asked, eyebrows raised in open curiosity.

"He won't talk about that. Adventure, rumors of gold, family trouble of some sort? I don't know for sure, but I do know he regrets it and wishes he hadn't. He's told me that much, in a roundabout way, more than once."

Holding the mug in her lap, she continued. "He and a friend came out here together. Somewhere along the way, they heard about some lost Spanish gold. Years before, the Spaniards passed through here, fought the Indians, found gold—or stole it. Then, they lost it when they were attacked in return."

She motioned with a wave of one hand. "There's supposed to a cache or two hidden somewhere on the ranch, up in the hills, or on one of the mesas. There are hundreds of caves all over, some large, some small. If the stories are true, the treasure could be anywhere."

She pointed in the direction of the bookshelves. "Some of those volumes hold tales of lost mines—some ancient, some not so ancient. Franklin has talked about some priests—friars or some such. I'm not familiar with all the Catholic stuff, but he claims a couple of them came through here while he was still alive.

"One was old and crippled, the other was younger, but they told about some kind of buried treasure. Called it a 'treasure beyond price', if I remember right. Seems, they thought it was somewhere up in what we now call Flatrock Canyon.

"Anyway, they never found it; the old priest took sick and died. The young one disappeared—probably, killed by Indians; least, that's what Franklin thinks. He may have got lost and died in the desert. A lot of folks have, down through the years.

"Anyway, for whatever reason, Franklin left his family, his patients, and his pulpit. Out here he found wilderness, mountains, dry desert, thousands of square miles of open range—and Indians."

"Did Franklin ever find any of the gold?" Will asked.

"Don't know if he did or didn't," she answered.

"Why?" Jake broke his silence. "Won't he talk about it?"

"Well, he says he found some gold, found something, but he can't remember what it was or where it was. We do know from some letters that he wrote his wife, Patricia; he found something. We don't know what. Many of the letters and papers are lost."

Pausing to take another drink of the chocolate, she smiled and added, "I haven't reminisced like this for a very long time."

She placed the mug on the side table. "Anyway, when Patricia arrived here in 1849, along with their two children and a couple of her brothers and their families, they brought cattle, horses, and such, along with enough money to establish what became this ranch. He had already made claim to the land before they arrived."

"What happened to Grandpa?" Will asked.

"We don't know exactly," Amelia replied.

"Won't he tell anyone?"

"Says he can't remember."

"A ghost with a bad memory," Jake mused.

Amelia nodded in response.

"Here's what we do know—what he can remember," she continued with a solemn look. "Soon after he and his friend arrived in the area, they came across a young Indian boy. One of the local Apaches—a child it seems. He was all alone in the desert and dying from snakebite. A rattler had got to him somehow. Franklin's partner wanted to leave the child to die, or kill him outright. Seems he hated Indians." She grimaced as she said the words.

"To make a long story, short—Franklin kept the child, nursed him back to health, and then, returned him to his father, who was some type of chief. The man was very grateful and offered his friendship. Eventually, they went through some type of sacred ceremony to become blood brothers.

"In fact, the chief was so grateful that he granted Franklin full use of the land that constitutes most of what makes up this ranch..."

Will's mouth opened in a wide yawn that he attempted to cover with his hand.

Amelia stopped in mid-sentence.

"Sorry, Mother," he mumbled. "It's been a long day. Gunfights with a ghost and all that, you know. My eyelids don't want to stay open any longer."

"You're right," she replied. "How rude of me to keep talking like this. Time for bed. You certainly had an interesting time coming out here. Rattlesnakes and gunshots all in one trip."

"The night in jail wasn't too much fun either," Jake added.

"Jail," Amelia's eyebrows went up. "What were you…"

"Fleeing from bad guys with big guns," Will rushed to explain. "A certain deputy sheriff didn't like the way us 'big city boys' came into her town, so we were given a night's free lodging—courtesy of the county."

Jake added, "Ricky, the sheriff, took care of things the next morning. Everything's all right now."

"Ricky—Sheriff Richard Red Wolf—our sheriff's brother, Sara's brother. He's the one made you spend the night in jail?" Amelia sat forward, raising her voice in consternation.

"Yes, ma'am. And, to make it even better, he's an old shipmate of mine, we served in the Navy together." Jake's face broke with a big grin. "To be truthful, though, it was his deputy that put us in the brig, not him."

"I'll certainly have a word with him in the morning, anyway. Locking my son up as if he were a common criminal." She spoke in a tone that boded ill for Sheriff Ricky Red Wolf.

She changed the subject. "Now, as for you two, breakfast

is always at six around here. You two might be able to find something left by seven—depending on what kind of mood the Singh brothers are in. And, if the ranch hands leave anything.

"Oh, also, our phone system is computerized so if anyone calls you, it will ring through to your individual rooms. And, I gave Tracie the extension number for your room, Will."

"Put'm on hold, whoever calls," Will mumbled through another yawn, his hand over his mouth. "This city boy needs his beauty sleep, and he needs it now."

"Beauty sleep," Jake quipped. "It'll take more than a few hours to fix you up." He turned to Amelia, "May we escort you to your room, ma'am?"

Chapter Three
Death in the Desert

Sleep came to Will with reluctance, and when, at last, it did, restless, disturbing dreams arrived with it:

The two gunfighters faced each other, a few yards separating them. The unrelenting sun burned down from a cloudless sky. Here and there, mesquite trees and yucca plants broke the monotony of the barren landscape. In the distance, a lone coyote sang its mournful song. Far-flung mountains sat distorted by heat waves rising through the air. Dust devils whirled and danced across the thirsty plain.

Both men stood, impervious to the remorseless heat that bore down on them. Each had thoughts only for the other.

Rancher Watson, the fastest draw in the west, faced the

The Ghost of Grandpa Wills

evil gunman, known as Dead Eye Dan, bank robber, murderer, and ravisher of women—a heartless and cruel villain. Watson waited. He always waited. Let the other man draw his weapon first—that, after all, was the 'Code of the West.' Now, live or die, Rancher Watson would stand by it, even if this varmint was the very one who had left his beloved wife, Nellie, dying in her own blood.

The Killer's hand moved, a blur in the noonday sun.

Rancher Watson slapped his hand to his gun, yanked it free of the holster, thumbed the hammer back, aimed, and squeezed the trigger—all in one single fluid motion. He felt the weapon buck in his hand. Heard the loud explosion as the shot was fired. Saw the heavy slug crash into the villain's chest.

With great satisfaction, Rancher Watson watched the man crumple onto the desert floor. It was over. The vile creature was destroyed.

Justice was done.

Vengeance, satisfied.

Someone was calling his name. A woman's voice. His beloved? But, no, she was gone; he would never hear the beautiful sound of her voice again...

"Mr. Willie, please. You wake now," a high-pitched voice roused him from his dream. He opened his eyes. They slowly focused on a woman of short stature, slight build, and Asian features, standing near the foot of his bed with a tray in her hand. He recognized her as one of the Singh women he had seen the night before.

"Missy say go wake Mister Will, now. Take coffee." Her small face was wrinkled with a frown of concentration. "You come quick, maybe not have breakfast. No time sluggards this house. Sheriff come vely soon now. You not be late."

Having delivered her message, she placed the tray on the dresser top, smiled, gave a polite bow, twirled around, and disappeared through the doorway.

Chapter Four
Breakfast, Then Questions

With his hair still damp from the shower, Will found his way into the breakfast room at the rear of the main wing. Morning sunlight streamed in through a large window that framed a spacious stone-paved patio, bordered by a manicured green lawn. Several large trees cast their shade across the area.

Craggy, multi-hued hills and barren plateaus rose up in the distance. Will paused, seeing himself riding alongside John Wayne or some other cowboy hero, exploring the rugged hills.

"Those are cottonwoods, in case you didn't know," a voice broke through his reverie. Will swung around to see Jake sipping from a large coffee mug. "Waited for you, Littl' Bruthur', 'til they told me I might not get somethin' cause the cowboys don't usually leave more than crumbs." Pointing to an empty chair, he grinned up at Will. "There's sacrifice, an' then, there's sacrifice. So, I heeded the friendly warnin' and had a bite."

Jake smacked his lips. "Those Singh brothers can make omelets that truly be worth singin' about. I hope you'll pardon the pun." He wagged a finger at Will in emphasis. "I took the liberty of already ordering a plate for you. Now, get your coffee, get seated, and I'll inform you as to what is to be a happenin' today."

No sooner had Will made himself comfortable with a mug of coffee, than the door to the kitchen swung open and one of the Singh wives entered, laden with a large tray overflowing with plates, glasses, and other requirements for breakfast. She was followed by the other Singh lady bearing a load of covered dishes.

"Twins?" Will asked. "They look identical."

"Oh, you noticed," Jake laughed. "They are identical, just as are their husbands; twin brothers married to twin sisters as a matter of fact."

The two women laid out the plates and other items with care and precision, bowed, and left the room.

"I thought you had already eaten," Will looked over at the omelet on his friend's plate, every bit as a large as the one on his.

"That was more than two hours ago, Littl' Bruthur, and I've already been out to the stables, taken a short ride, and been to their private firing range to familiarize myself with the gun you used to shoot holes in your bedroom wall."

He gestured with a well-buttered biscuit held in one hand. "It seems your mother wants her newfound son to know a little something about how to handle guns, so I'll be starting you off with that old six-shooter..."

"I..." Will tried to interrupt, holding a forkful of omelet midway between his plate and mouth.

"No time for questions or comments," Jake interrupted. "The Sheriff and Miss Amelia's lawyer team—both of'm—are on their way as we speak. Once they are finished with the two of us, we shall, then, be taken on a tour of the house—the first of many tours, I assume. This is one enormously huge domicile and a sprawling piece of property as well. There's definitely more than one day's worth of looking to see all there is to see."

Between mouthfuls of omelet, Jake continued explaining. "They're, also, firming up the plans for getting Tracie and the kids out here as soon as possible. Your mama is very anxious to meet her newfound daughter-in-law and grandchildren."

Jake raised his eyebrows in emphasis. "She's like some youngster awaitin' for Santa Claus to arrive." Raising his mug to his lips, he commented, "This is some of the best coffee I've ever tasted—have to find out where they get it from. Anyway, we need to finish 'cause we'll both be answering lots of questions, and it ain't polite to talk with your mouth full." He took a big bite of buttery toast, slathered with homemade peach jam.

Will took his friend's advice and dug into his food. Along with the omelet, came a stack of waffles which he drowned in a variety of dark honey. He was on his third coffee when the dining room door slid back, and the sheriff strode in, a deputy close behind her.

Instead of yesterday's uniform, she wore a blue denim skirt, a short-sleeved white cotton blouse, and western style boots. Her shiny black hair, instead of being in braids, hung straight down, flowing well below her shoulders, front, and back. With her copper colored skin, dark hair, and flashing eyes, she left no doubt as to her true natural heritage. The gun hanging from the belt around her waist with the accompanying badge left no doubt as to the authority she carried.

Jake and Will rose to their feet.

Amelia followed in her power chair, with Maria at her side, trailed by the lawyers, Jimmy and James. As if by magic, both Singh women appeared, pushing a serving cart laden with more coffee and accoutrements. They also cleared away the remains of Will's and Jake's meal.

Amelia spoke first. "Everyone be seated and get comfortable. Sara has some things she wants to say, questions to ask, and thoughts to share."

She turned and waved at the tall lawyer. "Jimmy, please pour me a big mug of that hot chocolate. Everyone else, help yourself, and then we'll get started."

Jimmy obeyed Amelia's request before filling two additional mugs with steaming hot coffee. He kept one and handed the other to Sara. Will watched and saw the sparkle in the sheriff's eyes as she took it from the big guy's hand. He thought of Tracie and wished she were with him. He found himself longing to see his family again.

The sheriff interrupted his thoughts. "This is what we know at this time..."

James had been quiet up to this point but now he jumped up from his chair, slapped both hands on the tabletop startling everyone, and spoke in a solemn tone. "There are several points which we must examine and consider in a very serious light. First, Will and Jake were both placed in danger by certain parties, identities as yet unknown, when a pair of rattlesnakes were placed in their vehicle while dining."

He raised his hands and crossed his arms across his chest, taking a defiant, authoritative stance. "Second, they were attacked while on the open road again, by parties unknown who first attempted to run them off the highway. Third, they were then shot at..."

Scowling down at James, the Sheriff bent forward and took control of the conversation. "After discussions with my brother in Sandlot, as well as with the Texas Department of Public Safety, who by the way, found what they believe to be the black SUV used in the attack located very near the Sandlot exit.

"The vehicle in question was stolen in Dallas. Soon after the attack on the two of you, it was wrecked, burned, and abandoned. Evidence indicates the SUV skidded and rolled several times after leaving the roadway."

She paused and glanced around the room before continuing, "The badly charred remains of the driver were found, still buckled in behind the steering wheel."

Sara looked directly at Will. "The DPS also found the remains of a large truck tire on the freeway, at the spot where the crash occurred. That tire is probably what you ran over while still entangled with your assailant."

With this new revelation, both Will and Jake tensed and leaned forward.

The sheriff continued. "We feel it is safe to assume, at least for now, that the same SUV was used to drop off the snakes in Sweetwater as in the highway attack. Also, there was a carjacking less a mile north of where you two were attacked. We think the cases are related. The hijacked car was most likely used as a getaway car for the perp or perps, that survived the crash."

With a dark frown creasing her forehead, she continued.

"The driver of the hijacked vehicle was severely beaten and left lying on the side of the road. Her condition is considered critical."

"A woman," Maria exclaimed wide eyed.

"A mother of three children," Jimmy added his forehead furrowed in anger. "Whoever did this was both desperate and vicious."

Sara turned to Jimmy. "Please tell everyone what you discussed with Miss Amelia just a few minutes ago."

Jimmy stood, cleared his throat, and his deep voice filled the room. "An important point, a possible motive, of which we have been reminded is that under the terms of the will as originally written by Miss Amelia—before she discovered the existence of her son—there was another beneficiary. Said beneficiary has now been cut out of the new will. We believe it worthwhile to investigate this as a possible connection."

"Who might that be?" Will asked, with an edge in his voice.

James spoke up, "An organization known as the Marfa Arts & Historical Society..."

Jimmy interjected, "They at one time had a museum somewhere on the outskirts of Marfa. According to local newspaper records the building was destroyed by fire about twenty years ago..."

James broke in again, "The original museum building was never rebuilt, the society went bankrupt, and we believe has since existed only on paper due to a lack of funds and public support."

"Most but not all of the board of directors are dead," Jimmy added with a scowl.

"However, Miss Amelia now has a living heir which means that that organization and any surviving directors have been prevented from having any share of Amelia's estate. Therefore, we have concluded that it is reasonable to believe someone for whatever reason, did not want the two of you to get to this ranch." James emphasized his point by waving a finger in their direction.

Will asked, "What other evidence is there?"

"Nothing concrete as yet," the Sheriff replied. "But I shall keep looking."

She turned to Will, "Also, I will be taking your DNA samples before leaving the ranch today, Mr. Watson. This will be an official, legal analyses that will stand up in court. Do not leave this room until I have the sample."

"Now," Jimmy's deep voice again filled the room. "Who knew the two of you were making this trip? Name every person you talked to, both of you, and what you said to them from the time you met James and myself in your office until you left and were actually on the road." He thumped the table with his big index finger. "We also need to know, Mr. Watson, as much as is possible, who your wife and children may have talked to."

Two hours later the sheriff drove away, towing Will's battered pickup on a trailer.

"Lunch will be served at noon," Amelia announced. "Afterwards, we begin showing the two of you what this old place is about. Meanwhile, I'm taking a short lie-down."

Chapter Five
Around the Old Home Place

As the plates and other dishes were cleared from the lunch table, Will took a last big swallow of iced tea and handed the glass to Mrs. Singh. He nodded with a word of "Thanks" and turned to his mother.

"We'll begin our tour in the kitchen," she said. "I've seen the two of you eat, so I know you'll be very interested in where all that good food comes from." She turned to Maria, "Would you care to take a break, my dear. I'm sure these two men can be trusted not to attack me in your absence."

"Thank you." Maria hesitated. "I..."

"We promise to behave ourselves as proper gentleman should, Miss Gonzalez," Jake interjected with a smile, his eyes on her pretty face.

"I...well...okay—I do have some paperwork to catch up

on."

"I wish you would just relax, Maria," Amelia replied in a caring tone. "You've not taken any time off since coming here. Now please, go and relax. No paperwork. That's an order."

As the nurse turned to leave, Will chimed in with, "I've been told no one ever says 'No' to Miss Amelia either."

"Who told you that?" Amelia snapped back at him.

"I think," Will answered with a grin. "I think, it was that big tall lawyer friend of yours—the one with the deep booming voice."

"I'll have his hide for making up such lies about me," she answered, but there was a twinkle in her eyes as she spoke. "Now, let's stop wasting time. Follow me, but one of you will have to get the doors." With those words, she swung the power chair around and headed for the kitchen door.

It was the largest kitchen Will had ever seen. Laid out in an 'L' shape with two aisles and a series of work tables and counters down the center, there was a bewildering array of sinks, stoves, ovens, refrigerators, mixers, and other items he could not identify.

"You could serve an entire ship's crew from here," Jake commented.

"We often feed all the hands and their families from here. You met several during lunch just now. I also entertained a lot before my cancer, and we used to have the entire church out here along with all their guests quite often, you know." Her voice lowered and Will detected a quiver in her words. "Now, however, my cancer has changed all that…"

She coughed lightly, cleared her throat, and continued

speaking, "Even so, my son, I'm planning something special as soon as your family arrives." She smiled again. "I intend to celebrate my newfound family in proper West Texas style. We will be inviting people from all over two counties."

She paused for a breath. "Our ancestor who originally built these two sections of the house was big on impressing other folks. Also, a century or more ago the ranch was very isolated, no paved roads, most people traveled by horse and buggy. It took days to get here from anywhere. And back in the late eighteen hundreds, this was a layover station for the stagecoach and freight wagons that ran south to El Paso all the way into Mexico."

Both of the Singh brothers along with their wives and families were lined up along the right side against the sinks and work spaces. Will saw several younger copies of the older Singhs plus a few older ones as well; they all looked almost identical to his eyes.

"Their children, their parents, and their grandparents," Amelia proceeded to pass down the line introducing each by name leaving the two newcomers totally confused by the end of the line.

Later when alone, Will and Jake would debate the numbers of both junior and senior Singhs they had met. "I counted ten children and seven older folks," Will would argue."

Jake countered with, "Naw, nine kiddos, and ten of the older folks. I'm sure there were some great-grandparents and maybe an uncle in the mix as well. I think maybe your mama's been running her own immigration service here."

The Ghost of Grandpa Wills

With the introductions concluded, Amelia pointed to two doors at the east end of the kitchen. "The left one leads to their private quarters; they occupy almost all of the south wing. The right door opens into the pantry with a large walk-in cooler and freezer."

Amelia turned to Will with a stern look in her eyes. "Feel free to wander in there anytime, but if you make a mess your blood will be on your own head. I, myself, enter only with fear and trembling." She glanced at Singh Loh, who responded with a polite bow and pleasant smile.

"You've already seen some of the library," Amelia led them down the aisles, among the bookshelves. "Feel free to read any of the books and use all the facilities available. Many of our volumes are first editions; some are rare collectibles. Most, but not all are concerned with Texas, West Texas, and local history. I have also collected a lot of material about the Apache and Comanche who once roamed through this area." She added with a strong emphasis, "That is some of your heritage, Will."

Will opened his mouth to respond but was distracted as they stepped around the end of one of the many bookcases.

"There's my office," Amelia explained.

At the southern end of the library the wall curved into the room, in a large convex arc with a very solid looking wooden door centering it.

Amelia passed a key ring to Will. "Open it, please—my son. Her voice cracked, then lowered to hoarse whisper. "It's my office. At least it was until...well...I just can't do as much as I once did." She looked away as though studying the contents of what had once been her inner sanctum. Will saw a tear on her cheek as she turned away. Both men followed her as she rolled through the doorway.

Will estimated the room to be about thirty feet in diameter, the interior cluttered with furniture, bookcases, and file cabinets. The centerpiece was a large, antique desk made of carved oak, sitting toward the west side of the room. A large aerial photograph hung on the wall behind it.

"That's the ranch property," Amelia explained pointing. "Taken about twenty years ago."

A wrought iron staircase rose up from the floor to Will's left. Following the curvature of wall, it disappeared through the oak ceiling high above. A worn cowhide covered the center of the stone floor, but the desktop was bare—not even a telephone. Dust lay everywhere.

"Haven't been in here in a couple of years," she said in a soft, quiet voice. She paused looking at the far wall, seeing nothing. It was not the wall she was peering into; it was the past.

She dropped her eyes before adding in a soft voice. "Can't do it anymore, you know—manage the business, run the ranch, or anything else. That's why I hired a manager. Took on Mr. Phillips about two years ago."

She looked up at Will tears still on her cheeks. "Always wanted a son—to take over some day. A lot of responsibility in this place. Several families depend on it for their livelihood."

A faint smile crossed her face. "There's a lot to learn, you know. Not much time to learn it in."

Will looked down at her. This aspect of discovering his mother had not occurred to him before now; things were moving fast, very fast. He opened his mouth to speak, but no words would come, he reached down and took her hand instead. She clasped his hand in both of hers, pressing it against her damp cheek.

"We've seen enough in here," she whispered.

Outside the library, Will pointed to a set of doors on the opposite side of the entrance hall. "What's over there? Behind those big double doors?"

Amelia hesitated before answering. "The old ballroom. Remember I told you about an ancestor who had high aspirations, fancy ideas, and liked to show off. Well, he included it when this wing was built."

"Can we see it?" Will asked, and started toward it. "I've never been in a real ballroom."

"Not today, my son," she said, with hesitation. "It, it's not used much anymore." With her eyes downcast, she added, "No parties at all, none since…"

She looked away for a brief moment. "Well, not for a long time—a very long time."

Again, Will sensed a veil of sorrow passing over her. He started to ask what was so upsetting, but she spoke again. The dark mood seemed to have passed.

"The elevator's over there. Let's see what's up on top." She toggled the chair's control lever and moved in that direction.

The roof was a broad, flat expanse of tar and gravel interspersed with A/C units, chimneys, and satellite dish antennae. From his vantage point, Will saw in the west a towering bank of dark clouds rising up behind the distant mountains—an army gathering its forces before launching an invasion.

A strong breeze whipped the few thin strands of Amelia's hair, what little remained of it after the ravages of the cancer treatments. However, she ignored the storm, turned, and powered over to the eastern parapet, wheels crunching across the crushed gravel. Turning parallel to the low wall, she stopped and looked out over the battlements.

Will and Jake joined her as she described what they were seeing.

"Our eastern boundary runs over beyond those mesas." She pointed. "Can't see it from here, though. There's an old highway out that way. Used to be the main route to Marfa and on down to Presidio. It's seldom used now."

"The railroad has a train about once a day, maybe. Was once a store and gas station over there, also. Anyway, don't need to worry about that. I guess you'll see it all someday.

"The buildings over to your right are our maintenance sheds and horse barns, plus some other buildings. The equipment barn is the nearest. We keep our trucks, ATVs, and other mechanical things in there. Mr. Phillips has his office in there. I offered him space somewhere in the house, but he said he needed to be closer to where the work is. I guess he's right."

She hesitated for a short moment. Will thought he heard uncertainty in her voice. "He seems dedicated to his job. He's really taken over since I got so sick. Takes care of everything now."

She pointed east-southeast to a large flat-topped mesa with its rugged cliffs rising like the walls of a great stone fortress. Will thought it had a dark, threatening look about it with its steep sides rising up in precipitous broken faces, interspersed with black crevices.

"That big rock there is called *Diablo Montana*," she said, staring out into the distance.

"Montana?" Will questioned.

"Spanish for Devil Mountain," Jake offered.

"There's a cave on the south side of the mountain and the ruins of an old stone building. Legend says an old Apache shaman lived there, an old rogue who was both feared and hated by Whites, Indians, and Mexicans alike. Lots of stories about him and the cave; none of them nice."

Amelia turned back to look at Will and Jake. "The cave is called *La boca del diablo*."

"The Mouth of the Devil," Jake translated.

"None of the ranch hands will go near the old ruins. Some won't even go up the south side of the mesa." She waved a hand in the general direction. "But there are lots of stories about the mountains around here, many going all the way back to the Apache and Comanche that once roamed these parts. Your Uncle Ben knows many of them. He used to enjoy scaring me with some of them when I was growing up as a kid."

Will started to ask who this Uncle Ben might be, but Amelia laughed and kept talking.

"I was almost tempted to go in there once. I was a teenager and liked to do crazy things like that. Anyway, your Grandpa scared me away from it. He talked like it was just what its name says—the Devil's Mouth."

Turning to the northeast, she continued. "The big one there is Ghost Mesa, highest point on the ranch and the largest in total area. Most rugged as well. I don't know of anyone that's ever been up there." Pausing, she smiled up at them, with a gleam of mystery in her eyes.

Will felt the wind tugging at his clothing and hair as he

strained to hear her soft-spoken words.

"You've heard of the Ghost Lights of Marfa haven't you?" She waved toward the mysterious plateau. "Sometimes there are ghost lights similar to those down near Marfa but not as famous. Ours are seen only from here on the property. I used to come up to the roof to watch for them. I have seen them, once or twice, you know. However, no one has ever explained them."

She paused again, before facing north. She pointed to a third, large stone rimmed mesa. "That's Flatrock Mesa. There's an enormous flat rock hanging over the edge of the small canyon at the near end—the south end. Hangs out over a little lake that's formed back up in the canyon. We used to go up to the top for barbeques and the like—built a fire pit up there a long time ago—some picnic tables up there as well…" She fell quiet for a few minutes. "…we don't go up there now. Don't go much anywhere, anymore."

Will studied the 'Flatrock' as his mother talked. It looked no more inviting that did the other two. Dry, barren, hostile. *Probably full of cactus and crawling with rattle snakes,* but he said nothing to his mother.

"Maybe we can all go up there when Tracie and the kids get here," Will interjected, hoping to lift her spirits."

"Uncle Ben will be glad to take all of you up some time." A faint smile creased her face, although the spark had disappeared from her eyes.

"Let's go back down, Miss Amelia," Jake offered. "We can all have a glass of iced tea and a quiet rest. Maria's probably getting worried by now."

She managed another smile and looked up at Jake, "She's a sweetie, that girl. She sure is. Best nurse I've had out here. Don't know why some nice fellow hadn't snatched her up and married her."

Turning back toward the elevator, Will pointed north. "What about that section of the house over there? It looks like all the windows are boarded up."

The north wing, almost a mirror image of the south, sat dark, silent, and foreboding, even though the sun had just passed its midpoint in the sky. Every one of its cast iron window shutters were closed tight. Will remembered the vultures perched atop the battlements from when he and Jake had first arrived. A chill crawled up his spine. His mother broke into his thoughts.

"It's the oldest part of the house, the original section that was built back before the Civil War," Amelia explained. "It's been locked up for a long time. Something bad happened there a long time ago, way back before I was born. They closed the shutters and chained the doors. Inside it was walled off from the rest of the house. "I have never been in there. It was forbidden when I was young. No one ever goes that way." She shivered, even as she sat there in the sun.

"Come, ma'am," Jake urged her. "Let's go on down where it's cool and outa this heat."

Chapter Six
Larson Building, Midland, Texas

Staring through the sliding glass doors, Larue Larson stood in the living room of his penthouse apartment, situated above the offices of his law firm. Far below, the streets of Midland lay in shadow as the sun touched the horizon out beyond the neighboring city of Odessa. High above, cirrus clouds streaked across a darkening sky; in the lower altitudes, cumulus formations crowded together while the rays of the setting sun painted them in hues of red, gold, white, and grey.

Immersed in a dark mood of black anger, Larue saw none of it. His recent trip to the big Choctaw casino, north of the Red River in Oklahoma, had not gone well. Lady Luck, fickle as only she could be, turned against him soon after he arrived. His losses had not been light.

"Flaming redskins." The words boiled out of him.

The Ghost of Grandpa Wills

"Grandpa was right. Custer should've won." It was all their fault—the Native Tribes of America—of that Larue was positive. He cursed them aloud, every member of every tribe and nation from the Apache to the Sioux. Somehow, he was certain, the cards had been purposely stacked against him. His bitterness boiled deep within his soul, a deep-seated hatred learned from both his father and grandfather.

The thought of his ancestor reminded him of his prized memento, left to him by that cold, hard, old man. Passed down through several generations it had become an obsession for Larue Larson.

Turning toward a large framed oil painting that hung on the wall Larue snatched a pair of white cotton gloves from a drawer in a side table. He reached the painting in a few quick strides. Still carrying a dark scowl, he tugged hard on a lower corner. The portrait swung back on silent hinges, slamming against the wall. It revealed a keypad framed by a dull gray metal door. He quickly punched in a series of numbers. The door clicked open. With gloved fingers, he carefully withdrew an object sealed in a clear plastic bag.

Sliding back the zip seal, Larue reverently removed the contents—a leather-backed book, old, worn, weather beaten, sweat stained—the pages yellow with age. The dark scowl dissolved as his fingers caressed the antique volume with a tenderness never shown to any living creature, neither man nor beast.

Larue leafed through the familiar pages as he walked back toward the glass wall. Each time he read the faded, spidery handwriting, some of which was almost indecipherable, he felt that the author, long dead, spoke direct to him—as if the words, penned more than a century and a half earlier, had been written for him personally.

Lawrence Larue Larson was certain that the spirit of his long dead ancestor was reaching out, straight to him through this journal. Justice. The ancestor wanted justice. And revenge! Moreover, it was Larue's sworn duty to exact that justice—and find a treasure in the process.

His brow and his face darkened in an angry scowl as he thought of the cruel injustice done to his family so long ago. He closed the safe door and swung the portrait back into position.

"I will have what is rightfully mine, what should have been yours." His eyes fastened on the portrait in front of him. He spoke to the old man in the painting, the original owner and author of the journal. "I will have it back for you. That I solemnly swear." It was not his first time to utter this oath.

His new cell phone vibrated in his shirt pocket, breaking into, what was for him, a sacred moment. Snatching the device out, he punched it with a finger, held it his ear, and sneered, "You're late."

His face grew darker as he listened.

Larue snarled into the phone, "Ferrell, you are not paid to make excuses, you are paid to get results. Next time you call, you best call with good news. You want the rest of your money, you finish the job." He threw the phone to the carpeted floor and stomped his foot with all his strength. "Idiots! Imbeciles! Fools! Why must I put up with such inept stupidity?"

Chapter Seven
Jake and Grandpa.

Amelia had done little more than taken a sip of her iced tea when Maria insisted on taking her up to her room for a nap. She asked Will to accompany them, so Jake found himself alone and decided to explore the library.

Jake wandered up and down the aisles for a time before stopping at a large aerial photo of the ranch, a composite of several smaller ones that had been collaged together to make a detailed whole, larger than the one in Amelia's office. Mounted on the east wall, it reached from the floor to above his head and stood wider than his outstretched arms. He was studying it when he sensed the presence of someone behind him. The air grew icy cold. He gritted his teeth. "*Keep calm, Ol' Man.*" Light shimmered to his right; and the ghost appeared.

The hair on the back of Jake's neck rose and goose bumps crawled up and down his spine. He fought the urge to bolt and run. The apparition stood beside him. "Right fair-sized spread, is it not?"

"Yeah, that it is," Jake replied, wondering how one was supposed to carry on a normal conversation with someone who had been dead for more than a century and a half. "Gets lonely in here all by myself. No one comes by except Amelia."

"Yes, sir, I guess it would."

"Call me Franklin if you would, sir."

"Uh, okay, ah, Franklin. Call me Jake, please—if you would." *Never been on first name terms with a ghost before.*

"You are a Navy man; I heard them say."

"Yes, sir," Jake answered, surprised that the ghost would know such details.

"So am I, or was, I guess. Served in the Navy and proud to say I did. Saw combat, I did." Jake saw his expression change; his voice hardened. "Against the bloody Redcoats, it was."

"Redcoats." Jake's eyebrows rose. "You mean the British?"

"Well, of course. Who else? Indians did not go to sea." The ghost turned to look Jake in the eye. "Yes, sir. I served proudly under Captain Charles Stewart; that I did. Started out as cabin boy then went to gunner's mate."

"Cabin boy? When did you serve, may I ask?"

"Was a lad of thirteen when I signed on. Things were different back then." He paused for a moment, with a faraway look in his eyes. "War of 1812 they call it now. Captain Charles Stewart was as fine a commander as ever stood on the deck of any ship anywhere. A real gentleman, he was."

"What ship did you sail on?" Jake asked with growing interest, almost forgetting who, or what, he was talking to.

"What ship, you ask? That is her there, sir, over the fireplace." He pointed. "Finest fighting ship ever sailed in the United States Navy."

Jake immediately turned and walked over to the fireplace. He halted in front of the huge, natural stone fireplace and looked up at the large oil painting. It depicted a wooden hulled, heavy frigate in full sail through rough seas.

Jake stood, unmoving, and whispered in awe, "That, sir, is the USS Constitution." He turned back to stare at the ghost. "You served on the USS Constitution?" he asked in wonder and deep admiration.

"Ol' Ironsides, we called her." Franklin's voice rang with pride. Jake thought he saw the ghost increase, grow in size and height. "I was there when we captured both the HMS Cyane and the HMS Guerriere. I witnessed the British cannon balls bouncing off her sides."

Jake stood, speechless and in awe. He pondered how to respond until he suddenly snapped to attention and saluted. "I thank you, sir. And I salute your bravery and your service to our country. I am proud to make your acquaintance."

Chapter Eight
The Reluctant Cowboy

Earlier, as they stood together on the roof, Amelia had pointed in the general direction of what she called the horse barn, but down here on the ground, things looked different, so Will could not be sure where he was supposed to meet the mysterious Mister Wayne Phillips, manager and foreman of the Wills Ranch. She had said little about the man except that he now ran almost everything on the property and was seldom seen—except when he needed something or was giving orders to someone. He never ate with other employees in the dining area, kept to himself, and was always telling everyone that he "had a ranch to run" and "no time to waste."

All the ranch outbuildings stood southeast of the house, the nearest a football field's length away. Surveying the scene, Will ruefully decided that, with his lick, it would be the one farthest away.

Will's attention was caught by one of the ranch hands in the distance, speeding toward a clump of mesquite in one of the ranch ATVs. In his imagination, he immediately pictured himself in the driver's seat of one the little four-wheel drive vehicles. He had never been in one but felt certain that something so small would be easy to handle—and a real blast as well. In fact, the more he thought about it, the more he liked the idea. *"Maybe this won't be such a bad day, after all."* He switched on his MP3 player, plugged in the ear buds, and started walking:

"Ten-Forty, read ya loud and clear." Boss Watson thumbed the radio off, dropped it onto the seat, and turned to Jose, the ranch hand sitting beside him. "We'll get'm this time. These crooks're 'bout ta learn you don't rustle cows off the Wills ranch." He deftly threaded the speeding machine in amongst the trees. "Yahoo…"

Boss Watson was soon distracted from his heroic ride by his feet. The expensive new footwear may have looked fancy in the store, but they certainly did not feel such as he trudged along in the dusty heat of West Texas.

Ahead, a rider approached at a slow walk, trailing a horse bearing an empty saddle. The stranger reined his mount to a halt just at the edge of the lawn and sat watching, making no sign of greeting or recognition. He sat motionless in his saddle, face shadowed by the wide brim of his hat.

Will drew closer, the cowboy remained silent, still watching, without dismounting. He felt as though the man was sizing him up and did not approve of what he saw.

At last, the stranger spoke, "Miss Amelia wants you to see the ranch." His words slid past a toothpick protruding from his mouth. "You can start on horseback." He extended the hand holding the reins to the extra mount.

With his smile gone, Will accepted the reins. His heroic dreams of bounding over mountain and plain in a fancy ATV were now destroyed—dashed upon the sharp rocks of reality.

"Too much to see in a day, even a week." The man waved an arm toward the east, emphasizing the vastness of the property. "You can use one of the ATV's another time—if you know how." He sat, looking down. Will stood, looking up, feeling as though he were under a microscope, being investigated, searched for flaws—and found lacking.

Abruptly he rider asked in a mocking tone, "Ever been on a horse?"

"Not much," Will answered. "You Wayne Phillips?"

The cowboy answered with a sneer. "You're looking at him." Twisting in the saddle, he pointed back to the other mount. "Best way to learn is to get your butt up in that saddle and just do it. A man has to start somewhere. So saddle up. Don't have all day—got a ranch to run."

Will moved around to the horse's side as Wayne continued. "She's named Feetlebaum."

Will stared back at the cowboy, "Featle—what?"

"Old story about a race horse that always came in last." Phillips smirked. "Can you mount up by yourself or do you need a boost?"

"I can manage." Will moved toward the mare, hoping he sounded more confident than he felt.

"I recommend you try mounting from the nearside. That's what they're used to," Phillips cautioned. Will paused and looked up at the man who still wore a smirk, enjoying his confusion. In a voice heavy with scorn, Phillips added, "Her left side."

Will stepped the mare, feeling more foolish with each move.

"Safer to go around in front so that they always know where you are." Phillips scowled, working his toothpick from one side of his mouth to the other. "Ever been kicked by a horse?"

Will shook his head and answered, "No, not as I can remember."

"Well, you'd remember if you had." The manager hawked and spat phlegm off to one side. "It's bound to happen sooner or later if you work around horses very much. You won't enjoy it when it does. And this ol' mare here, she may have a few years on her, but she's still got a lotta kick in her." His expression left Will with no doubt that Mister 'Ranch Manager' Phillips would enjoy seeing it happen.

He continued talking as Will struggled to put a foot into the stirrup. "Once you're in the saddle, grip with your knees. Hold the reins with both hands. Sit up straight. The horse always knows when the rider's a newbie, a nervous greenhorn; then they get nervous. If they sense you're a greenie—they'll want to take charge."

Will pulled himself up, threw a leg over, and sat in the saddle. "Which way from here?"

"The mesa over there; you can see it as we round the old north wing. That direction." Wayne pointed to the northwest. "It's called Flatrock Mesa."

Will rode in silence, following the ranch manager until he saw the red sandstone cliffs rising in the distance, their colors a stark contrast against the pale blue, cloudless sky.

He eyed the barren crags and overhangs with a mixture of wonder and suspicion. He saw their raw beauty while feeling threatened at the same time. He remembered his mother's words from yesterday about riding and picnicking up on the top. "Mother said they go up to the top sometimes."

Phillips answered without looking back. "Trail's around and on up the back side, north, then west.

"And what's up there when we get there?" Will asked, not feeling enthusiastic about the idea.

"The view," Phillips answered. "When you get up there you'll see most of the ranch as well as the lake down in the canyon."

"Lake?"

Wayne laughed and spat again. "Yep, small spring fed lake. Not much more than a cow pond actually, but it's supposed to be quite deep. Spring comes down from the cliffs at the head of the canyon. Dammed up by a big rock fall, long time ago. You'll see it when you get up there."

He turned to look at Will from under the shade of his hat brim. "You drove across the streambed when you came in."

"You keep saying 'you.' What about when 'we' get up there?" Will asked, afraid that he already knew the answer.

"Not going," Phillips responded with a snort. "I have a ranch to run."

He tightened the reins to turn his horse and added, "Even a greenie like you shouldn't get lost." He pointed. "Like I said, just ride north till you see the mesa. Then, turn back south when you're ready to come home. Besides, that ol' mare there, she'll know which way the hay barn is, even if you forget.

"Now, give her a real gentle kick with your heels and flick the reins real careful—light like this." He demonstrated again with his own. "Don't want to spook her." With those words of encouragement, Wayne Phillips spurred his mount, swung her around, and cantered off to the east.

Will watched the manager disappear into the mesquite. He pulled his ear buds from a pocket and stuffed them in his ears. They reminded him of Katie. He realized that he had not called home as promised—every morning before everyone left for school—and every night before bedtime. Too late now, though. Besides, Phillips was probably waiting for to him to either turn around or fall off.

With that thought, Will gritted his teeth and decided, *Not this 'greenie.' I'm on this horse, and I'll show big man, Phillips, I can do it.* With his mind made up and his determination set, he flicked the reins. "Giddy up." Relief flowed through him as Feetlebaum plodded forward.

The reluctant cowboy and his loyal steed rode off into the barren desert.

The countryside stretched around him, parched and thirsty all the way to the horizon. Years of drought had sucked the moisture from plants and soil alike.

The sun burned down with relentless fury.

Dust devils danced across the dying prairie.

The tortured air shimmered with heat rising from the barren wasteland.

Ranger Watson reined his sweat soaked mount to a halt and wiped his brow with a bandana, as he scanned the horizon. Squinting against the unyielding sun, he shaded his eyes with his hand as he searched the land. He saw no sign of Black Jack Jim, notorious killer, and the most wanted man in all of Texas. Nevertheless, the fearless Ranger knew the coldblooded murderer was out there, somewhere; and he would find him.

Neither heat of day, nor cold of night, would stop Ranger Watson—never had, never would!

Ranger Watson would get his man—always had, always would!

It was not for nothing that he was known as the "Relentless Ranger."

Chapter Nine
Uncle Ben

As the sun approached the midway point in its journey across the sky, Will sat slumped in his saddle. Without guidance, Feetlebaum had wandered from one tuft of dry grass to the next, threading her way between the trees and cacti.

Pain woke Will out of his reverie. Cramps gripped his legs. His throat was scratchy with dust and heat. Every muscle in his body screamed for relief. In addition, the fancy, high-priced, best quality cowboy boots were killing his feet. With a groan, he pulled the buds out of his ears and looked up to survey the countryside.

Panic seared through him as if a bolt of lightning had struck. The cliffs were not in the right place—not where they were supposed to be. In fact, they were nowhere in sight. The stalwart hero, the *Relentless Ranger*, realized he was lost and a long way from where he wanted to be. There was no sign of his destination, nor could he see the place from whence he had come. Nothing in sight but trees, rocks, cacti, and flat-topped mountains. Surrendering to utter despair, he knew he was irretrievably lost in the desert, without water or food and with no idea of which direction to go. Shouting, he yanked on the reins. "Whoa, stop." The mare ambled to a halt, head hanging as if asleep.

Only then did the "Relentless Ranger" think to turn in the saddle and look behind him. Relief flowed through his body when he saw the dark shape of Flatrock Mesa rising above the mesquite, but it was a long way off—in the wrong direction. There it sat, thrusting skyward, dry, hard, threatening, and ominous; here he sat, thirsty, tired, and sunburned. Back home, packing sunscreen had never entered his mind. After all, heroes do not need such sissy stuff.

Remembering his mother's words about the old Catholic Friars and others that had disappeared into this vast wilderness, Will panicked. Cursing aloud the encircling wilderness, he jerked on the reins. Shouting, he pulled hard and kicked with his heels. "Giddy up, you hunk of dog meat."

A large bird broke cover from a small scrub directly beneath the mare's nose. With a loud cry and a furious fluttering of wings, the feathered fowl darted, running across the rocky earth, weaving in and out amongst trees and cacti. The semi-somnolent mare exploded into action—but not exactly as her rider had intended.

The old horse shot straight up in the air and hit the ground running. Will rose with her, higher than did she. With arms and legs akimbo, spread to the four points of the compass, he completed a full, mid-air, backward somersault.

Feetlebaum landed on her feet—but not her erstwhile

rider. By the time Will touched earth again, his faithful mount was several yards northeast of his landing point. He came down hard on his back, in an ungraceful sprawl across the drought-stricken remnant of a desert shrub. With a loud, explosive grunt, all the air gushed from his lungs.

The *'Relentless Ranger'* lay gasping, fighting to suck air into his tortured lungs, wondering how many bones were broken, whether he would ever walk again, and if he might ever see his beautiful wife and wonderful children—all the while staring up at a cloudless blue sky.

Many thoughts ran jumbled through his mind:

No one knows where I am.

They will look for me in all the wrong places.

They will miss me but not until after supper, when it's dark.

Is there a moon out tonight? There was one the other night, wasn't there? Was that a week ago or another lifetime?

Darkness…

Nighttime…

Coyotes…

Mountain Lions…

Snakes…

Buzzards—huge birds that will peck out my eyes. (That happened in a movie once!)

How will I die? Thirst or eaten by coyotes?"

Will closed his eyes against the scorching heat of sun, but the bright light still burned through. He heard a loud roar accompanied by the sound of a very large something crashing through the dry brush, rushing toward him!

I'm dead! Too young to die!

Filled with dread, Will braced himself for the very worst—savage teeth rending his tender flesh.

Darkness came over him. Something now blocked the sun.

He heard a gruff voice speak. "Alive, must be. Lips're movin'. Lik' fish outa wat'r he be. Might he be havin' bones broken?"

Will felt strong hands take hold, one under each armpit. Caught in a rough vise-like grip, he was jerked to his feet. Pain shot through every fiber of his body. At last, he found enough breath to moan.

The voice continued, growling out orders. "Stand, young fella'. Straight. See what manner man ye be."

Blinking, Will opened his eyes to stare at the dirtiest, ugliest face he had ever laid eyes on. Startled, he stepped back and would have fallen, again, had his rescuer not caught and held him steady.

Watery blue eyes stared back at Will, jaundiced whites streaked with red. Tanned and burnt by both sun and weather, wrinkled and creased, the face looked like old parchment that had been soaked, wadded up, and dried many times. A mop of grey hair and beard—long untouched by comb, brush, razor, or shampoo—encircled the broad, round face. A wide, crooked nose centered the face. The lips, what could be seen of them through the untrimmed moustache, were full but chapped and cracked—the teeth, large, yellowed, and worn.

An old-fashioned pith helmet, battered and stained with sweat, sat atop the mess. The stranger's well-worn shirt and pants, tattered and patched, were made of non-descript denim and looked no cleaner than his hair.

"Heh, hey, think maybe he'll live, maybe he might." The stranger muttered and moved close to Will's face. "Can he talk?"

Will blinked and sucked in a deep breath, glad to be able

to breathe again.

"Yeah," he gasped. A sharp, stabbing pain in his ribs almost paralyzed him. "I think I can…W…who are you? You real?"

"Real, asks he." His rescuer snorted. "Course, real I be. Think I be a ghost 'r sumthin'?" He slapped his thighs and hooted with laughter. "Ghost cain't pick people up when down they fall. Real I be, an' know who he be. He knows not who I be." He continued his raucous cackling as he stepped back—much to Will's relief.

The old man scanned Will up and down. He once again felt as though he were under a microscope. "You be a hurtin' abit." The stranger made it a statement, not a question. "Right good fall that were. Not best way fer gitt'n off horse. Never done thata way meself."

"Wasn't on purpose; she jumped, threw me off," Will answered, feeling embarrassed.

"Hee, hee," the old man was still snickering as he turned toward the mare, who now stood nibbling at a clump of grass about twenty yards away. "Ass over tea kettle, you were. Feet skyward. Hope not hurt old mare none. Ornery as they come, she be. Friends we be, many year, since 'fore you be hatched."

Not wanting to hear the old man's prattling, Will looked around and saw the source of the racket he had heard—a battered ATV with two seats and a cargo bed filled with a jumble of items. Wanting to sit down or, at least lean against something, Will tried to take a step. He winced and bit his tongue to keep from crying out. The old man was right; he was in real pain. Forcing his legs to move, he took one step, then another, and limped over to the machine to lean against it while watching the old man approach the mare.

The stranger mumbled in tones Will could just hear, but

not understand. The horse whinnied and moved toward him.

Grabbing the reins, the old man led the mare back to the ATV. Now, Will saw the horse was limping and that the old man no longer wore a smile; a frown clouded his grizzled face.

He looked Will hard in the eye as he came near. "Be right skittish w'strangers, 'specially greenhorns." He bent down to inspect the animal's left foreleg. "Why be a riding you ol' gal? Eh, why they be a ridin' ya?"

Backing against the mare's leg, he pulled her hoof up between his thighs.

"Com' her', Greenie," he demanded. "Looksy. See what it is ya be doin'."

Will staggered over, keeping one eye on the animal, the other on the stranger—not sure which of the two might be the more dangerous.

"Down," the old man ordered. "Take a looksee what ya done." He reached out and with a grip of iron, pulled Will closer to the injured hoof.

Will, never having seen the underside of a horse's hoof before, had no idea what he was supposed to be seeing.

"Rock," the old man rasped out as he pointed with a finger. Releasing Will's arm, but keeping a firm grip on the foreleg, he glared up. "Knife."

"Huh," was the startled response.

"Knife. Pocketknife. Bowie knife, any kinda knife. Did greenie greenhorn come all way…no knife?" The grizzled face glared up at him.

"No, I didn't bring one," Will confessed. In fact, at this moment he had no idea where his pocketknife was. Tracie had given him one for his last birthday, but he had put it away somewhere after cutting himself while trying to trim his fingernails.

"Toolbox. Red. Screwdriver. Git it. He do know screwdriver, don't he?"

"Maybe," Will mumbled. "I think I've seen one before."

After retrieving the requested tool, Will watched the old man pry the offending stone from the mare's hoof, his voice kind and his caresses gentle as he worked. At last, with a grunt of satisfaction, he tossed the stone aside and lowered the injured limb to the ground.

"In," he ordered, looking up at Will and gesturing to the ATV passenger seat. "Cain't be a ridin' her now. Shouldn't been ridin' her afore. Old gal—old as you be." Raising a fist in the air, he declared, "Young for man, old for horse."

"I didn't chose her," Will protested as he climbed in, moving boxes of shotgun shells out of the seat and shifting the gun to point away from himself. "She was chosen for me."

Will sat and watched the old man remove the saddle and reins. As gruff as he had been to Will, he spoke with tenderness to the mare before dropping the tack into the ATV's cargo area clambering into the driver's seat.

"We go slow; she be followin'. There be feed. She be knowin'." He twisted the starter key, and the engine clattered into life. The old man shifted into gear and let the machine crawl forward.

They rode in silence for a few minutes until Will spoke up. "Who are you, and how do you know me? We've never met before."

The old man gave a low chuckle. "Benjamin Franklin Wills, that be who I be." He thumped his chest with one hand. "Youngest son of one Franklin Percival Wills, Fourth. He be father of one Franklin Percival Wills, Fifth—who be father of Miss Amelia Priscilla Annette Wills."

He turned to stare at Will, "Mr. William Wordsworth Watson, I be Great-Great Uncle Ben." He ended with another chuckle and turned back to watch where they were going, just in time to give a twist to the steering wheel to miss a small mesquite tree.

They moved at a pace to match that of Feetlebaum. Will still wished his new-found uncle, would pay more attention to where they were going and dodge some of the rocks and holes. Grabbing a metal handle on the dashboard, he held tight.

"I, I didn't know I had an uncle," Will stammered and ducked as another tree limb bounced off the windscreen before swinging back to slap him on the top of the head.

"Not know mother, did he not," came the reply.

"What should I call you?"

"What? Why, Uncle Ben, a'course. Tho' some 'round here call me Looney Ben. Not t' me face. But, I know what they be a sayin' b'hind me back; that I do. `Deed I do. Ol' Crazy Ben knows much as what goes on in these parts." He ended with another chuckle.

"Where do you live? Here on the ranch? With the other hands?"

"Course I be here on the ranch. Ain't one of the other hands. Amelia's uncle, I be—your uncle, too."

He braked the ATV to a sudden stop, twisted around in his seat, and pointed back to the northeast. "That'a way. There be my place, young Willie Boy, nephew mine."

Will looked back, wincing in pain as he twisted around, to see where his new found uncle pointed—the forbidding edifice his mother had named Ghost Mesa.

"Ghost. Ghost Mesa. I be close up under Ghost, Nephew. There be trees. There be water. There be my castle. Sometime maybe he come, hey? Man's home be a castle. Hey. You know."

He released the brake, and they rode in silence for a long while before Will asked, "Why is it called Ghost?"

"Heh? What ghost?"

"The mesa. Why's it called Ghost Mesa?"

"Cause," Ben replied with laughter. "'Cause they be ghosts. Lights, noise, in the night, new moon, in the darkness. Sometimes, full moon. Come some night. He be seeing. Maybe watch from rooftop, sun goes down. Yes, see from Castle top."

He turned to stare at Will, eyes boring into him. "Maybe afeared of ghosts ye be. Scary they be. Young fella, afeared maybe he be?" A strange light came into Ben's eyes.

"I never met a..." Will stopped in mid-sentence remembering two nights before when he had met a ghost and not liked it—not even a little bit.

"Never a ghost has he met, did he say?" Ben completed the unfinished statement.

"That's not what I was going to say."

Ben responded with another low chuckle.

They finished the ride in silence. The old man stopped the ATV behind the house, at the edge of the quadrangle, and waited while Will staggered down from the vehicle. Every muscle, every bone, every joint in his body complained with each step.

The backdoor flew open before Will could reach it. One of the Singh wives ran to him, calling in her high-pitched voice, shouting in a language he could not understand. She was soon joined by her sister and the two brothers.

"Mr. Willy," one of the men exclaimed. Will couldn't tell which it was. The four rushed to help him. One of them exclaimed, "You awful." He had to agree—if he looked as bad as he felt.

At the door, he was greeted by Jake.

"Good grief, Littl' Bruthur. What…?"

"Old horse threw me."

It was a matter of a few minutes for them to get the invalid up the elevator. The Singhs attempted to carry him, but he fought them off, groaning every time someone touched him. Jake got him into bed, on his stomach, with shirt and boots off.

Just as Will thought it could not get any worse, his mother rolled into the room with Maria right behind her.

"Oh my," Maria exclaimed. "What happened?"

"Fell off the horse," Jake explained.

"Thrown off," Will countered, his voice ending in a moan.

"My dear, Will, what has happened?" Amelia questioned. "How badly hurt are you? Is anything broken?" Her concern and excitement showing in her voice. "Must I call an ambulance? Should we drive you to the hospital? He's bleeding! Maria, Mr. Jacobson—do something!"

Maria moved around to the bedside opposite Jake and began her examination. "When you fell, what did you land on, Mr. Wills?" she asked.

"My back," came the terse reply.

"That's very obvious, Littl' Bruthur," Jake interjected. "But, you came down on something that tore holes in both your shirt and your hide. Now, we need to see if you'll be needing stiches and if you broke any ribs. You'll definitely be having some lovely bruises come morning." He prodded in a few places, much to his patient's discomfort.

Under Amelia's watchful eye, Maria and Jake administered first-aid to her newly-found son. Once they were satisfied that no bones were broken, and pain pills duly dispensed, the patient was left alone with strict orders to lie quiet and go to sleep.

Struggling to breathe, Will rolled onto his side enduring sharp pain. He sensed that he was not alone and opened his eyes.

There stood the figure from two nights before, but without the gun in his hand.

"W—who? W—what?" Will stuttered and struggled to push himself up.

"Do not get yourself up, Grandson," the ghost responded in a quiet voice. "You rest now. We shall be watching out for you. Rest easy."

Franklin floated over, closer to Will's side. "However, you will be needing to learn a thing or two concerning horseflesh. About people as well. I believe that we may be making a rancher out of you yet."

The ghost paused and stared down at his grandson for a moment. "But there is still much work to be done" He disappeared.

'Make a rancher out you'—the words played through Will's drug fogged mind. *Didn't come out to ride horses and raise cows.* The pain killers took over, and the reluctant cowboy passed into oblivion.

Chapter Ten
Music in the Night.

Sometime during the dark hours of the night, Will woke from a pain-filled dream only to realize that the hurting was not all in his imagination. Now there was another discomfort adding to his misery. He struggled to sit up, fumbled for the lamp switch and gathered his will power for the arduous journey ahead. The bathroom was only a few feet away but it might as well have been a mile, considering how he felt at the moment. He staggered and stumbled there and back, before falling facedown onto the bed. He lay there gasping until he had gathered the strength to pull the sheets up.

Then, he heard it.

Music.

An orchestra playing and a man singing—sounds drifting in from somewhere. Somewhere nearby? Or far away? Was it real? Or was the gun toting ghost, now raising his voice in song?

Not frightening either. Rather, the music was plaintive and beautiful. Very beautiful!

"I need your love.
God speed your love…
…I hunger for your touch…"

The music filled him with a deep longing and loneliness. Staring into the darkness, he missed Tracie as never before. He remembered, with shame, that he had not phoned that day, as promised. In addition, they had fought the night before he'd left, after he came home with his mouth full of that stupid tobacco, and he'd left without saying, *"I love you,"* or had he? He could not remember. *When was the last time I said those three, simple little words?*

All the while the song continued, repeating itself again and again—until he drifted into another pain filled dream.

Chapter Eleven
The Next Day.

A knock on his bedroom door, followed by a cheery, "Good morning, Mister Will," aroused him from troubled slumber. Without waiting for a response, Flower Singh entered gracefully balancing a coffee tray on one hand. "Time you wake up," she sang out in her high soprano voice. "Breakfast thirty minutes. You not come, you no eat." With that stern warning, she laid the tray on the night stand, twirled, and disappeared through the doorway.

Taking the mug with him, Will limped toward the bathroom and the shower, hoping the hot water would relieve the soreness in his back. He groaned aloud when the stinging spray hit him.

He winced with pain as the towel touched his back and saw blood stains on the cloth as he hung it back on the rack.

The Ghost of Grandpa Wills

Choosing his oldest shirt from the few he had brought, he slipped into it and fastened the buttons. Forgetting there was an elevator, he made the arduous trek to the dining room down the stairs—leaning against the bannister, every muscle complaining, as he descended.

Jake was already at the table. "Welcome and good morning, Littl' Bruthur. How're we feeling?"

"Like I've been thrown off a horse, then stomped on."

"Let me look," Jake ordered, rising from his chair.

"Sure you want to look before breakfast?"

"I've seen worse, Willie, my friend, much worse."

"How do you know? If it looks as bad as it feels..."

"You're still alive, Littl' Bruthur. You're still alive and kickin'. That's how I know."

Will gave no response. He removed his shirt and let his friend make his examination.

"Some beautiful bruises back here. In addition, you are oozing blood. Need some bandages. I'll fix you up after we eat. Want some omelet?"

As if by magic, Blossom appeared from the kitchen with another mug of their fabulous coffee. Jake ordered breakfast while Will slipped back into his shirt and lowered himself into a place at the table.

"Did you hear the music last night?" Jake asked.

"You heard it? I thought maybe it was another trick of the ghost. Kept me awake a little while. Made me feel kinda lonely and sad."

"It was '*Unchained Melody*' by the Righteous Brothers. An old song from back before either of us was born. One of my favorites. Or it used to be, that is. Now it just makes me lonely and sad. Reminds me of...Reminds me..." He hesitated and looked away, at a loss for words.

"I wondered if you were playing a CD or something," Will added. "Thought it'd never stop, went on and on, over and over. But, I finally went back to sleep."

"Not me, Littl' Bruthur." Jake cleared his throat and looked back at Will. "Not me, and I don't think it was your ghostly grandpa either. I got up and went down stairs. It was coming from behind those big double doors across from the library, what your mother called *the ballroom.*" His voice took on a softer tone. "I thought I heard someone crying as well—a woman." He paused for a brief moment before adding, "I think it was your mama."

They looked up to see Maria standing at door.

Jake rose to greet her.

"It was Miss Amelia." She closed the door behind her. "Thank you for not intruding on her sorrow. She goes there often, late at night when the pain is too great. She plays that song, over and over. It was their song together, you know. She has never forgotten him, and it helps take the pain away—for a little while."

Stepping up to the coffee urn, she paused to fill her cup and then turned to face them. "He swore to come back, you know. She vowed to wait for him. She is still waiting—just as she promised she would."

"Who?" Will asked, gesturing with his palms up. "Who's coming back? Who's she waiting for?"

"Your father, Mr. Watson." Maria's dark eyes bore into him. "She promised to always wait for your father, and she still keeps her promise."

"My father," Will replied in a hushed tone. "But he's dead. Dead for...for a long time. He can't come back."

"Don't say that, Mr. Watson." Maria put down her mug and looked straight at him. "Don't you ever say that to her.

The Ghost of Grandpa Wills

You will break her heart."

Her eyes washed over Jake and back to Will. "He vowed to come back for her—someday. She promised to wait.

"So, she plays the music. Over and over. And she weeps. She is lonely, very lonely. She never forgets."

Her next words cut straight to Will's heart. "They were in love, Mr. Watson. She still is. Do you have someone to love?"

She looked past his eyes, into his soul, into the depths of his very being. He recalled the pain in his heart from last night.

He hesitated.

She waited.

Finally, he broke the stillness and confessed in a low voice, "Yes, I do…"

There was silence until Jake put down his mug, jangling some silverware. He coughed and cleared his throat before speaking. "Morning, Maria. Would you be joining us for some breakfast, I hope?" He moved a chair and held it for her.

"Yes, please, if I am not intruding," was her reply as she accepted his invitation.

The two Singh sisters made another magical appearance—this time with a plate of huevos rancheros along with a fresh urn of coffee.

"How do they do that?" Will asked.

"What? Ohh, they have a secret recipe, won't reveal it to anyone," Maria answered.

"No, I mean, how do they manage to arrive with what you want, just when you want it, without asking?"

"I don't know, but they do, and it sure tastes good, however, they do it." She looked at him with her eyebrows raised. "Now, how's your back? We'll take another look after we've eaten."

"Jake's already checked," Will assured her.

"He'll need new bandages," Jake said. "Still bleeding some but I expect he'll live—until his next ride at least." A big grin spread across his face as he raised a forkful of omelet to his mouth.

Chapter Twelve
The Big Flatrock

With breakfast finished and Will's back examined, doctored, and bandaged, the duo made their way out to the maintenance barn. Jake carried an ice chest and a small canvas backpack.

"The ATV's are out here," Jake explained. "I asked Jose to have one fueled and ready for us. And, I'm driving." Will acquiesced without protest.

Jake threaded the machine amongst the trees and around the clumps of cacti and dried grasses. Will rode without his earbuds, paying attention to his surroundings. They followed a rough trail around the east side of Flatrock Mesa and true to the ranch manager's description, it was narrow and steep but not impossible. Jake kept up a running commentary on the countryside, the vegetation, and the wildlife they came across.

"How do you know so much about all this stuff?" Will asked.

"I read, Littl' Bruthur. Lots of research. I have a curious and enquiring mind so I study about where I'm going before I go. Saved my life more than once, especially back when my chopper went down where it wasn't 'sposed to. Besides, there's the big aerial photo on the wall back in the library, as well as the one you saw in your Mama's office. They picture the entire property. I studied them while you were out falling off the horse."

"Thrown off. I was thrown off!"

They rounded a large, jagged outcrop of granite and passed through another grove of oaks. Jake came to a halt and said, "Look behind you."

Will sat amazed at what he saw.

"That's the Davis Mountains directly to the north," Jake explained. "The low country is part of the Chihuahua desert, largest in North America. It stretches from here into Arizona and way down into Mexico. Wild it is and has its own beauty but not a place to get lost. I read of some that did and have still never been found."

Rugged granite peaks rose up from endless miles of cacti and mesquite-strewn dry plains stretching to the distant horizon where everything faded into a pale blue. It was impossible to tell where the sky ended and desert began.

"Over that way is Mount Livermore, the highest peak in Texas, just a bit over 8,000 feet. Com'on this way. Let's keep following this track. The ranch hands sometimes bring their families up this way for a picnic. There's an old shack up here somewhere, but they usually bring tents and such. You have to carry up all the necessities including water.

"Let's head on to the south end, but keep close to the east rim so we can see the ranch. I expect it's possible to see most of it from up here."

Chapter Thirteen
Flatrock Canyon

"We don't want to get too close to the edge," Jake cautioned. "The ground's uneven, and the cliff looks undercut in places. Let's park this thing in the shade, over under those trees."

They each grabbed a bottle of water from the ice chest and leaned back against the ATV, talking as they did.

"Well, Littl' Bruthur, no snowcapped peaks, no pine trees. But what d' ya' think?"

"I'd probably break my neck if I ever went skiing anyway."

Their musings were interrupted by the clatter and roar of another vehicle speeding across the mesa behind them. They turned to see an ATV bouncing over the rough terrain, heading their way.

"Who in the…" Jake asked.

The Ghost of Grandpa Wills

"Uncle Ben. Otherwise known as Benjamin Franklin Wills, younger brother to the father of my mother's father."

"What?"

Will was interrupted as the approaching ATV slid to a halt next to theirs. Dust billowed around them.

"Never mind. He drives like a lunatic." Jake jumped out of the way as Ben's machine sprayed them with dirt and gravel.

"He's also known as Looney Ben," Will added, a wry smile creasing his features.

"I won't bother asking why," Jake cried.

Uncle Ben was out of his ATV and loping toward them with a pair of field glasses hanging around his neck, banging against his chest. "See be about, havin' looksee."

Jake offered his hand in greeting but was ignored. The old man continued with a rapid-fire narrative, talking as he walked, not waiting for their response. "You be Jake Jacobson. I be Benjamin Franklin Wills. He might call me Ben. You be Navy. I be Army, OSS."

He led them to the eastern edge where a spear of granite thrust out over the plain below. "Be about 200 feet down straight," Ben explained with a chuckle. "Ain't Grand Canyon, still big drop all way down. Be small lake, hundred acres maybe." He pointed in a southwesterly direction. "Canyon wall came down, made lake. 'Fore Ol' Ben being born, it was. Big flat rock over there. Now be seein' Canyon Flatrock. Someday rock be fallin'." He finished with another chuckle.

The large rock formation was obvious, a huge slab jutting out from the mountainside. From where they stood, it appeared to be almost flat on the top with an underside shaped like the prow of a wide bottomed, shallow draft boat.

"Take these, Nephew, look east—look south." He handed the glasses to Will. "Big house that way. Landing strip there. Far away be highway north ta south. Gas station, house, store, hotel. Old days, trading post. Bought gas, long ago…"

Ben paused. Will thought he saw a far-away look in his uncle's eyes. "She was pretty littl' gal; that she were. Gone now." A deep sigh escaped from the old man. "Most ever'body gone away; long time be gone now."

Will did not know how to respond so he said nothing—just handed the glasses to Jake who searched the area for a few minutes before asking, "Is that a railway out past the highway?"

"That it be. Surely be. Twice week. Long ago, ever' day."

He paused again before blurting out, "There be treasure out there, out here. Buried gold. Lost mines. Maybe this canyon. Maybe out there. Legends. Tales. People come, people look. Ol' Ben tells'm, 'Vamoose, go 'way.' Now you look. You see. Wills Ranch. Someone wants it."

He fell silent, reached for the glasses, and turned back to his ATV.

Jake spoke up as they watched him roar away.

"You do know how to pick some interesting relatives, Littl' Bruthur; that's for sure. First, the long-dead ghost of a grandfather. Now this somewhat unusual gentleman, for an uncle. How old do you think he is? He's not another ghost, is he?"

"Huh? Oh, no, he's quite real; he's alive. Picked me up off the ground after I was thrown off the horse. Don't think a ghost can drive an ATV either. I don't know how old he is, but I reckon he's gotta be somewhere around ninety or so."

"At least, if he's telling the truth," Jake agreed. "The

OSS was the Office of Strategic Services formed in World War II, predecessor to the CIA. You do know how to pick'm."

"That hill over there, the big one, is Ghost Mesa," Will pointed. "Uncle Ben says he lives in that patch of trees near the base."

"How'd he know who I was?" Jake asked.

"Don't know. Yesterday, he knew who I was and how old I am. Don't know who he's been talking to." He turned back toward the ATV. "Let's get back to the house. My back is killing me."

Amelia greeted them as they entered. "I had Singh keep some lunch for you both." She led them into the dining room where the two Singh sisters appeared, carrying trays of sandwiches and iced tea.

Somewhere between mouthfuls and small talk, Will asked his mother, "Who is Uncle Ben? Is he really my uncle?"

"So he found you, did he?" she answered. "He always does things his own way, in his own time. And, yes, he really is your uncle. I guess great-great-uncle would be more accurate, and he's as real as they come."

"Was he actually in the OSI or whatever it was, back in World War II?"

"He most certainly was, only it was the OSS, precursor to the CIA. He has the medals and commendations to prove it, as well. But, he never talks about that, unless he trusts you. I'm the only living person he talks to much anymore. I think he also spends a lot of time with your Grandfather whenever he's here at the house."

She added, with a stern look on her face, "And, if you ever laugh at him, he'll most likely never speak to you again."

"How old is he?"

"Somewhere in his late nineties. He's served in every conflict from World War II up until the Gulf War. He was wounded more than once; always went back until the last time, when he was shot in the head. That left him a little mixed up. Don't let that fool you, though; he's fluent in several languages, been on all seven continents, and more than a hundred countries. There's a lot of smarts under all that grey hair, although most people don't realize it."

"Why does he talk so funny, like he doesn't know where to put his words and all?"

"That happened after his head injury. He sometimes even mixes in words from a foreign language with what he's saying, not so much now, as he used to, though."

The afternoon passed. Will wandered around the house and nursed his sore back with more pain pills. Most of his time was spent in the library where he found a doorway into another room that his mother had not shown them. There, he discovered display cabinets, encased in glass and locked, containing coins, guns, and various other artifacts. He wandered the aisles, amazed at what he was seeing. History had always been boring when he was forced to sit through the mind-numbing classes during grade school and afterwards. Taught by bored football coaches who were there only until they could get out to the athletic field, history had been nothing more than endless lists of meaningless dates about people, long ago dead and buried. However, this stuff was real, and he could almost touch it. *Katie will love this*, he thought and remembered it was, again, past time to call his family.

Chapter Fourteen
Duel at Midnight

Sleep came hard for Will that night. Trying to keep up with Jose and the other ranch hands at the supper table had not been one of his brighter ideas. They seemed to think that the hotter the salsa, and the more one consumed, the manlier you were. Machismo was the word Jake used. Will made a mental note to look it up someday. Katie probably knew what it meant; that was embarrassing; his nine-year-old daughter knew more Spanish than he did. For that matter, even his son in first grade knew words he did not.

Two big swallows of that foul tasting pink stuff—chalk with the artificial taste of cherries—plus a few antacid tablets settled some of the demons in his belly. More pain pills eased the fiery misery that kept running up and down his backbone.

As he lay on his side, shapes cast by the moonlight

filtering through the curtains moved slightly; perhaps it was the A/C stirring the air, perhaps not. As a child, his imagination had always seen ghosts and witches in such shadows that had often left him quivering in fear beneath his bedcovers. This time he just mumbled, "G'night Grandpa." He closed his eyes and, at last, sleep came. Fitful, uneasy, and filled with vivid, lifelike dreams.

The two gunfighters faced each other, twenty yards between them. The full moon shone down from a cloudless sky casting silvery light across the dry, almost treeless plain. Here and there, the monotony of the barren landscape was broken by a lonely mesquite tree or yucca plant. A coyote sang its lonesome song in the distance. Far-flung mountains sat enveloped in purple shadow. Stars sparkled and glimmered above. However, neither man gave any attention to the wild beauty surrounding them.

Each had eyes only for the other.

Marshall Watson, the fastest lawman in the west, stood facing down the evil gunslinger known as Black Jack Ben.

Watson waited.

He always waited.

Let the other man draw his weapon first. That, after all, was the Code of the West and live or die, Marshal Watson would stand by it.

The Killer's gun hand moved, a blur in the moonlight. In one fast, lightning-like response, Marshall Watson dropped his hand to his gun. But the weapon would not leave its holster. His hand would not grip the pistol. He could not use his fingers.

The killer laughed aloud, a hideous cackle. He aimed

and fired.

BANG. BANG. BAM. BAM. The Killer fired again and again-

It all disappeared in an explosion of light. Marshall Watson heard someone screaming his name.

Chapter Fifteen
Back Home

Will crashed back into wakefulness as Jake burst into the room, hitting the light switch and shouting. "Willie! Bruthur Willie! Wake up! Tracie's on the phone. Com' on, wake up. Somethin's happenin' back home. She's tryin' ta get you, but somehow the call came through to my room. She sounds scared, upset, or somethin'. Hurry."

Sleep disappeared, and the fog dissipated from Will's head. "What? What are you yelling about?" He tried to push the covers back and roll over, but his right arm was numb. He cried out, as feeling returned. "No wonder I couldn't draw my gun." He had been lying on his arm as he slept. The full meaning of Jake's words came to him. "What are you talking about? One of the kids hurt or something?"

"Don't know, Littl' Bruthur, but you best hustle your

caboose in there real quick like. She's waitin' on the phone, and there's definitely something wrong."

Will untangled himself from the bed covers to stumble out of the bed and across the hall. Entering Jake's room, he snatched up the phone.

"Tracie! What's happened?" He screamed into the phone. "You okay? The kids hurt? What's going on?"

"Will!" Will realized she was crying. "Someone's shooting at us. They shot out windows, and there are bullets in the walls and the furniture. It's terrible. Bullets in the bedroom. The kids are hiding in the closet and..."

"Tracie, Trace!" He shouted into the phone. "Are you okay? Anyone hurt? Did you call an ambulance? How about the police? Call 911 now. Trace, talk to me..."

He felt Jake's hand on his shoulder. "Easy, Littl' Bruthur. Cool your jets down a bit. Slow down and listen so's she can answer your questions." Jake's touch had a calming effect.

Will heard Tracie saying, "We're okay but scared and hiding in the closet. The police are on the way. I hear the sirens now. And, we don't need an ambulance. Will, I've never been so scared in my life. Why would anyone do this?" She paused for a minute, "The police are here. Gotta go. Bye."

A click; a dial tone. She was gone.

Will sat for a moment in stunned silence until Jake broke into his thoughts. "Take a deep breath and then talk to me. Tell Bruthur Jake what's happened. First off, is anybody hurt?"

Will sucked in a deep breath. "No one's hurt, but someone did shoot up the house-"

He was interrupted by shouts from the hallway, "What's happened this time? Will, you haven't shot out another mirror have you? You must learn how to use a gun properly. Now, where are you?"

Amelia's shouts were accompanied by more voices. Maria came running in to see about her charge.

Jake's voice boomed out, "Everybody's okay. No one's been shot or hurt." He looked at Amelia, "Tracie tried to phone Willie here, but the call came through to my room instead. Now, I suggest we let him tell us what's happened."

He turned back to face Will. "Littl' Bruthur, you start talkin' and say it all nice and slow so's we can understand you."

Will took another deep breath. "Someone shot up our house, knocked out some windows, and left bullet holes in the walls and furniture. Even in the bedrooms." He continued talking, accompanied by exclamations of surprise and dismay from the women.

Amelia broke in, her brows furrowed in anger. "Why, Will?"

She leaned forward in her power chair, fiery with emotion. "Why would anyone do such a thing as that? What kind of neighborhood do you live in anyway? I told you to bring them out here with you."

"We live in a quiet area," Will responded. "It has always had a reputation for safety and low crime. Besides, if they had been with me they would still have been shot at and had to fight rattlesnakes as well."

Amelia glared at him and asked again, "Why? I ask you again, can you think of any reason why?"

"I don't know, Mother. I really do not know."

"Hand me that phone, son. We can't get to Dallas right this minute to help them, but we can't just sit here and do nothing either." Grabbing the phone, she punched in some numbers.

"Jimmy. Is that you? Of course, I know what time it is. Now, listen up..." She gave a quick explanation before adding a long list of instructions.

After hanging up, she turned back to Will. "You call that sweet wife of yours and tell her 'Help is on the way.' We can't be there right now, but Jimmy knows some people in the security business. They will be arriving on her doorstep real soon.

"You tell her we are coming to get her and the kids tomorrow, today rather, as it's after midnight. Although, I don't think we can get there before afternoon."

"Afternoon," Will cried out. "It'll take two days at least to drive that distance—if my old truck'll even make it. Besides, the Sheriff still has it."

"Truck? Who said anything about driving? Let me have that phone back," She ordered.

"You still have it in your hand," Will replied.

"Oh, yes. I guess I do." She punched in more numbers.

"Del," she shouted into the phone. "Yes, I know what time it is, and you've had enough beauty sleep for one night. It doesn't do you any good anyway, and Brenda Lou doesn't need it 'cause she's already the prettiest gal in the county." She paused to take a breath.

"Now, you listen here; how quick can you get a plane out here to the ranch? We have an emergency on our hands. We need to get to Dallas and fly some people back here today, soonest." She paused to listen before blurting out another set of orders.

"When? Right now. Quick. This is an emergency."

She paused before continuing, "There'll be at least four going both ways—that includes Big Jimmy.

"I know, he counts for two, but James only counts for half. Anyway, there'll be an additional adult and two children, with luggage, lots of luggage, coming back."

She paused again. "That's why you're going there—to pick them up. And, we'll be needing transport when we get there. A couple of limos should do. How soon can you be out here at the ranch? This morning?"

She paused again.

"No. That's not soon enough. But, if that's the best you can do... And of course, you'll put it all on my bill."

Another pause.

"No I can't go; can't fly anymore. Now you get here as soon as possible. You hear me?"

She disconnected again and handed the phone back to Will. "Now my boy, you call that girl of yours like I said, and you tell her that help is on the way and to pack her bags. Furthermore, I'm not prepared to take 'No' for an answer." She turned to her nurse.

"Now, Maria, where's that Singh? Tell him I need some hot chocolate."

"Yes, ma'am," came the quiet reply.

No one ever said "No" to Miss Amelia.

Chapter Sixteen
Rescue!

They finished breakfast just as the sun rose over the distant mesas. Amelia rushed Will and Jake out to a waiting ATV, instructions pouring out of her. "The plane will be here shortly. Del promised. You get out there and bring your wife and my grandbabies here where they'll be safe. Now get!"

Jose was waiting with one of the four-seater ATV's. They piled in as the Singh brothers ran out carrying a large ice chest which was loaded behind Will and Jake. As they prepared to speed off, Will heard his mother call out, "Plane's on the way. Be here soon."

They bounced over the ground, Will hanging on to the vehicle with both hands. They slid to a halt at the west end of the long patch of flat ground they had seen from the mesa top the previous day. It did not look as smooth and level up close as it had from above.

Almost as soon as Jose had killed the ATV engine, Will heard another sound. Searching the sky, he saw a small dot growing larger and beginning to take shape.

"That's not a jet is it, Jake?"

"No, Littl' Bruthur, not a jet. But it does have two engines, and if it's what I think it is…" He paused, listening.

"What?"

"If it is, then we are about to ride in a real classic that's probably older both of us put together."

Will looked over at his friend who wore a big grin on his face.

"And, arguably, the best made aircraft ever constructed."

The aircraft in question came into full view, losing altitude with the landing gears dropping into position. The upper half of the fuselage was a bright fire engine red and gleaming white beneath. In the bright morning sun, the plane appeared to be enveloped in flames. The name, "*RoadRunnerAir*," was emblazoned above the windows in Royal blue. At the tail, the vertical stabilizer sported the caricature of a bird, also in royal blue with a yellow beak, very much like a certain cartoon character of the same name.

"It's a beaut, that one is," Jake exclaimed. "C-47 in the military. DC-3 for the civilian crowd, but I've never seen one this bright and new looking—like it just rolled off the assembly line or even better. It may be older than I am, but it looks in a lot better shape."

He glanced over at his friend, who wore a deep frown.

"S'matter, Littl' Bruthur? You lookin' worried?"

Will gave no reply, refusing to take his eyes off the dry earth.

"Say now, you're not afraid are you? You ain't afraid of

flying, are ya? Hey, don't tell me you never flown before?"

Will looked up, hesitant to make eye contact. "Never." He felt as though he was confessing some dark, shameful secret. "Only been to an airport once, back when I was a kid. What if I get airsick?"

By now, the plane was on the ground rolling toward them, billows of dust rising behind it.

Jake chuckled, raising his voice to be heard over the roar of the propellers.

"That's what barf bags are for," Jake laughed. "And I'll just eat your share of the goodies."

"I don't think it's funny."

"Just keep your thoughts on Tracie and the kids," Jake added in a more serious tone. "Think of this as a rescue mission. You're the hero comin' to save them."

"Jake, stop it. I've never done anything heroic in my life." He had to shout to make himself heard.

The aircraft braked to a smooth stop. Silence came as the pilot hit the kill switch; the props wound down and stopped.

They waited, and the dust settled; the side door opened, and a set of metal steps were quickly lowered to the ground. A head appeared through the dark opening, and a deep voice bellowed out, "Welcome aboard." A hand waved in greeting. "Hand up your luggage first, and then climb in."

"Oh no," Will muttered, "Not those two."

Jake bent and grabbed his ever-present briefcase with one hand and a handle of the ice chest with the other.

"Cool your jets, Littl' Bruthur, they're the only two lawyers I've met that I like, and they're on our side. They're here to help you—and your family. Don't you forget that."

They handed up the two items and climbed aboard where they were greeted by a tall, wiry woman dressed in red coveralls, the type that sprouted pockets everywhere. She had "*RoadRunnerAir*" embroidered on the right breast pocket and across her back. Flame red curls fell across her shoulders and spilled down below her shoulders, front and back.

"I'm Brenda Lou Wilkinson. Welcome aboard *RoadRunnerAir*, Flight 001, to Dallas and back. I'll be serving as your co-pilot and sometime flight attendant, today. Please allow me to show you to your seats."

Will stumbled as he made his way through the doorway. The aircraft was an old tail-dragger which meant that the entranceway leaned to one side. Once within the passenger area, he had to hold on to the chair backs as he followed her down the sloping aisle. She placed him in the second row with Jake in front. There were four columns of seats, two down each side of the aisle, twenty-four seats total, all large and comfortable looking.

Big Jim sat in the first row, opposite Jake. Will found himself seated across the aisle from James who had not left his seat to greet them nor had he spoken. His eyes carried a wild look that startled Will.

Scared? Is the cocky little guy afraid of flying? Will smiled, realizing that the idea gave him a perverse sense of comfort.

Once they were all aboard, Jimmy, bending low, manhandled the folding stair ramp up into its storage position and secured the door.

A man appeared behind Brenda Lou, also tall, thin, as wiry as she, and dressed in similar fashion. But, in contrast, was totally bald. "Del," he said. "Your pilot for the flight. Bren's kind enough to let me drive this thing ever once in a while."

"As long as you behave yourself, Del Boy, Momma will

The Ghost of Grandpa Wills

let you play." Will heard but did not like her use of the word 'play'; the sour feeling in his gut meant this was no game for him.

Del continued speaking, "Let's get this chest buckled in somewhere and everyone strapped in as well."

He grabbed the cooler, carried it toward the tail area, and proceeded to strap it into one of the rearmost seats. As he made his way forward, near the front of the passenger compartment he exclaimed, "Brrrr. Ouch, where'd that cold air come from? All the powers off. That's really weird." He shrugged and disappeared into the cockpit area.

Will turned around, looking to where the pilot had been standing, saw nothing, and looked at Jake, who was, also, staring at the front area. Jake shook his head and shrugged his shoulders, palms upward, which Will took to mean he had seen nothing unusual, either.

The seats were large, plush, and very comfortable—not the original factory equipment.

Brenda Lou bent over him, her long curls brushing his face as she checked his seat belt. She smelled of soap, shampoo, and flowery perfume—a pleasant mixture that made him think of Tracie. Again, he remembered they had quarreled the night before he left. And he had not called as promised. Now she and the children were in danger, and he was hundreds of miles away.

Terrible, disturbing questions tumbled through Will's mind. Questions with no pleasant answers—*What if they are attacked again? What if the plane crashes? What if—what if I never see them again?*

Brenda Lou finished with him and moved forward to check on Jake. She then proceeded to give a short lecture about the plane and their coming flight.

"Our plane, in case you were wondering, is a refurbished Douglas Aircraft DC-3, one of the later models manufactured in 1948 and since updated with a strengthened airframe, more powerful engines, and long range fuel capacity. The DC-3 was one of the most reliable aircraft ever built. The one we are flying in is truly a 'Grand Ol' Lady of the Air'.

"We have the ability to fly from here to Dallas and back without refueling, but we will be topping-off at our turn around anyway. Our maximum flying speed is just under three hundred with cruising speed a little less. Our projected flying time is about two and a half hours, but that is subject to change due to the possibility of unexpected weather conditions. This is Texas after all, and you all know what late spring is like in this part of the world."

There was a loud pop and a metallic whine accompanied by strong vibrations. All of which was followed by a tremendous roar and a cloud of smoke. One of the propellers began to spin. Just as the vibrations smoothed out, another series of pops, whines, and roars erupted from the other side of the plane accompanied by more smoke.

Will wanted to release his restraint, jump out of the seat, and flee the aircraft as he saw fire and smoke belch from the engine nacelle just outside his window. However, as neither Jake nor Jimmy showed the least concern he held himself in check and watched in fascination and fear, as the propeller began to rotate until it became a blur.

Brenda Lou raised her voice until she was shouting, continuing her spiel. "These are not the original seats. First built to carry just over thirty passengers we have opted for comfort, safety, and long distance. Besides, it is very difficult to find comfortable seating for a certain gentleman sitting over to my right."

Big Jim nodded and smiled, "Your consideration is appreciated."

"You are most welcome."

She turned back to the other passengers. "We have also installed the very latest in communication and navigation equipment. Furthermore, we now have a brand new autopilot with the latest software and GPS positioning. At least, we won't get lost and end up somewhere in Mexico; although Cancun is supposed to be very nice this time of year.

"Please keep your seat belts buckled at all times while in your seats. The seat backs must be in full-upright position during both takeoff and landing operations. Also, keep your seatbelt tightly buckled during any air turbulence.

"The restroom is through the door in the rear. I do not recommend its usage during periods of turbulence. That is the one seat on the plane without a safety belt.

"In addition, there is definitely no smoking on-board at any time. Please enjoy your flight."

With those final words of encouragement, she wheeled about and hurried into the forward area to take her place in the copilot's seat leaving the cockpit door braced open.

The roar of the engines increased, the vibrations intensified, and they began moving. Will clenched every muscle in his body, his knuckles white on the armrests. He could not take his eyes away from the window as he stared at the world outside, a safe world, firm and solid (forgetting about the rattlesnakes and gunshots for the moment). That solid world moved—at a slow crawl at first. Suddenly, without warning, that solid, firm realm began to fly by.

We're spinning in circles! Will's heart almost stopped beating. *Crashing on takeoff, I'll never see Tracie again!*

But he felt no crashing jolt, no explosion of fire and pain, no rending of metal and flesh; save for the noise and vibration of the engines, all was, soon, calm again.

Daring to look through glass where he had once seen the North Wing of the house, Will now saw Big Ghost Mesa in the distance. Realizing Del had just spun the plane around, he berated himself. *Of course, you ninny, the runway's that a way.* Leaning back against the soft cushions of the seat he continued chastising himself for his own foolish fright.

Millions fly every day and live through it. The aircraft paused for a few minutes. Will held his breath, the butterflies in his stomach were having a field day as another thought came into his mind, *Not in planes twice their age.*

The engines roared, reaching a crescendo of noise, and the vibrations intensified until the entire aircraft shook. Will squeezed his eyes shut and shrank as far back into his seat as possible. He waited for death to take him away!

However, death did not come to Will Watson. The takeoff was smooth and without incident. As soon as they were level, the vibrations decreased to a less fearsome level, and he relaxed enough to suck in a big breath of air. Releasing the death grip on the seat arms, he glanced across the aisle at his fellow passenger.

James sat straight and stiff, corpselike, staring at the seatback in front of him. When he turned to return Will's stare, his eyes stood wide open, unblinking, as if ready to pop from his head.

He's scared silly. He's even more afraid than I am. Again, he found a perverse sense of satisfaction in knowing that someone was more miserable than he.

Chapter Seventeen
An Uninvited Guest

Del appeared through the doorway, moved to the aisle, and announced, "Weather reports some thunderheads ahead in what normally would be our route. We don't have the capability to fly over them. They usually reach upwards of about 33,000 feet, and we max out at about 23,000. We could fly through them though—provide some entertainment for our passengers."

Will's heart sank down into his stomach. His pulse rate doubled.

The pilot continued with a wicked smirk on his face and, looking straight at James, continued, "Or we can go around them." He shrugged his shoulders in a nonchalant manner. "After due consideration to the sensibilities and proclivities of certain of our esteemed passengers, we have decided on the latter course of action. Also I don't want the hailstones and lightning strikes to mess up our brand new paint job.

"I caution you though; we will still, most likely, experience some turbulence. Unfortunately, quite unavoidable." With that, he proceeded aft to the restroom, returning a few minutes later whistling a merry tune as he took his seat in the cockpit.

Will now wished he had some antacids and painkillers; both his stomach and his back were torturing him. After a few minutes, he became restless and decided to get out of his seat and risk moving around. He also realized that Mother Nature was calling. All was peace and quiet, so he decided that now would be the time to answer her summons. The possibility of stormy turbulence lay ahead. Thus he decided, *Do what you gotta do; do it now, and do it in peace.*

Nearing the restroom, Will stopped just rearward of the last row. Sure that his vision was playing tricks on him, he blinked, rubbed his eyes, and looked again. Sure enough—there was a man's backside protruding from the wall of the aircraft into its interior—the bottom half of a man's body from the waist down, legs spread into the cabin area.

His first thought was that this was a crazy joke; someone with a weird sense of humor had gone to the trouble to make it appear as though a man was kneeling with half his body outside the airplane. Then he recognized the ancient, worn-out, dirty trousers. "Oh no," he moaned and hurried over. He reached out to grab something; he knew not what. *How do I get a grip on a ghost?*

"Grandpa. What are you doing here?" he hissed hoping not to be over heard. His hands found nothing solid to latch onto, even though he did feel the bone-chilling cold.

The ghost moved, withdrawing back into the cabin area.

The Ghost of Grandpa Wills

With his eyes wide with exhilaration, Franklin exclaimed, "Hot dang, Grandson. This flying in an aero plane is sure something. Nothing like it." He floated above the deck, waving his arms in his excitement. "Never seen anything from way up here be…?"

"Grandpa!" Will interrupted in an angry tone. "What are you doing here?"

"Why, I wanted to ride in one of these flying contraptions," Franklin replied dropping arms to his side, taking affront at Will's less than gracious tone of voice.

"I have read about them and seen them on the television. But I never rode in one," he answered in an innocent tone. He stood straight with his hands on his hips, floating in midair and glaring down at Will. "Just came along for the ride. That is all I have done."

Now, he tilted himself forward until the two were almost nose to nose and demanded, "And how, may I ask, is it any of your business anyway? This is still a free country, is it not?"

"You're not supposed to be here."

"And why not? There is no law that says I cannot."

Will was not sure about that statement. *How would the FAA rule on the question of having a ghost on board?*

"Mother said you weren't supposed to ever leave the house. This is not the house."

Much to Will's relief, Franklin pulled himself back allowing more distance between their noses. The ghost leaned backward until he looked down his nose at his grandson. "Son, I know this flying machine is not a house, and she never said I could not. She just said I never did, like as if I never could. But I never said I could not and never said I would not neither. So, when I do want to go, I go."

A fiery light shone in his eyes as he spoke. "Besides, I

am old enough; I do not have to ask anyone's howdy-do when I want something." Crossing his arms in front of his chest he looked over Will's shoulder.

"Who are you talking to?" Will heard Jake's voice and turned to see him standing close behind.

With a frown Will replied, "Grandpa's onboard. I caught him with his front side hanging outside and his backside hanging inside."

"That must have been a pretty sight," Jake chuckled.

"Not funny, especially if it freaks out our pilots upfront."

"I am not scaring anyone," came the angry retort.

Will scowled at his grandfather.

"What's he saying?" Jake asked.

"Promised not to cause any trouble. Now I need to get somewhere fast, if you don't mind." Will turned back toward the restroom.

Chapter Eighteen
A Bit of Air Turbulence

Will turned off the water and reached for a paper towel to dry his hands just as the floor fell out from under him. Immediately, thereafter, he found himself being thrown hard against the rear bulkhead of the tiny restroom. Landing on his back he gasped as air was forced from his lungs.

Lying on his back grimacing in pain, and wild eyed with panic, he found himself looking up at the restroom door. Disoriented, he struggled to right himself until he was somersaulted onto the ceiling, which was now where the floor should have been. To his horror, he now stared into the open bowl of the stainless steel toilet—where he had been sitting just a few seconds before. *Sure glad I flushed it,* was the thought that ran through his mind.

His world shifted again. This time, Will was thrown hard

against the door. It burst open with a crash and the sound of splintering wood. Out of control, he landed on his backside, sliding feet first, down the center aisle. Screaming, he snatched at seat mountings, pant legs, and whatever else came into reach—all to no avail. He came to a bone-jarring halt with one foot against the back of the copilot's seat and the other against the base of the control pedestal. He heard Del and Brenda Lou, in panic-stricken tones, shouting to each other, along with more screams coming from the passenger compartment.

Will had no idea what had just happened. However, what he did know at this precise moment, was that the same rear-end he had seen back near the tail section, now protruded from the base of the control panel just below the throttle levers. He realized they were in serious trouble.

"Grandpa," he screamed reaching out with both hands, thrusting them deep into the ethereal figure. Cold seared through him, but he ignored it as he flailed his hands around. "Franklin Percival, come out of there before you kill us all!"

In one quick movement, the ghost backed out of the control panel. The plane leveled off before going into a nose-up attitude to begin a steep climb. Will, still on his back, slid toward the passenger section. He was well on his way when a hand grabbed him by his oversized belt buckle.

Chapter Nineteen
Level—At Last

Jimmy kept a firm grip on Will's belt until the plane leveled out.

"Thanks," Will gasped. The big guy released him. He struggled to his feet and, holding to armrests and seat backs, he wobbled his way back to his own seat and buckled himself in place. Looking around, he saw James sitting stiff and unmoving, head pressed against the seat back. He had turned a deathly white pallor and bore a close resemblance to a corpse. Will hoped the little guy was still alive. "Jake, you okay?" He called, in a hoarse whisper.

"Yeah, still hangin' in there. That was some ride. Never heard of air turbulence doing that."

"Doing what? I was flying all over the place. What all did happen? But, I don't think it was turbulence—least not the kind you're talking about."

"We did a complete loop and then lost altitude real fast. Thought we were goners for sure. What makes you think it wasn't air turbulence, anyway?"

Will loosened his straps and leaned forward enough to keep their conversation more private. "'Cause Grandpa decided to visit the cockpit, that's why."

"What?" Jake's head whipped around, his eyes wide and his mouth open in amazement. "Are you sure?"

"Yeah, you better believe I'm sure—very sure."

They were interrupted by Brenda Lou, who staggered from the cockpit, pale and wide-eyed, looking as if she had just looked death in the eye.

"She don't look as peppy as a while ago," Jake commented.

"Don't blame her," Will responded. "I've felt better myself."

"Is everyone okay?" she asked, bracing herself against the back of Jimmy's seat.

"We're all alive," Jimmy answered in a weak tone.

"You might check on James," Will pointed. "He's looking a little pale."

"I, I'm okay," James responded in a quivering voice, barely heard above the cabin noise. "Anyone care to explain what just happened? Felt like we were upside down for a while."

Brenda Lou came down the aisle to stand between Will and James. With her feet apart and continuing to brace herself, her eyes shifted from one to the other. Her gaze settled on Will. Feeling as if he was under a microscope, he shrank back into his seat. After a moment's scrutiny she asked, "You okay?"

The Ghost of Grandpa Wills

"Yeah. I think I'll live. Few bruises is all—I hope, but I'm sore all over."

"You get checked out when we get back," she said in an authoritative tone as though she were used to giving orders. She bent forward, coming close to Will's face and demanded, "What was all that yelling?"

Releasing the seat, she brought her hand up to wag her finger in his face. "Sounded like you were shouting something about your Grandpa. I don't see any old folks on board. Hope you weren't talking to that ghost that's supposed to be haunting the old Castle. Were you? We don't need any dead folks on board."

Will forced a chuckle and then answered, "Of course not. That's just an old story. I've never believed in ghosts anyway. How about you?"

There was deep suspicion in her expression as she stood straight. "I have no time for such tales."

Will forced a laugh. "Yeah, same here."

Jake kept his head down and his mouth shut. Will fell back into his seat and tightened his seat belt.

As Brenda Lou passed, Jimmy's voice boomed out above the engine roar, "What did happen back there, Bren?"

She paused a few seconds. "Must be a bug in the software for that new autopilot system. It's disabled now. We'll be having it checked out completely before using it again. We're flying manual rest of the way in.

"Everything looks calm all the way into Love Field. The storms have moved east. We're well north of them so we should have a smooth ride the rest of the way in. Forecast looks great for the return flight as well."

James found his voice and squeaked. "How about the plane? Is it okay? Anything broke?"

"Course not," she laughed. "We're still in the air, aren't we? She's a tough ol' gal; this gooney bird is."

I think I see a tinge of green in the little guy's face.

Chapter Twenty
A Heart to Heart Talk

Will sat for a few moments before getting restless again. He was angry and becoming more so by the minute; *Grandpa almost crashed the plane!* Moreover, the ghost was not supposed to be on board, and what will happen when Tracie and the kids came on board? He was certain that none of them would like flying with a ghost as a fellow passenger.

Will sat thinking for several more minutes. *"How do you make a ghost behave himself? How does Mother control him?"* With those thoughts still running through his head, he made up his mind, unbuckled, and moved to the last row, where he paused and looked around. He saw nothing unusual, but still sensed a presence. He remembered the same feeling other times when his grandfather had been nearby but unseen.

Sliding into the starboard seat, he spoke in soft but firm

tones, hoping no one—no one living, at least—would hear him, "Grandpa! Grandpa! Show yourself. Let me see you—no one else, just me."

A long pause.

"Grandpa. I know you're here. We need to talk. Now, stop acting like a spoiled kid. Show yourself."

The air grew cold around him and shimmered. He watched his grandfather materialize, floating in the window seat with the upper half of his body showing above the cushions. The sight gave Will a creepy feeling; he wondered whether he would ever get used to it. It was weird, having a ghost for a grandfather—talking to someone who had been dead for more than a century and a half.

"Talk, Grandson. No one else can see me, but they might wonder if you have taken to mumbling to yourself."

Will hoped the engine noise would hide their conversation. "Why," he asked?

"Why what?"

Will answered while trying to hide his anger. "Don't play games, Grandpa. This is serious."

"I told you. I wanted to ride one of these flying contraptions." Franklin kept his eyes on the window as he talked.

Will wondered, *is he watching the clouds pass by or avoiding having to look at me?*

"I wanted to see how they work. Not being alive does not mean I am not curious. I get bored always staying in the library-"

Will broke in, "You aren't supposed to be here!" Forgetting himself, he raised his voice and gestured. "You aren't supposed to leave the house."

Now Franklin turned to face Will. "Why? Says who?"

The Ghost of Grandpa Wills

"Mother, for one thing. Besides, ghosts aren't supposed to ever leave the place where they died."

"Grandson, for someone who does not believe in ghosts, you certainly seem to consider yourself an authority all of a sudden."

"That's what it says in the books I've read," Will responded.

"Books," Franklin responded with a huff. "Young fellow, you have been reading the wrong books. As for me, I am talking experience—firsthand experience. Besides, the house is not where I died anyway."

Will's eyebrows went up in surprise. "What? Where then? Where did you die?"

This is bizarre, asking someone where they died.

"I do not know," Franklin answered. "I cannot remember. The house had not been built as yet—nary a stone of it."

"Well, where then?"

"I do not know where; somewhere dark is all I can recall. I believe that to be why I fear the darkness." There was a strange, lost expression on his face. "Have you ever heard of a ghost being afraid of the dark?"

"Ahh, can't say that I have, but then, I confess, I don't know much about'm—never having met a real one before." Frowning in concentration, Will added, "Maybe the dark place is your grave, where they buried you. Most people are afraid of being buried."

"No," Franklin replied in a solemn voice. "I was never buried. Nor was there a funeral. I do reckon I would remember my own funeral."

Now, the ghost stared, not at Will so much as through him, looking back into the past, searching for something, but he knew not what.

"There was no funeral because they never found my body. It is lost, off in some dark place somewhere. It was dark where I died."

Will did not know how to respond. He saw pain and sadness in his grandfather's eyes and wondered, *Can a ghost cry, actually shed tears?* He realized that he felt empathy for his grandfather. *He really is hurting.*

"Grandpa," he said, his anger gone. "I'm sorry about getting so mad, but you did almost kill us all."

"Will not happen again, I swear." The ghost held up his right hand.

"Yeah, okay. But what about Tracie and my kids?"

"Huh," Franklin looked surprised and hurt as he replied to the implied accusation. "I will not hurt them. I do not—have never—hurt a child," he added emphatically.

Will remembered his mother's story about Franklin caring for the young Apache boy.

Franklin continued, "And I do not wish to frighten any women folk—especially my own family and kin."

The ghost paused a moment, looked Will in the eye, and asked, "Is she a pretty lady?"

"Huh? Who?" The question caught Will off guard. "You mean Tracie?"

Franklin said nothing but frowned as if he considered that a foolish question.

"Of course," Will answered, as he pictured her in his mind—*Bright smile, blue eyes, long golden curls, petite, every bit a most beautiful woman.*

"She's very pretty; she's beautiful," he affirmed, looking at the back of the seat in front of him.

His thoughts went back to Tracie. He again realized how

The Ghost of Grandpa Wills

much he missed her. No more than a few days had passed, but so much had happened it seemed more like weeks or months. They had never been apart for more than a day before now, and how he had always taken her presence for granted—and the kids as well.

"Might you have a photograph? No such things in my day, just daguerreotypes; I saw one of them before." Will thought he heard his grandfather sigh, or was it a sob?

Franklin went on. "Nothing to remember them by, now." He spoke so quietly that it was difficult for Will to hear the words above the noise of the aircraft. Again the ghost looked past Will.

He's staring at something faraway, far off in another place, another time.

"Nothing to remember them by," Franklin repeated. "Just my memory, and it is not too good anymore."

Will wondered what to say, how to reply when his grandfather turned back to look at him.

"Have a picture to show me?" Franklin asked again.

Will reached for his billfold, found his photos of Tracie and the kids, and displayed them.

"Do you tell her?" Grandpa broke into his thoughts.

"Huh?"

"Do you ever tell her how pretty she is? You ought to, you know." Again, that same faraway look. "I never did, you know. Now it is too late. Too late to tell her anything now—too late."

Will thought he heard a sob as Franklin continued. "Been too late for a long, long time."

The ghost floated by Will, toward the center aisle, looking at the aircraft wall opposite them. "You know, I never told her I loved her either; never said so to my children neither. Then, I went off to Texas." His grandfather paused. Will opened his mouth to reply but the ghost interrupted. "I got myself killed before they arrived. Tried to talk to them afterward, but they were always scared real bad."

He turned back to face Will. "My own family, blood kin, too afraid to talk to me."

Will thought back to his last night with Tracie, the argument about that stupid tobacco and the ridiculous clothes he had chosen, and how disappointed the kids were about not going to the coast. How he had made all the decisions—without including them.

His grandpa floated there, staring at him. Will felt transparent, as though Franklin was looking right into his innermost being. *Is he reading my mind?* With reluctance, Will confessed, "Not in a while, I guess."

"No, I never said, 'I love you' neither—then it was too late—way too late." The old ghost wavered, becoming almost transparent. When Will looked up, he saw tears running down his grandpa's cheeks

"Not going to scare anyone; at least, I surely do not want to. I would like to give them all a hug, a big hug." He sighed again, as he looked away—far away into the distant past. "But that will not be happening. A ghost cannot hug people; people cannot hug a ghost." He twisted back around to look at Will, eye to eye. "I shall stay out of sight. I will not wreck this flying machine. Nor will I be frightening your lovely lady and harming my grandchildren." With those last words, Grandpa Wills disappeared.

Will sat alone in the rearmost seat, lost in thought when Jake's voice broke in.

"What ya thinkin' 'bout, Littl' Bruthur?" Jake stood looking down, with anxiety written across his broad, round

The Ghost of Grandpa Wills

features. There was concern in his voice. "You look as though you just got some real bad news or somethin'."

Will glanced up at his best friend then looked down at the floor. "He said he'd never told them he loved them, never said 'I love you; now it's too late'."

"What?" Jake asked in a puzzled tone. "Who said they don't love you? Who've you been talking too?"

"No, not about me. He was talking about his wife and kids. How he never said he loved them. Then, it was too late. Too late to say anything."

Will took his eyes off the floor and stared at his best friend. "We argued, Tracie and me, fought actually, the night before I left." He added in words so soft that Jake leaned in close to hear. "I can't remember when's the last time I said that to any of them; told'm I love'm."

Jake waved Will over to the window seat and made himself comfortable next to the aisle. They rode in silence for a few minutes, both saying nothing but sharing each other's presence while staring at the seatbacks in front of them.

"You been talkin' to your Grandpa?"

"Yeah," Will looked at his friend for a moment before casting his eyes to the floor. "He told me how he never told'm he loved them, just ran off to Texas; never saw them again. At least, while he was still alive."

Jake sat, also, looking down as if counting the rivets in the floor plating. He cleared his throat and spoke.

"Littl' Bruthur, I'm gonna tell you sumthin' I've never told another livin' soul."

Will turned to his friend and saw moisture forming in Jake's eyes.

Jake's gaze met Will's. The words came slowly, hesitantly, and with effort. "We'd been ridin' a while. Kids were getting' restless like kids do on a long trip."

Jake paused and cleared his throat. His voice grew hoarse. "Caroline was asleep, her head propped against the window with a pillow." He stopped talking once more, shifted his eyes, and stared out the plane's window, but it was not the clouds he was seeing.

"They started fightin'; the two of them did. Yellin' and all. I knew they was hittin' each other like always happened."

When Jake looked back, Will saw big tears rolling down his cheeks. "I turned back to yell at them. I was real tired—had a bad headache. Hadn't wanted to make this trip anyway, and so I was already angry. So I—I yelled at'm. Took my eyes off the road for just a second to scream back at them."

Jake coughed and cleared his throat while he wiped his eyes with the back of his hands.

Will sat speechless, hurting for his friend, the one he considered his only true friend.

"That's when it happened you know—when I lost control." Jake sat forward with his elbows on his knees and covered his face with his hands.

He continued speaking through his fingers. "Something happened. Never knew what. We rolled over and over. Don't know how many times we rolled."

Through sobs Jake said, "The last words they heard from my mouth was 'Y'all sit down an' shut up.'" Tears streamed down his cheeks. "Those were the last words they ever heard their daddy say. And Caroline—Caroline, my Caroline, she never heard anything…ever again…"

After a pause, Jake wiped the tears away with his hand, turned to face Will, and added, "Littl' Bruthur, you always tell'm you love'm!"

Jake's dark eyes burned deep into Will's soul. "Don't

you ever stop tellin'm how much you love'm."

With those words, Jake rose abruptly and walked slowly back to his seat.

Will sat without moving, looking out the window and seeing nothing, overwhelmed by his friend's confession.

Time passed, crawling by. Occasionally Will reached up to wipe the moisture in his own eyes. His thoughts were on Tracie and his children when Del's voice boomed out over the intercom, announcing their impending arrival at Dallas Love Field.

Chapter Twenty-One
On the Ground.

Ground transportation came in the form of a very long stretch limousine. Jake claimed shotgun position. "I know where we're going and the quickest way to get there."

As soon as he was buckled in, Will grabbed his cell phone and punched the speed dial for Tracie. She answered after the first ring.

"Hello—Will? Her tone told him she was on the edge of tears. "Where are you?"

"Trace, we're at Love Field in a limo and on our way to pick you up; be there as soon as possible. Don't worry, everything's going to be all right."

"All right? Will, somebody shot at us."

The Ghost of Grandpa Wills

Is that anger or fear in her voice? Or both? Probably, the latter, he decided ruefully.

"Police are all over the place and some armed security people as well." Her words spilled out, running together. "I had to take the kids out of school early and ask for time off. What's going on?" She asked in a tone that left no doubt about her anger. "Will, are you in some kind of trouble?"

"I…" He did not know how to answer that question, at least not in a few short words over the phone. "I'll explain when I get there. I'm not alone. Jake is with me." She always seemed to take comfort in Jake's presence.

"Trace, I…I, Tracie, I…I love you. I've really missed you a lot. You and the kids, I've missed all of you."

"Will—what? You're scaring me now. What is happening? You've never talked like that before."

"I know; I'm really sorry. But, but—it's all going to be okay, and you'll love my mother. The kids will too. Tracie, they have a grandmother—a real live grandmother. And there's horses they can ride. Cows as well."

He heard a young girl's voice come through the phone from somewhere behind Tracie. "No, you can't have that. It's mine; so put it back!"

The voice in the background became a shout. "Mom, Robbie's taking my stuff." Will recognized his daughter's voice. With his grandfather's words running through his mind, he thought—*Katie, dear, I love you, and I'm going to tell you so when I see you.*

"Will, I've gotta go." Tracie's voice broke into his thoughts. "Need to help the kids finish packing. How much can we bring?"

"Lots and lots, Trace. Don't worry about that. Mother hired a private plane just for us." He heard a shrill, angry scream arise in the background. "Mom. Mommmmm. Make him stop. Now!"

"Gotta go. Duty calls. Will, I love you, too. Bye." The phone went dead.

Chapter Twenty-Two
Home Again

Will's heart skipped a beat when they pulled up in front of his house. He saw the police cars and an SUV parked at the curb. Hearing Tracie talk about it on the phone was one thing, but now the reality of the attack came home. This was not his imagination; this was real. With his heart thumping, he was unbuckled and out of the limo before it stopped moving, running hard as soon as his feet hit the ground.

As Will approached the front door, a tall, burly man dressed in a dark suit, opened the front door of the house and blocked the entrance, his left hand held inside his jacket, just above his waist. He opened his mouth to speak when he was struck from behind and roughly pushed aside.

Katie and Robby fought their way through the space between the man and the doorframe. "Daddy! Daddy!" Will was almost to the steps when they reached him. Going to his knees, he wrapped them in his arms, hugging them tight. Words spilled out of them— "afraid," "scared," "guns," "shot," and "mommy crying."

"It's all right," Will tried to reassure them. "I'm here. Uncle Jake is here. Everything will be okay." He hoped he sounded more confident than he felt. *Why is all this happening?* The question kept running through his mind. Still holding them tight, he added, "I love you. I love you with all my heart."

He heard other voices and looked up to see Tracie standing there—dressed in a short-sleeved blouse and her favorite pair of old, faded blue jeans, with her golden curls wafting in the light breeze. Rising to his feet, he disentangled himself from his kids saying, "Let me say 'Hi' to Mother."

Stepping forward the first utterance out of his mouth was, "I'm sorry." More words tumbled forth— "You're beautiful. I love you. I've missed you. I was so afraid I'd never see you again." Tears filled his eyes as he pulled her close, squeezed her tight, and kissed her.

As she returned his hug, she heard him give a sharp gasp of pain. She pushed away to arm's length. "What? Are you hurt?"

"Bruises."

"Will. What…"

"I, ah, I fell—was thrown—off a horse. Just some cuts and bruises on my back. I'll be all right in few days."

A familiar voice called out from behind her. "Yeah, if only he had landed on his head it wouldn't have hurt him." Tracie swung around and she saw Jake, a kid hanging onto to each hand and a big smile on his face.

"Jake!" She released Will and rushed over to give him a

big hug before backing off. With hands on her hip and steel in her eyes, she demanded, "Someone tell me what's going on. Now!"

"We'll talk about it on the plane," Will responded.

"We really do need to hurry," Jake added.

"Yes, ma'am, he's right. It would be best if we could get back to the plane as soon as possible." Tracie looked around for the owner of the strange, deep voice. She saw two strangers, one quite tall and the other quite short, standing next to the big burly guy, along with a uniformed police officer.

Will spoke up, "I guess introductions are in order." He waved a hand toward the pair and said, "James Smithson and Jimmy Smith—Mom's lawyers."

"Just call me 'Jimmy,' please ma'am, if you would," the tall one said, his voice rumbling like a volcano about to erupt. He smiled down at her and tipped his big Stetson in polite greeting. "That's my little brother, James." He pointed.

"Pleased to meet you, also," James spoke up. "We're here to see you get to the ranch safely."

"Safely?" she protested. Resuming her authoritative stance, hands on hips, eyes blazing, she again demanded, "I want to know what's going on, and I want to know now." She turned back to Will. "All this talk about packing up and flying off into the wild blue yonder; what about our home and all our belongings? We can't just leave everything and run off to somewhere at the other end of the world."

"Hey, mister, are you Batman?" a small voice piped up.

Everyone stopped and looked down to see Robby standing in front of Jimmy, head bent back, staring up at the big man.

"Sorry," Tracie hurried to explain. "That's Robbie, and

we watched a Batman movie on TV last night. Now he wants to meet him and see the Bat Cave."

Jimmy smiled, showing his big gold teeth, and lowered himself to one knee on the grass. "No, young fella, I'm not Batman, but I can show you some real cowboys and horses when we get to the ranch."

"Cowboys?" the youngster exclaimed. "With real 'paches and G'romeo?"

"Well," Jimmy laughed. "I can definitely show you some real live Apaches, but I'm afraid Geronimo'll be a bit of a challenge." He took Robbie's hand in his as he stood. "Now come on, let's get this show on the road. We want to get to the ranch before dark." He bent low to speak to the boy. "Besides, your grandmother's real anxious to meet you and your sister." With those words, still holding the little hand in his big one, he started for the house, turning to Tracie as he did so.

"This property will be guarded and under surveillance all the while you are gone. Arrangements have already been made—by direct order of Miss Amelia."

Tracie looked at Will, eyebrows raised, "Who?"

"Mother," he answered with a big grin. "And no one ever says 'No' to Miss Amelia."

Chapter Twenty-Three
Questions in the Air.

"Will," Tracie spoke with a sense of urgency in her voice, "those two lawyer friends of yours, they have guns. I saw them under their suit coats. You know I don't like guns. Anyway, aren't they against the law on airplanes?"

"This is a private plane, and we're in Texas—or over Texas, and they are both licensed to carry concealed weapons. I think both Del and Brenda Lou are probably armed as well."

"Licensed or not, I don't care. Guns are bad. They're dangerous. Why do they need guns here anyway?"

They were about fifteen minutes into their flight and sitting together well toward the tail section. Both kids had chosen to go forward. Katie sat next to Uncle Jake; Robby had taken a real liking to Big Jimmy and was peppering him with questions about "'paches and G'romeo". The big guy looked as though he were enjoying himself while Robby sat entranced, not taking his eyes off his newfound hero.

Loosening his seat belt, Will turned to face Tracie. He took her hands in his and said, "There are some things you need to know, but I didn't want to talk about in front of the kids. It would scare them."

Her eyes went wide open. "Scare them; you're scaring me now. What's going on? You make it sound as though someone's trying to kill us."

She withdrew her hands and with a frown creasing her brow continued, "Just because some idiots were stupid and careless the other night doesn't mean they were trying to kill anyone."

"True." He continued in what he hoped was a calm voice. "If that was the only thing that has happened."

Those words rocked her back into the seat cushions. With her voice rising in both volume and pitch, she demanded to know, "Will Watson, what do you mean by 'the only…?'"

"Shh, shh." He tried to wave her down before the kids heard the tension in her voice. "Everything's okay, now. Let me talk."

He paused, brushed a loose curl away from her eyes. "Have I ever told you how beautiful you are?"

"What," came her startled response? "No. I mean, yes. Just a little while back. Why are you acting so weird all of a sudden? Now tell me what's going on."

"Okay." He sat back, cleared his throat, and fixed his eyes on her. "Well, you are very beautiful. This is what happened, some of it, anyway…"

"No. I want the whole story, all of it." The look on her face told him there would be no compromise on this matter.

"It's a long story."

The Ghost of Grandpa Wills

"It's a long flight, Buster; so start talking." She turned to face him and, now, sat with arms crossed and a cold fire in her eyes that warned him to tread lightly.

So—he told her everything—almost.

"Rattlesnakes? You got shot? You didn't tell me?"

"Shot at. The truck's full of bullet holes, not me. And, I'm telling you now. So, when you and the kids were shot at—we all decided not to take any chances."

"Is that all? Any more life and death episodes I need to know about?"

"Well, there was the 'air turbulence' on the flight out," a voice interrupted them.

"What?" They both looked up to see Brenda Lou standing over them. "Sorry, I couldn't help but over-hear. You weren't talking in whispers.

"I really wanted to ask about refreshments. Miss Amelia packed a bunch of stuff—cold drinks and all. Anyone hungry? Del and I, we have our own stuff. We're vegans."

"Vegans," Will replied, "Where's that?"

Tracie laughed. "Not a place, Dummy—a who. They're strict vegetarians, no animal products in their diets."

"Yeah," Brenda Lou added. She waved at the big ice chest bucked into the seat behind and across the aisle from them. "And I'm sure Miss Amelia has packed a ton of steak and beef sandwiches for all of you—probably enough for a jumbo jet full. So, don't hurt her feelin's; everybody get to eatin'." She turned and walked back to the front.

"So, what's this 'air turbulence' stuff?"

"Ahh, she said earlier that it was the autopilot, and then they switched it off. Everything was okay after that. A real smooth flight.

"Let's see what's there." Will unbuckled and started to

get out of his seat.

Tracie grabbed his arm and held on. "Not yet, Buster, you haven't told me why yet."

He sighed and sat back down, "We don't know why. It may have been a bug in the autopilot or the bad weather. Who knows?"

"Not that, you doofus. Why did someone shoot at you and try to kill you?"

Forgetting about the ice chest for the moment, he sat back down and looked past her, seeing white clouds sailing past the window. He rubbed his eyes with his fingertips and took a deep breath. "The sheriff thinks someone didn't want me to get to the ranch." With palms up, he shrugged. "I don't know why. Why should anyone care where I go?"

"You can't figure it out?" she asked, looking him right in the eyes, almost nose to nose, "Will Watson, how big is this ranch?"

"I don't know. It's huge."

"How much is it all worth?"

"With oil wells and cattle—lots, a whole lot."

"And your mother is sick?"

"Yes—cancer."

"Is she dying?"

"Well—yes, they say she is. The doctors say so, that is."

"Are you her only child? Her only heir?"

Will stared at her, eyes open wide.

Tracie demanded, "Will answer me. Who will inherit all this when she passes away?"

"I hadn't thought about it," he confessed.

"Well, start thinking about it. And, think about what might happen if you weren't here to get it? That just might give you some clues about who's been shooting at us."

She pointed forward. "Maybe 'Big Jim' up there has some ideas he can share with you. Just send Robby back to me. I think we'll go ahead and take a peek in that snack box."

Robby did not want to leave Jimmy's side but relented after being offered a peanut butter sandwich.

"What can I do for you, Mister Watson?" Jimmy asked as Will squeezed into the seat next to him.

"Call me Will, please, if you will."

"I will, Will, if you will call me Jim."

Will moved around to the window seat and made himself comfortable

"Yeah, well, any ideas why anyone would be shooting at me and my family?" he asked, looking up at the big guy.

"A few ideas, yeah, theories—no hard evidence. How about you?"

"Well, I think I remember you saying something about someone not wanting me to get to the ranch."

"The thought has occurred to me—and Sara, as well," Jim continued; a frown creasing his forehead.

"Why?" Will asked, "Why try to stop me from getting to the ranch?"

Will gestured with his hands out, palms up, and fingers extended. "What's the big deal about me seeing my mother when I didn't know she was my mother?"

"In case you haven't figured it out, you are now her sole heir—except for some bequests to her employees and a few charities. You get it all—after the estate duties, that is."

"I haven't even thought about an inheritance, Jim. Why, I'm glad to even have a mother after all these years. I hadn't considered anything else. I don't want her to die."

Big Jim sighed, "Neither do I, Mr. Watson, ah, Will; neither do I. She's been like a mother to both James and me ever since we both can remember. We were orphans, too, you know. Until she—well until she filled that empty spot in our lives. So, I share your feelings."

There was a short pause before Will asked, "What if you hadn't found me? What would have happened to everything?"

"This is just between you and me. Understand? Actually, I'm not supposed to discuss any of this without Miss Amelia's say so." He twisted in his seat to face Will.

"She hasn't said 'Don't' but then, she hasn't said 'Okay' either. So I'm stickin' my neck out a bit here. My little brother back there." He jerked his thumb back over his shoulder as he spoke. "He will probably have a hernia when he finds out. He's a real stickler for details. So mum's the word; you hear? But you and your family are the ones being shot at, and we all want to keep you safe."

Big Jim shifted in his seat. "You may remember that we discussed much of this back at the Castle. Let me clarify the matter for you."

Will listened, chewing on his lower lip while the lawyer reiterated the past events that lead to the present situation.

As Jimmy finished his monologue he reached up with a big finger and poked Will in the chest. "And by the way, if you don't have a will, you need one—ASAP."

"So, any chance someone connected with that society didn't want me to show up?"

"We're lookin', Mister Will; we're certainly a lookin'. We have contacts, you know. Some people who owe us a favor or two."

Jim turned in his seat. "Now, my advice for you is keep your eyes and ears open and your head down."

The Ghost of Grandpa Wills

After a moment of silence, Jim cleared his throat and continued, "Now, I have a question or two for you."

Will sensed something unpleasant was coming. "What?" he asked with apprehension.

Jim continued with a strange look on his face. "When you came slidin' down the aisle and made that very graceful entrance into the cockpit—then came slidin' back again." A deep chuckle escaped from inside Jimmy as a huge grin spread across his face. "I do wish we had all that on video. You looked so graceful.

The grin disappeared replaced by a somber expression, "Anyway, I heard you screamin' somethin'—somethin' that sounded a lot like you were shoutin for that legendary ghostly Grandpa of yours. Maybe I misunderstood you? Do you think?"

Will forced a little chuckle and asked, "Surely, you don't believe in ghosts, do you?"

"Didn't used to. Now? Well, let's just say that lately I've become a bit more open minded on the subject. So tell me, is your ghostly grandpa on board this plane?"

Will hesitated for a moment, cleared his throat, and looked out the window before replying. "Unfortunately—yes."

"Did he cause all that ruckus with the autopilot?"

Will turned back to face Jim. "Afraid so. He was curious about the controls so he stuck his head inside the electronics—just to take a look. Messed them up a bit."

"A bit!" Jimmy tensed up. Will wondered whether the big guy was going to explode. "That's an understatement; he almost killed us all!"

Will responded, wanting to be diplomatic and pour oil on troubled waters. "It all straightened out as soon as I got him out of it. Mother says he can work a computer the same way—if he doesn't mess it up first. But, he's learned how to use them and has his own back there in the library. She unplugs it if he doesn't behave."

Will found he wanted to defend his grandpa—despite all the trouble he had caused. *After all, he is my grandfather—even if he has been dead for a century and a half.*

"And what do we do now? Take his airplane away from him?" The big guy's voice dripped with sarcasm.

"I had a long talk with him, and he promised not to do it again."

"Well, why was he here on the plane anyway? I thought ghosts couldn't leave the places they haunted."

"I asked him the same question. He said I had been reading all the wrong books and that no one's ever told him he couldn't go anywhere."

Will shrugged and gestured, palms up. "He's never been in an airplane before so he decided to come along." He added in a stronger tone of voice, "He promised to behave on the way home—not cause any more trouble."

Jimmy looked around as if he expected to see the ghost hovering close by. "Is he here, close to us? Right now? Listening to us? Can you see him?"

"Not at this moment. He can show himself to family or to everyone, or he can hide from everyone. But, I'm learning to know when he's around. Sort of sense his presence."

"The ice cold feeling I get sometimes when I visit your mother in the library?"

"That's only if he touches you or gets real close. I just have a feeling when he's around. It's a family thing I guess."

"And what will your wife say when she learns about your ghostly ancestor?"

Will admitted. "I don't think she'll be too happy, so I'd appreciate it if you don't say anything."

It occurred to Will that Tracie enjoyed reading ghost stories and spooky novels—especially those about pretty young women living in old stone houses—stuff that he had always thought silly. He wondered what she would think about such stuff in real life. *After all, she is quite pretty and going to a stone house, haunted by a ghost.*

"Yeah," Big Jim nodded. "You going to tell her, or let her find out the hard way?"

Will looked at the big man for a moment before turning to stare past him to where Jake sat reading on the other side. He turned back to Jim, "I haven't quite figured that one out yet."

"Well," Jim said, a rueful smile on his face. "I'm sure she'll be finding out one way or the other. That's one secret that won't keep very long once we're back at the ranch."

Will excused himself, released his seatbelt, and moved back to where Tracie sat. Robbie was more than happy to get back to his new found hero. With a cookie in one hand and a can of soda in the other, the boy hurried forward.

Will searched the cabin area looking for his long-lost ancestor—part wishing he would never see him again, part hoping for a quick glance—if only to know where he was. Seeing no sign of the ghost, he slid in next to Tracie. She had her electronic notebook out, ear buds in place—reading and listening to music.

"What ya readin'?" he asked, trying to sound casual as he lowered himself into place.

"A book," came her reply as she removed the ear buds. She looked up at him with suspicion written on her face. "Why? What's wrong now?"

"I never said anything was wrong. Just asking, that's all." He studied the back of the seat in front of him.

"You never asked before—except when you want to make fun of what I'm reading."

He turned to face her. "Well, I'm just curious that's all. You like those ghost stories and such. Is that one of 'm?"

"Look, Will, it's been a hard few days, and I just wanted to relax without an argument. You make up your stories; you read what you want, so let me read my ghost stories. Okay?"

"I was just wondering if you actually, really did believe in ghosts; that's all."

She lowered the notepad to her lap and looked at him, "Okay, spit it out. Something's bugging you. What are you talking about?"

"J—just asking, that's all." He shrugged his shoulders and looked away.

Her eyebrows came together in a frown as she looked hard at him. "Ghosts. You're not trying to tell me the ranch is haunted?"

Chapter Twenty-Four
The Truth Is Out

"Well, ahh," he stammered, "It, well, not the whole ranch—just the house. And he's not a bad ghost. He's promised not to do anything bad or scary. He really loves kids. And he promised-"

"What? He promised…" she exclaimed gesturing with hands in the air and a wild light in her eyes. "You're trying to tell me you've been talking to a ghost? You expect me to believe that? You're the one that doesn't believe in spirits and ghosts and such."

She raised a hand causing Will to flinch, as he feared the worst. Her index finger poked a staccato rhythm into his chest bone as she emphasized her irritation one syllable at a time.

"Garbage and nonsense is what you always say. Laughing at me for what I read, and now you sit here and tell me that you've been talking to one?"

She leaned back, her voice dropping low, but her eyes still blazing. "I suppose next you're going to tell me you're on a first name basis with it. What do you call it? Charlie? George? Or Freddie?"

She changed to high, mocking tone. "Hey, Freddy, want to come out and play Halloween?"

She paused to catch her breath, allowing Will a chance to break in and say something.

"I call him Grandpa because he's my grandfather," he blurted out. "Actually, my great-great-great-great-great-great-grandfather. On the other hand, maybe it's five greats. I never can remember if it's five or six."

"What? You're crazy. You have lost your mind. You must have landed on your head when you fell off that horse."

"No," he responded with force. "It wasn't my head; it was my back. And I didn't fall; it threw me off."

She stared, open mouthed.

He continued. "His full name is Franklin Percival Wills, but don't call him Percival or Percy; he doesn't like that. Franklin'll be okay—or Grandpa. Yeah, you can call him Grandpa. I think he'll like that."

She sat unmoving for several more minutes not taking her eyes off him. Her blue eyes, usually mysterious and inviting, flashed with cold anger.

She shifted in her seat and spoke, biting off the words one by one.

"I'm going back to the restroom. You get me a cold soda out of that ice chest and tell your ghost of an ancestor to stay away from me—far, far away." With those words, she rose from her seat, squeezed past him, and turned toward the restroom.

"Yeah, sure." He turned to call after her. "Trace, please be careful. That's the only seat on the plane without a seatbelt."

Chapter Twenty-Five
Back at the Ranch—At Last!

The sun was low, hanging over the hill tops when the Grand-Old-Lady-of-the-Sky rolled to a gentle stop at the end of the grass runway. Miss Amelia, along with Maria, sat waiting in the big six-seat ATV. The entire Singh clan and most of the ranch hands were gathered around as well.

Will was surprised to see his mother struggle to her feet with Maria's help and stand as she waited to greet her new family. He saw a wonderful smile on her face, accompanied by a sparkle in her eyes that he had not seen before. There were also tears, but he knew these were tears of joy.

Amelia opened her arms wide and embraced him. He hugged her tenderly, afraid of crushing her frail body. She released him and turned to Tracie, standing next to him. The children hung back, shy in the presence of so many strangers.

The Ghost of Grandpa Wills

"Mother, this is Tracie, my wife." He then turned to his children. "That's Robbie with Big Jim and Katie with Jake."

Amelia turned to Tracie and reached out, stumbling as she did. Tracie caught her as she fell. They held together, arms tight around each other for a few seconds in unexpected intimacy.

Amelia looked up at her newfound daughter-in-law and spoke with hesitation, "I, I'm afraid I must apologize for my clumsiness. I had hoped to welcome my newly-found family standing on my own two feet."

Tracie saw tears on her mother-in-law's cheek. "No need to apologize." She helped Amelia back into the ATV. Holding Amelia's hand, she squatted down beside her, a smile on her face. "I, I've always wondered what it would be like to have a mother-in-law; never had one before."

Glancing back, she added, "And the children, they're thrilled to have a grandmother; although, Robbie's not sure what one is." She stood, pivoted, and called out, "Katie. Robbie. Come and meet your grandmother."

Chapter Twenty-Six
Together Again.

"It's almost midnight." Tracie fought to stifle a yawn. "You must be exhausted."

"Yeah, and I don't know how Mother made it through the day as long as she did."

They were not in the same room where Will had shot out the mirror. This one was much larger but also, with its own bathroom in the suite. The children had been given a room across the hall.

Tracie stood and turned a full circle, studying the room and its furnishings.

"Will, this house is enormous—absolutely the largest I've ever been in."

"More like a castle—which is what most people call it. And you haven't seen nearly half of it. Neither have I for that matter."

"Do you think the kids will be all right?" Tracie asked. "This is such a huge old place. It's more than a little bit spooky out in the hallway—even without a ghost roaming through the place." She paused before asking, "Will, are you really sure?"

He came to where she sat on the side of the bed.

"Look, Trace, Grandpa promised not to scare or hurt either you or them. He likes kids, too. He misses his own, you know. He told me so, even had tears in his eyes when talked about them."

"Tears. Are you serious?" She looked at him in surprise. "I never heard of a ghost shedding tears—at least not real ones."

She swung her head around, her eyes sweeping the room. "Furthermore, where is he right now? Listening to us while we talk about him? Watching us? How am I going to change clothes? Get ready for bed? Take a bath? How do I know he won't be watching me?"

He took both her hands and looked her in the eyes. "Grandpa is not a Peeping Tom. He's a real gentleman, used to be a preacher and a doctor, a medical doctor, before he came out here to Texas."

"This is crazy. Do you really expect me to believe all this stuff you're telling me? You've never believed in ghosts. 'Dead all over' is what you always said."

"Just like Rover," he completed the old rhyme. "But then, I met Grandpa face to face—nearly scared me to death." He saw her eyes go wide and realized he had said the wrong thing.

"What do you mean?"

"Okay, I mean he played a little trick on me, but he promised not to do anything like that to you or the kids." Will rose to his feet. "Okay, I have an idea."

"What? she asked suspicion in her eyes.

"Best way to ease your mind is for you to meet him. Get to know him personally."

"What?" She shied back away from him. "Oh, no. You're crazy. You've lost your mind." She scooted back on the bed leaning farther from him. "I don't want to 'get to know' him—or any other ghost for that matter. I sure don't want to know him on a personal level."

He grabbed her hands before she could move out of his reach.

"Trace, he's family. He's my grandfather."

"Family! He's dead, you moron." She tried to pull her hands away from his, but he held on tight. "Been dead for a couple of hundred years, you said."

"Only about a hundred sixty or so," he corrected her.

"Who cares?" she responded with her voice rising in volume and pitch. "A hundred or two hundred or even a thousand—dead is dead. He's a ghost, and I think this is the craziest conversation I've ever had in my life."

Keeping a firm hold on her hands, he stood, pulling her up with him.

"Come on," he urged.

"No. Where?"

"The library. That's where he stays at night. He has his own computer down there. Watches movies, looks at the news, that kind of stuff."

"Will—I don't want to do this."

"He won't hurt you. I wouldn't suggest it if I thought he

would. I think you'll like him once you get to know him."

"You have got to be completely out of your mind."

"Now, be quiet." He pulled her to the door. "We don't want to wake the kids."

Chapter Twenty-Seven
Pleased to Meet You, Ma'am

The house was silent, but far from being in total darkness; Amelia had left extra lights on for the benefit of her newfound grandchildren. Will led Tracie down the main staircase, squeezing her hand in his.

"Please, you're hurting me. My fingers'll be turning blue if they don't get some blood flowing."

"Sorry," he whispered, relaxing his grip. "I just hope he's here, that's all."

"I thought you said he stayed in the library all the time."

"No, just a lot of the time—most of the time. He gets bored and wanders around sometime, mostly during the day. I think he stays here during the night. Mother leaves the library lights on because he's afraid of the dark."

"What?" she halted on the bottom step. "Now I know

you're either crazy, or you think I am. He's a ghost, and he's afraid of the dark?"

"I think he's got claustrophobia 'cause he remembers dying in some small, dark place somewhere." He eased her toward the library door. "We talked about it on the plane, you know. He was real upset and had tears in his eyes just like when he talked about his wife and kids."

Will turned the handle and pushed the door open. It swung back without a sound as they entered. The lights were on but dimmed, except for the corner where the painting hung. Weird shaped shadows stretched across the floor and crawled up the sides of the bookshelves. He pushed the door shut, reached out, and flipped all the switches on. Bright light flooded the room. He led her over to one of the big leather reading chairs and offered it to her.

"No, I think I'd rather stand. Will, I'm really…this is giving me the creeps." She moved closer and clung to him.

"Yeah, I know. Did me, too, the first couple of times. But then nobody had bothered to introduce us properly the first time we met."

He put his arm around her shoulders, squeezed, and spoke in a loud whisper. "Grandpa. Grandpa. Are you here? Come on out, and show yourself. I want you to meet my wife. Come on now, don't be shy. Let her see you're nothing to be afraid of. Remember, she's like I was—never seen a ghost before."

Silence.

He felt Tracie trembling in his arms.

"Grandpa. Come on, please."

He felt the tingling sensation crawling up and down his arms, the hairs on the back of his neck stood up, the temperature dropped. The air shimmered in front of them.

Tracie tried to hide in his arms and whimpered, "Will, please…"

"It's okay, Hon; everything's okay. Now just relax, turn around, and open your eyes. Say 'Hi' to Grandpa. He's standing right there."

Speechless, Tracie stared, mouth open.

The ghost tipped his hat. "Hello, Miss Tracie, ma'am. I am truly pleased to meet you. I certainly do not mean to frighten you. I am right sorry about that."

Tracie stared at the ghost, awe mixed with fear written across her features. Maybe it was the light and the shadows, but his body seemed to change, sometimes, it was almost transparent, then, almost solid.

"Will, is this real?" she looked up at her husband with a dark frown creasing her forehead. "Or a trick of some kind? You're not trying to fool me, play some kind of joke or something? If you are, I'm not laughing, and I'll never forgive you."

"Trace, Hon, this is no joke, and he's as real as it gets. And I promise you that I would never, never ever try to play this kind of trick on you. Not ever!"

The ghost stood watching and listening for a moment before he spoke again. "No tricks, ma'am. I learned my lesson from your man there. He shot me. Right through the heart, that he did." He gave a light chuckle and continued, "He would have killed me, too." Another chuckle. "If I were not already dead, he certainly would have killed me."

She turned to look at Will, eyes wide with shock, "You shot him? With a gun?"

"It was an accident." Holding her shoulders, he faced her. "I, I didn't mean to. I actually tripped, and the gun went off. I was even more frightened than you are right now."

The Ghost of Grandpa Wills

He turned back to face his grandfather. "Grandpa, stop fooling around. This is no time for playing games. You're scaring her. I told you; she's never seen a ghost before."

The chuckles ceased. "Sorry. Miss Tracie, I am forgetting my manners. I really do not wish to frighten you."

With a shy look on his face, Franklin added, "You are right pretty, you know." He fumbled with his hat which he now held in both hands. "Even prettier than that picture your Will showed me."

Tracie glanced over at Will with an unspoken question on her lips.

Franklin continued talking. "I like children, always did. Should not have left mine, but—like a fool—I did."

A smile broke across his face. "Your boy is going to look just like you, you know. The little girl, now, she is the spitting image of mine when I left them."

His smile changed to a deep frown. "Do not ever leave them, Grandson. Do not ever let go of them. Protect them! Always take care of them!"

His tone deepened as he turned to look Will straight in the eye, "You take care of Miss Tracie here! I can see that she is a real blessing from above."

Will was startled to hear words like that. Unsure of how to respond, he stammered, "Y, Yeah, I know. I, I'll…"

He was interrupted as Tracie found the courage to speak, "Thank you, Mister…Mister…?" She hesitated. "You're the only ghost I've ever met or talked to. Sorry, I…"

"Just call me Franklin." He held his hat at waist level and gave a slight bow in her direction. "You might call me Grandpa if you wish. We are family, you know."

As he stood straight once more, Tracie saw the glint of moisture in his ghostly eyes. "It's been right lonely around here, just Amelia and me, especially, now, that she is sick and frail. She was so strong and spry before. And, she is one of the few who has never been afraid. Always treated me like one of the family, she has."

Will spoke up, "Grandpa, I'm sorry, but it is late—after midnight, and it's been a very long day. We need to get to bed. Gotta say 'good night' if you don't mind."

The ghost looked at them for moment. He spoke in a soft, quiet voice, tinged with sorrow. "Yes, I surely understand." He disappeared from sight.

Turning to Tracie, Will offered his arm. "I hear the bed calling, ma'am."

Chapter Twenty-Eight
Sleepy Discussions

"You shot him!" she exclaimed, as soon as they were back in their room with the door closed. She stood there, hands on her hips, glaring at him as he closed the door.

"I wanted to tell you about it back on the plane..."

"Well, you didn't, Buster. So tell me now—all of it. And everything else as well—anything and everything. What else have you conveniently forgotten to tell me?"

"I didn't mean to shoot him. It was an accident." The old feeling of intimidation returned.

"Oh, yeah," she sneered. "The old 'I didn't know the gun was loaded' story." She wagged her head from side to side. "What were you even doing with a gun? You've never owned one—not even a BB gun."

"It was an old thing that had been lost. I found it up in

the top of the closet. Mother didn't know it was there. It belonged to her father or his father; I don't remember which."

"Okay, it was old, it was lost, and all that. So what were you doing with it anyway? And how did you manage to shot your grandfather? Or, his ghost rather, or—or whatever?" She shook her head. "So, why shoot a ghost for crying out loud?" Her voice rose again in volume and pitch. "It's already dead."

"Hon, please, hold it down a bit." With his palms down, he made quieting motions at her. "You'll wake the kids, scare'm."

"Will Watson. Don't you dare try to shush me!" With hands back on her hips, she tossed her head back, sending her curls flying. "How many more guns are there around this house—all lost and forgotten? Just waiting to be found by two young kids—namely ours."

"Hon," he started to say something but went over to sit on the edge of the bed instead. After a pause he sighed and went on to explain. "Okay, it was high up on a shelf way out of their reach. I found it by accident when I threw my suitcase up there."

"Threw your suitcase, huh. Yeah, that sounds about right for you, Will Watson. Crash, bang, bam, just stuff. Don't need to be careful with it."

"Okay, I'm sorry. It had been a long trip, and I was tired. The suitcase was empty anyway. So, I found the gun, and I was looking at it over by the bed when he appeared out of nowhere." Will expressed himself with his eyes wide, arms out, and palms up. "I mean, one second he's not there, next second he is. And he held a gun in his hand—pointing the thing at me."

"He was pointing a gun at you?" she exclaimed. "He was going to shoot you?"

"It wasn't real. His gun, I mean. He is a ghost and all that. He was wearing whatever he had on when he died, but I don't think the gun will actually shoot bullets—not now anyway—but I didn't know, then. Seems another lifetime ago. Anyway, I didn't know who he was at first; sure didn't know he was a ghost."

Exhaustion caught up with him. He exhaled and deflated before her eyes.

Her anger subsided. "Let's go to bed."

Later, with the two side lamps on, they lay in bed looking up at the ceiling. Tracie whispered, "I still find all this hard to believe, and it's more than a little scary even if he is a member of the family."

She rolled onto her side to face him. "I've never been on first name terms with a ghost before. At least, no one was hurt and no damage done."

"Well, not exactly," Will replied.

Her response was immediate and loud, "What?" Rising to one elbow, she struck him on the chest with her other hand. "Who got hurt? You said no one was hurt."

He gasped and yelped as her fist connected with his bruised ribcage. "I was hurt. I fell down, and you just hurt my broken ribs."

"Oh, Will, Hon—broken ribs? You didn't tell me about that." She sat up next to him, with anxiety on her face. "How bad is it? Did your grandfather do that? How does a ghost break someone's ribs?"

He answered her through clinched teeth, "It wasn't Grandpa—it was the stupid horse. She threw me off when she got scared by some kind of bird.

"And, I was trying to say that the only damage was the old mirror."

Tracie twisted to sit with her legs folded beneath her. "Old mirror?"

"Yeah, the bullet went through Grandpa and shattered the glass mirror behind him."

"Will—just how old was this 'old' mirror you broke? Was it a very big mirror?"

"Oh, it was old enough, about a hundred years or more. I think it measured about six feet by four."

She stared back, eyes wide and mouth open before adding, "Will, when you do it, you do it good. An antique mirror…"

"Yeah, and it once belonged to her grandmother, too."

She looked down at him for a few seconds before saying, "Will Watson, you are... I mean, disaster follows you around like a puppy wanting its supper."

He tried to raise himself to one elbow before moaning and falling back again. "Trace, Hon, I've never been so frightened in all my life. I was afraid I'd never see you and the kids again." He lifted a hand to brush her curls and caress a cheek. "Then, last night someone was shooting at you, and here I was more than six hundred miles away, and I couldn't help you. I wasn't there when you needed me."

She clasped his hand between hers. "You got there as soon as you could, and you brought the cavalry." A smile lit up her pretty face. "And, I think the big shiny airplane was a whole lot neater than some old knight on a white horse."

Her hero's only response was a light snore. She sighed, turned out the lights, and was asleep, almost, as soon as her head touched the pillow.

Chapter Twenty-Nine
Sunday

Two of the ranch hands, Jose and Stephen, were just walking out the door. Jake sat at the breakfast table, along with Maria, when Will and family arrived.

Jake greeted them. "You're late. It's self-service this morning. Milk and cereal's over there, along with bread, butter, jam, toaster, and such."

"What's happening?" Will asked.

"It's Sunday," Maria replied. "And the Singh's are working hard preparing a special celebration supper for later today. There'll be a light lunch of cold meats, salads, and a sandwich, for those who want it. Also, Miss Amelia did not sleep well last night; she's resting now."

"Anything wrong?" Tracie escorted the children over to the food.

"Nothing unusual, except too much excitement yesterday. She tires easily, and that causes her more pain. She'll be up for lunch, though."

"You do know the pastor's coming by after lunch?" Jake said, through a big grin.

"And we'll be having a devotional service afterwards," Maria added. "That will be followed by a big barbeque supper."

Will stopped in his tracks. "Pastor? Prayers? Here in the house?"

"Yes, it's all going to happen here at the ranch." Maria responded. "But, no, it's not going to be in the house, although the house will be open to visitors."

She pointed out the window. "It's to be out there under that big cottonwood tree."

Turning to Will and Tracie, she continued explaining. "While all of you were enjoying yourselves flying around all over Texas, Miss Amelia and I were phoning everyone in two counties, make that three counties, to invite them all for the big celebration barbeque."

"Celebration?" Will asked. "What are we celebrating?"

"You, Littl' Bruthur." Jake was pouring dark honey over a plate of waffles. "Or rather, all four of you. In case you haven't figured it out yet, Miss Amelia seems to think having suddenly discovered a hitherto unknown family as being something worthy of celebration."

Maria broke into the conversation. "The pastor, Howard Broadman by name, is from the Faith Community Church." She reached for her coffee mug. "Miss Amelia used to drive into Marfa every Sunday before she became ill. Now, one of the pastors and some of the members as well, come to the house for lunch and a devotional service almost every

The Ghost of Grandpa Wills

Sunday."

She watched the children as she sipped her coffee. "Today's very special because all of you are here, and she wants to introduce you. There'll be a bunch from the church, and everywhere else around the area. She's invited everyone.

"Some of the ranch hands are out back setting things up right now. The Singhs started preparing the barbeque hours ago—before sunup. They were actually working on it yesterday while you were gone."

Tracie spoke up. "We didn't pack our really nice clothes—just casual things. Everything was done in such a rush."

Maria laughed. "No fancy dressing allowed with this bunch. This is West Texas ranch country, and Faith Community is one of those cowboy churches. Some of them'll be showing up in their work clothes as well—those that work on Sunday, anyway. But they're very good people and really friendly."

By lunchtime, everyone was hungry again. An extensive tour of the horse barns and other out-buildings had left them looking forward to the big glasses of iced tea as well as the food—including homemade sourdough bread for the sandwiches.

"I'll be going up to rest a bit." Amelia sat back against her cushions soon after finishing a piece of sandwich and a glass of tea. "Remember to save room for the barbeque tonight."

Will called to his family. "Come on, follow me. Let's go look at the library; all the wonderful books and pictures."

Bill Tyson

Will suffered through the afternoon worship service which took place under the spreading branches of the old cottonwood tree. As Maria had said, people arrived from three counties, including the towns of Fort Davis, Alpine, Marfa, and everywhere in between. Afterwards, he and Tracie stayed very busy shaking hands until they both thought their arms would fall off. The children disappeared into the crowd.

As soon as there was a break in the introductions, Tracie turned to Will. "Where are the kids?"

"Don't know." He shrugged his shoulders as he searched the crowd. "They're somewhere around here, I'm sure. Let's excuse ourselves and go look."

Several minutes passed before Tracie touched Will on the shoulder and pointed toward the corral behind the horse barn. "Over there, Will. Who're the two old characters they're with?"

One was tall and thin, the other tall, but heavyset. Both appeared to be dirty and unkempt which, to Tracie's mind, meant unreliable as well.

"Those men don't look too trustworthy. I think we should go get the kids."

Looking to where she indicated, Will spotted them and felt his heart skip a beat as he realized exactly who the two "old characters" were.

"You can see both of them?"

"Of course, I can see them; they're standing right there in plain sight."

"Not the kids. I mean both the old men?"

"Yes," she answered with frustration rising in her voice. "I'm not blind. My eyes are as good as yours. Of course, I see

The Ghost of Grandpa Wills

them. Now, go get our children." At that moment, the tall, thin man turned and looked right at them, a huge smile on his face.

Startled, Tracie said, "Will, that looks just like your grandfather, the ghost we talked to in the library last night."

"You can see him?" Will repeated.

"Of course, you…" she started to say more when she realized what she was seeing—the ghost was there, out in the open—with her children. She clutched Will's arm, squeezing it hard. "It's your ghost, your dead grandfather, and you said he promised not to scare them." She kept her eyes fixed on her children. "What's he doing here? And who's the other one? Another ghost?"

Will hesitated for a few seconds before replying. "Don't panic. The kids don't look scared. But if you act scared, they'll get scared. So stay calm." He started walking. "The other one's not a ghost. That's Uncle Ben, and he's not dead. He's a weird old codger, but he's definitely alive—Mother's uncle, my great-uncle. Now, let's just walk up real calm like and act as if there's nothing unusual happening."

"My children talking with a ghost, and you tell me to act as though there's nothing unusual going on?

At that moment, Robbie turned to see them and came running, "Mom. Look, Mom. Dad. We found our grandpa, and he's a real cowboy."

Chapter Thirty
I'm Tired—Good Night

Tracie came out of the bathroom, dressed in her favorite pair of cotton pajamas. Will was already in bed but sitting up with his pillow between himself and the headboard, dressed in his favorite t-shirt and shorts.

"Well, it's been an interesting day, hasn't it?" He forced a smile hoping to lighten the mood.

"If you call hobnobbing with a ghost and a crazy old man, as well as hoping your children aren't frightened out of their minds. If you call that 'interesting' then, yeah, I guess it was." She frowned and flipped the light switch throwing the room into semi-darkness. "I've never been one to think of living with a ghost as such. And what if they had been frightened?"

"But they weren't," he answered. "They handled it better

than either of us. They enjoyed the whole thing. They like having a grandpa and, now an uncle as well."

"Well, it's going to take some getting used to. Now, are you sure they're in bed and settled down. No bad dreams or anything?"

He nodded in the affirmative. "Yeah, they're asleep."

"And what did you mean asking if I could see your grandpa? He was out there in plain sight, for everyone to see."

"Trace, not everyone could see him."

"What? I saw him. The kids saw him. That crazy uncle of yours saw him." She took her 'I'm-in-no-mood-for-argument' pose—brows knit together under a dark frown with her arms crossed over her breasts. In a voice that echoed her stance she demanded, "Explain, please, now!"

"Okay. He can hide from everyone, or he can show himself to everyone. But most of the time, only certain people can see him, like his direct descendants."

"Okay, so Amelia can see him," she commented.

"Yeah, unless he hides, but she knows when he's around."

"How does she know?"

"She just knows. She senses his presence, somehow."

"And you? You know when he's close by?"

"Yeah, I'm learning. He's not here right now. Besides, he promised he wouldn't do that kind of thing, and I believe him."

"You and the kids can see him."

"We're direct descendants."

"Your Uncle Ben?"

"Direct descendant."

"And all the other people that were here today?"

"None of them could see him unless he wanted them to."

"How can you tell the difference? When he can be seen by everyone or just seen by his descendants?"

"Ahh," Will thought for a second. "He looks more solid when everybody can see him. I mean it's hard to explain, but it's like he's a little transparent when just family can see him."

Tracie hesitated for a brief moment. "Okay, Mister Direct Descendant, so why could I see him out there when no one else could? Except for you and the family—all those direct descendants, that is."

"Ahh, I..." Will paused and cleared his throat before continuing. "I don't know. I really don't know." He looked her in the eye, grinned big, and said, "Who knows, maybe we're cuzins and don't know it?"

"What?" came her startled reply. "That's awful. We're married, and we have children."

"Distant cuzins, Tracie, my love," he hastened to allay her fears. "Very distant cuzins."

"We're going to find out," she declared. "I can't believe this is happening. It isn't enough that your life is threatened, and we get shot at, and then I find out there's a ghost in the family, and, now, you tell me I might be married to my own cousin."

"Hey, how about a 'goodnight kiss'? After all, we be 'kissin' cuzins'?" He puckered his lips with a big grin on his face.

"No! Now shut up, and turn out the light. I'm tired, and none of this is funny like you seem to think it is. Go to sleep. And there better not be any ghostly grandpas waking me up in the middle of the night, either."

Chapter Thirty-One
Larson Building, Midland, Texas

Larue Larson pounded his fist down on his desk. The glass top cracked and splintered with a loud pop. He cursed into the cell phone as a sharp pain stabbed up through his arm.

"Ferrell's a fool, and I'll deal with him when the time is right. No more mistakes, no more excuses. You will do what you have to do—no matter what!"

He watched blood drip from the gash on the side of his hand as he listened. A dark scowl clouded his fine cut features. He did not like the sight of blood, especially his own, and he liked even less the news he was hearing.

With the bleeding hand, he grabbed a handful of tissues from the ever-present box on his desk. Dropping the tissues, he rested his injured limb on the papers hoping to staunch the flow. He winced as pain shot up through his arm once again.

"Look, Phillips, as I told Ferrell, now, I'm telling you—I don't pay for excuses, I pay for results. As for that newfound son of hers, I want him gone, out of there. Don't care how you do it; just do it quick." With his thumb, he closed the call and tossed the phone onto the desk where it bounced and slid across the shards of broken glass.

He lifted his wounded hand to inspect the injury and saw a small sliver of glass jutting up from the wound. He cursed again and spoke aloud, looking up at a photograph on the wall. "That land was yours, and it should be mine—that thieving old geezer stole it from us, but I'll get it back—and the treasure as well."

Blood ran and dripped onto the broken glass as he held up his injured hand, doubled it into a fist, and, declared, "I'll get it back, that I swear!"

The photo, a reproduction of an antique daguerreotype, depicting a rugged man with long hair and beard and dressed in buckskins, made no reply; it only glared down with a stern expression.

Chapter Thirty-Two
The Grand Tour

Mrs. Singh woke them with a quiet knock on their door. She entered in a shy, respectful manner, carrying a tray laden with a pot of coffee, spoons, mugs, cream, and sugar. Katie and Robbie exploded into the room, immediately afterward, dressed, and bubbling with excitement.

"Hurry," was the first words out of their mouths.

"Uncle Jake said Grandmother's taking us for a trip, and we'll see all the horses, cows, and everything," Katie blurted out.

"Whoa there, Cowgirl." Will cautioned, his voice still heavy with sleep. "Slow down a bit. Your mother and I haven't had our coffee yet, and we're not going anywhere until we've showered and taken care of a few other morning necessities." He glanced over at Tracie, struggling to sit up against the headboard. She frowned and shrugged her shoulders.

Will turned back to his kids. "Now explain this 'trip' you're talking about."

"We're going to see the horses and all," Katie explained, dancing with impatience.

"Ride'm or just look at'm?" Will asked.

"Look at them, Daddy," Katie explained, as if he should have already known the answer. "We'll ride in the ATV."

"Daddy," Robby, after moving next to the bed, finally managed to make himself heard. "Don't want to ride TV. Wanna ride horsey."

Will laughed and ruffled his son's hair. "Don't worry yourself, my boy. We won't be riding on the T-V. We'll riding in an A-T-V. And the horse will come later—once we find one your size."

Putting a stern tone into his voice, he ordered them out of the room. "Now, everybody—both of you—out of here while your mother and I get up and get ready. We'll meet you down in the breakfast room where I'll be having one of Mrs. Singh's fabulous omelets before we go tripping out anywhere."

Down in the dining room, Amelia sat waiting for them wearing a huge smile on her face. "After we all have some breakfast, I asked Jose to ready two of the ATV's for us. We're going for a tour of the ranch—not the whole thing of course, that would take several days. We'll just take a look at some of what's close by. Dress light; it will be quite warm, and the sun is bright, so get your hats.

"There will be plenty of sunscreen, bottles of cold water,

and lots of iced tea along. The Singh's are also packing one of their famous picnic lunches for us, as well."

She turned to Will. "Son, I want you to drive the big six-seater for us. Jake has agreed to follow us with Maria in one of the smaller ones. They'll carry the food basket and my old wheelchair—not the power chair."

Chapter Thirty-Three
Diablo Montana

Will and Jake helped Amelia into a seat in the second of the three rows in the big ATV. Tracie took the shotgun position next to Will. Katie claimed the place next to her Grandmother while Robbie was left to possess the entire rear seat for himself.

"Where is Robbie?" Tracie asked, realizing he had disappeared. "He was here just a minute ago."

"He asked to go up to his room to get something he had forgotten," Amelia answered. "He did promise to hurry so I said it would be all right. I do hope that was okay?"

"He went to get one of his toys," Katie added in her superior "Big Sister" tone of voice.

Tracie bit her tongue holding back any comment, hoping her son's idea of "hurry" would not result in a long delay—

and someone having to go find him.

One of the Singh women opened the dining room door, shouting something they could not understand. Robbie came tearing past her with his cowboy hat on his head and a black cape waving in the breeze behind him. He held a Batman action figure in his outstretched hand as he ran.

"What is he wearing?" Will asked.

"That's the new Batman cape he got after you left. After seeing that Batman movie on TV, he's gone crazy," Katie explained, again using her big-sister voice.

With everyone aboard, Will pressed the starter button, shifted the gears, then they were moving.

The first part of the tour circled around the corrals and outbuildings—horse barn, workshops, storage sheds, and the large hay barn.

"We keep a good supply of hay on hand," Amelia commented. "Winters can be harsh at times, and we never know when there'll be a dry spell. Our last one was particularly bad. Then, there was the brush fire two years back, ruined a lot of good grazing."

Will drove slow and careful, thinking about his mother's frail condition. His own bruised ribs and sore back were also constant reminders for him to take it easy.

Amelia guided them among and around the mesquite where he learned, the hard way, to beware of their needle-sharp thorns. The painful red scratches across his arm and cheek reinforced the need for caution.

She led them across dry creek beds, up hillsides, and down into low valleys. They followed along the high rim of a rocky arroyo and found themselves on the edge of a large cluster of majestic old trees, standing part of the way up the sloping side of one of the mesas.

"This is called *Diablo Montana* in Spanish—Devil's Mountain or Mesa, in English." Amelia sat, casting her eyes around the area with a wishful expression on her face. Will wondered what she was remembering.

"Some think it's real spooky around here," she continued. With a smile she said, "I've always liked this big grove of cottonwoods, though." She pointed to her right, "Pull over under that large one where it's flat. We'll stop to catch our breath and have a bite to eat with something cold to drink. It's a bit warmer today than I had expected." She sighed and added, "I think maybe, I just feel the heat more."

Will and Jake were the first ones out and began unloading the food box and ice chest along with the wheelchair.

As soon as his feet touched the ground, Robby's first words were, "Daddy, need go peepee."

"Okay, my boy," Will answered. "You just hang on until we get your grandmother into her wheelchair. Then, we'll go find a suitable bush to hide behind."

Once Amelia was safe and comfortable, Will remembered Robby and looked around for him, but he was nowhere in sight. Alarmed, he moved toward the trees while calling the boy's name. Within minutes, they heard the child screaming in terror. Everyone turned to where the cries came from. Both Will and Jake had taken their first steps in that direction when a large animal burst through the trees.

Narrowly missing Katie, the creature dashed between Tracie and Maria before crashing into the underbrush behind them. Everyone came to a halt, mesmerized by the animal's grace and beauty; they momentarily forgot their concern for Robby.

"Oh," Amelia exclaimed, the first to find her voice again.

The Ghost of Grandpa Wills

"A white-tailed buck. A large one. Beautiful. Wonderful to see. I was afraid they might not return after the fire and the drought."

"And so close," Tracie added. "I've never seen one out in the wild before, just in zoos. It was so graceful."

She was reminded of her missing son as he burst back into the clearing shouting, "Mommy, Mommy." Seeing her, he ran straight into her arms.

"It's okay," she said in soothing tones, seeking to reassure him. "Tell us what happened. Are you hurt? Did something bite you?"

"Big thing. Knock me down." Leaves, grass, and dirt clung to the boys clothing, and his pants were unzipped.

"Now, Young Fellow," Will interrupted, with a frown, "what were you doing going into the trees without me—after I told you to wait?"

With a sudden pout, Robby hung his head. "Peepee, Daddy." The child looked up at his father with tears on his cheeks and sobbed, "It bump me."

Will knelt down, took the boy's shoulders and looked him in the eye. "Okay, Robbie, my little man. I apologize. It's Daddy's fault. I got busy helping Uncle Jake and forgot about your needs. I should have thought about you first." Will rose to his feet, taking his son by the hand. "Nevertheless, let this be a lesson, and don't do it again."

Will added, "Don't ever go wandering off by yourself. You were lucky this time; we all were. Your grandmother says that was a big deer, but it could have been a snake. It didn't want to hurt you—just wanted to get away from you—and all of us as well."

With excitement in his voice, Will suggested, "Now, how about we explore these deep, dark woods together?"

Lowering his voice to a dark tone he said, "Maybe, there's some real monsters out there somewhere?"

"Will Watson," Tracie broke in, her voice sharp with anger. "You stop that nonsense right now. He's already been frightened once. You'll have him too scared to go anywhere or do anything."

"Okay, okay," Will answered in a repentant voice. "No monsters, but there might be a rabbit or a squirrel. And I'll be with you so we can protect each other."

"Can I go too, Dad?" Katie chimed in.

Will turned to her with a bow and a smile, "Ah, most certainly, my fair lady. Come, please, come join us on this fair jaunt."

Raising his free hand high, he shook his fist in a victory challenge. "One fair damsel accompanied by two brave knights such as we, and there be no harm can befall us. Perhaps, yon Knave Jake, would deign to join us on our brave quest?"

"Knave, you call me. Don't I deserve the title of Knight, or at least 'Esquire'?"

"Okay," Maria broke in, "Knave or Knight or whatever—just remember that if any of you want something to eat, you best not be gone too long because we 'Ladies-in-Waiting' are hungry ladies, and we aren't in the mood to wait for long."

"And a warning," Amelia called out. "Stay away from that old shack and the bat cave up there." She pointed up the mountainside.

Robbie's reaction was instantaneous. "Bat Cave. Batman. Wanna see Batman. Go see Batman. Wow!"

His grandmother hushed him with a wave of her hand and continued explaining, "There's the ruins of an old stone shack up the hillside. It was built over one of the cave entrances a century or so ago by an old eccentric shaman, or some such. That's one reason folks call this Devil's Mountain. Some say the whole place is haunted—by evil spirits. They call the cave, *'La Boca del Diablo.'* That's 'the Devil's Mouth' in English."

Both Tracie and Maria frowned and glanced up in the direction Amelia had indicated.

Will's reaction to his son's excitement was more down to earth. "Whoa, Cowboy. Bat cave means bats, as in flying rodents. Kinda like rats with wings. And no, we are not going into some dark, smelly hole, full of snakes, spiders, and all that. We will not be going near it. You will do what your grandmother says."

"Dad, don't call them rats!" Katie interjected. "I think they're cute, and they eat all sorts of bugs and things. We studied them in science class."

"Okay, okay," Will responded in mock surrender. "So, they're not rats; they're still rodents, and I still think they're ugly, even if they can fly."

"Robbie," Amelia spoke up again. "We don't ever go near that place. Your daddy's right. That is a bad place—deep, dark, and dangerous. However, sometime we can come back around sunset and watch the bats as they fly out to go hunt the bugs Katie was talking about. Sometimes you can see them see from the roof of the house if you're up there at the right time."

Robbie stuck his bottom lip out and stomped his foot, "Wanna see Batman."

"No, sir," Will declared and grabbing his son's hand, headed into the trees in the opposite direction. "Come hither, Knave Jake, and give safe escort to our fair lady into the dark forest, that we might all explore its mysterious wonders." Without waiting for a response, he disappeared into the trees, heading down the slope, away from the evil bats and their dark lair.

Chapter Thirty-Four
Monday Night

"Do you think it was wise to let Katie drive the ATV home? Especially with your mother riding with us?" Tracie asked, once they were comfortably ensconced beneath the bedcovers. "She's never driven anything other than her bicycle, and that was a long way out to the mailbox and back."

"Hey, Mother enjoyed it, and I thought she did a really good job—especially for a girl."

He let out a yelp as Tracie smacked him full in the face with her pillow.

"Owww, what'd ya do that for?"

"Male chauvinist pig. Who's had more accidents? You or me? And don't go belittling our daughter."

"Joke, my Dear. It was a joke. And I told you, I thought she did an excellent job."

"Yeah, well, make sure you tell her that in the morning and make double sure she knows she's not to go out on her own. She must have an adult with her. Now, turn out the light. I'm exhausted."

Will lay there in the dark stretched out on his back, head on the pillow, with his hands clasped behind his head. Thoughts whirled about in his head, his imagination going wild—Devil's Mouth, Ghost Mesa, Ghost Lights, evil bats, dark caves:

"Hey, Boss." The ranch foreman he strode into the library, his spurs jangling as he clomped across the polished stone floor.

"Yeah," Boss Watson answered looking up from the documents he was perusing. "What ya need? Thought you'd be safe in bed by now."

"Them lights is back along with the weird noises. Sounds like the Devil hisself having a party up there. You told me to tell you next time it happened."

"Get the ATV ready. We're going up, gonna find out what all's a happenin' up thar. Bring a rifle." Watson gave the order and rose to his feet, a six-gun already strapped to his waist. "I was expecting sumthin to be a happenin tonight, it being a full moon an' all."

"Boss, I ain't a goin'," the foreman replied in a low voice, not willing to look his superior in the eye. "Not up thar. Not after dark. Not when them ghost lights be a runnin' an' all that devilish noise a goin' on. Ain't none of us here'd set foot on that mountain 'ceptin' Crazy Ben, maybe." The foreman backed away from the Boss' desk, eyes wide with fear.

The Ghost of Grandpa Wills

"Too rough and risky for an old timer like Uncle Ben," Boss Watson responded a somber expression on his face and his voice subdued. *'If you won't go—I'll go it alone. Besides, I ain't never met a ghost I didn't like..."*

The next thing Will was aware of was the earth rocking beneath him and someone calling his name. "Will, wake up. The kids are already up and gone to breakfast. We'll be the last ones there—again."

It was Tracie, shaking him awake.

"I've first claim on the bathroom, too," she added. "That's your punishment for tossing around all night. That must have been some dream you were having—rolling, turning, and mumbling strange stuff about ghost lights and mountains."

"Don't remember anything about it except a big mountain and some weird lights. Hurry, please," he begged. "I can't wait much longer."

Down at the breakfast table Tracie's first question was, "Anyone seen the kids? They were up and gone before we woke up."

"Came, ate, and outa here already," Jake put his coffee mug down.

"What? They just ran out of here without..."

"Okay, they're okay. Your Uncle Ben has them safe under his wing. They're just out back a ways. You can see them from this window." He pointed behind him. "Ben's showing them some young calves Miss Amelia had brought up just for that purpose. Go see for yourself."

Both Will and Tracie moved over and looked out toward the corral. There they could see the children along with two men. Both kids were sitting on the top rail of the corral fence, flanked by the men.

"Who's the other old…?" Tracie stared at the two characters.

Will touched her arm and whispered, "Shhh," while shaking his head.

"I think we'll just go out there with them for a minute. We'll eat when we get back. But I do want a big mug of that coffee to take with me."

Chapter Thirty-Five
Tuesday Lunch

Tracie strolled into the dining room where Will and the others waited for lunch. "Where're the kids?"

"I thought they were up in their room," Will answered. "Told them to get washed up before eating. Both were dirty, but Robbie needed a bath and a change of clothes. He looked and smelled as if he had rolled in cow manure."

"Hee, hee," Uncle Ben responded with a chuckle. "Young cowboy he be. Ride calf. Fall off. Back on. Brave, he is. Girl, she be ridin' 'm too. Stayed on, she did; surely she did. Some dirt be good fer'm."

"What?" Tracie exclaimed. "You put my kids on the back of those dangerous animals? They could have been injured, broken an arm or worse. Where are they? I want to see them, now."

"Okay. Okay, they be. Wash in the barn, they do. Washroom in the barn. Closer than house. No dirt in house."

"I'm going to look for them," Tracie stated with steel in her voice and fire in her eyes. "Who knows where they might be by now? They might've gone out looking for the bats or worse." Glaring at Will, she headed for the door before asking, "Are you coming or not?'

Will eyed the half-eaten sandwich lying on the plate in front of him. Reaching for it, he called to Tracie as she disappeared through the door, "Be with you in a minute." After refilling his tea glass, he took a bite out of the sandwich.

A sense of urgency drove Tracie toward the maintenance barn, an oversized, cavernous structure, opening at either end with large hangar like doors that slid back on rollers. They now stood open so that the interior could catch any stray breeze coming that way.

The wind whipped her hair, swirled dust, and stirred up the dry leaves. The branches of the old cottonwood thrashed about as she hurried. She ignored it all—feeling cold fear deep building within her. Something was wrong, she could not say what.

Tracie hurried through the opening at the west end of the building. "Katie. Robbie." Urgency, verging on panic, in her voice.

No response. Empty—no sign of the children.

Jose appeared through the east door, silhouetted in the bright outside light.

"Not here, Senora; I see them going that way." He pointed east.

"Walking?" she asked.

The Ghost of Grandpa Wills

"No, Senora, riding the big cart. "Su hija," he paused for a second, searching for the English words. "Your daughter, she drives very fast."

"What? Why didn't you stop them?" She was now angry as well as afraid. "Where is Will?" she shouted, alarm showing on her face and in her voice.

"I called, Senora. They did not stop." Jose answered in a defensive manner. "I think, maybe, you say they could drive the big cart. No?"

"No!" She replied in an angry tone. "And don't you ever let them do it again. Next time, you find me immediately; no matter what you're doing, you drop it, and come find me. Now, help me find them. Run up to the house, and get their father—and anyone else—especially Jake. Tell them all, what has happened. Now, run! Hurry!"

Tracie stood for a minute watching Jose as he ran up to the house, her mind racing about the dire possibilities of what might happen to her children. What should she do? Turning to the remaining ATV's parked off to one side, she made her decision and chose one.

As she sped out through the doorway, a dark figure stepped through a side opening and, from the shadows, watched her race eastward.

Chapter Thirty-Six
The Search Begins

Will was finishing his second sandwich and third glass of tea as he and Jake listened to Ben spin more yarns about his exploits around the world. The latest story concerned some adventure in southern Africa, places with names he could neither spell nor pronounce. The old codger seemed to have been everywhere and done everything.

Jose burst through the door. "Senor Will, you come pronto. Senora Tracie say you will come. *Su hija*—your childs—they gone away. Take big cart fast; go that way." The ranch hand pointed as he talked, words spilling out of his mouth. "Senora say you will come. Senor Jake, you come, too."

Will stopped with his last bite of sandwich halfway to his mouth. "Where is she? Where's Tracie?"

The Ghost of Grandpa Wills

"*Si*, she is at the big barn. She say I must tell you and Senor Jake. Your childs, they are gone ride in big cart. Gone alone. Senora Tracie, she wait for you in big barn. Say you must come now—*pronto, pronto*!"

Will lost all interest in the sandwich and his drink. "Jake?" he asked, looking over at him.

Jake was already sliding his chair back from the table. "I'm already with you Littl' Bruthur—with ya all the way." He turned to Maria. "Tell Amelia, please. Let everyone know to watch out for the kids." He followed Will out the back door.

Will ran to the maintenance barn and rushed in, with Jose close behind, to find no sign of Tracie. Will turned to him asking, "The ATVs? Did she take one of them?"

"*Si*, Senor. Your childs take the big cart. Your wife, she takes the leetle cart."

"Which one has a full tank?"

Jose pointed at the furthest one, in the corner.

"I'm taking it, now. Which way did she go?"

"There," he pointed. "They go there."

The ranch manager appeared out of the shadows as they spoke. "Saw your woman turn south after leaving the barn. She was driving real fast, especially for a greenie that's never driven one of these things before." He stared at Will with a cold look in his eyes.

"South. Why did she go south?" Will threw himself into the ATV. He was already through the doorway as Jake entered the barn, his breath coming in gasps.

Ben sat, watched, and listened as Jose explained everything. Rising to his feet, he hurried out to his own ATV. Forgotten by everyone else, he was determined not to be left out.

Climbing into his machine, he called out, "Franklin. Where be ye? Come here. Come now, old friend."

He pushed the starter button, and the engine rattled to life. The air next to him shimmered as the ghost appeared standing in the passenger area next to him, his lower half hidden by the ATV's seat cushions.

"Franklin, where she be? You know always where family be. Children, they be gone. Momma goes look for little ones."

The ghost seemed lost in thought for a moment as if he had not heard Ben's questions. When he spoke, his eyes were focused on something faraway.

"The babies, they have turned to the west. You must stop them. Their momma. She goes east and to danger. She seeks the children at the Devil's Mouth where the little flying demons lurk. There is darkness there. I am afraid. She will…" He hesitated again. "I must go to her. There is no time. Find the boy. Find the girl." He was gone, vanishing into the air.

Ben reached for his CB radio mike, keyed it on, and called out the alarm. There was no response.

Turn the page for
a sneak preview
of

Part III
The Ghost of Grandpa Wills:
Flatrock Mesa

*by **Bill Tyson***

Chapter One
Descent into Darkness

Tracie sped out of the barn, following the Jose's direction. She quickly realized that nothing looked familiar—everything looked the same, no matter which way she turned. Minutes after leaving the barn, she lifted her foot off the accelerator and allowed the ATV to roll to a stop. She stepped out of the machine and studied her surroundings.

Trees, cacti, dirt, rocks. She was in the middle of a dense thicket of trees. No mountains, no mesas, no house, no barn anywhere in sight.

Nothing looked familiar. Everything looked the same, no matter which direction she turned.

She recalled Jose saying and pointing, "East." She pivoted around. "Sun rises in the east. Sets in the west. Kids went east. I go east. Keep the afternoon sun at my back."

Up high in the western sky, dark clouds—thunderheads—

were building, an attacking army gathering for an invasion. She remembered Amelia saying storms always come from that direction. And this looked as if it might be a big one. The wind was already gusting strong, thrashing the tree limbs about. "Oh, why couldn't the drought last a day or so longer?" She clenched her fists.

Clouds building up—faint shadows. Keep the clouds to my back. Keep the sun to my back. She stepped up into the passenger's seat, searching for something familiar. Turning slowly, she saw something—the mesa they had visited yesterday. She thought she recognized the rocky cliffs rising above the tree tops.

The grove of trees where Robby was knocked down by the deer. Amelia talked about the bats in the cave—the bat cave, as she called it. Both kids clamoring to visit the cave and see the bats, heedless of the dire warnings.

Robby had lost his Batman figurine and cried when they couldn't find. He wanted to go find it.

The bat cave!!!

Regaining her seat behind the steering wheel, and with a prayer on her lips, she shifted the machine into gear, stomped on the accelerator and plunged ahead. Eventually, she spied a faint trail through the underbrush. Filled with desperation, anger, and fear, she dodged trees and boulders, and climbed into and out of ravines.

When she had almost given up all hope, she recognized the cottonwood grove from yesterday's picnic, just a few yards ahead of her. Easing up on the accelerator, she threaded her way up through the dense thicket until the machine could go no further. Killing the engine, she jumped down and continued on foot. Somewhere behind her, she thought she heard another ATV but dismissed it from her mind, deciding it was someone helping in the search for the children.

Scanning the area, she saw no sign of the kids—or any other living person for that matter. That thought brought a chill to her heart—no living person? There was a tremor in her voice as she called their names.

"Katie, Robbie. Answer me. Don't play games. Are you here?"

Silence.

She swallowed hard, forcing down the panic that grew within her.

With thorns tearing at her clothing and flesh, she broke through some low bushes and saw the old stone shack directly in front of her—weather-beaten, decaying, walls fractured and broken, with gaping dark holes where windows had once been. The roof was gone with only a few trusses still pointing upward like the bare ribs of some animal, long dead. Most of the chimney lay scattered and lost amongst the dry, brittle weeds. A small tree had thrust its way up through the floor of what had once been the front porch. The entire structure leaned against an ancient cottonwood tree. The only door hung crookedly on its single remaining hinge.

Without considering her own safety or thinking to search for signs that they had been there, she rushed forward, onto the remains of the old porch. The dry wood squeaked, sagged, and cracked under her weight.

"God, please don't let them be in there," she prayed aloud. "Surely they wouldn't go inside a place like this." She tried to reassure herself but had to know for sure. She grabbed the dried wood that barred her way and pulled. The entire door came loose, crashing against her legs. A sharp pain shot through her shin and right knee. Angry, she used both hands to toss it as far away as she could.

She stood among the ruins of what had once been someone's home. Dim sunlight filtered down past the tree limbs and remains of the roof as well as through holes in the wall. Dirt and decay lay all around her. Dust danced in the air, cobwebs hung in the corners.

From yesterday, she recalled Amelia's dire descriptions of the ruin's former inhabitants—tales of witchdoctors, evil spirits, and black magic. Told while the children had been away exploring with Will and Jake, the stories had been thrilling and fun to hear. Now, she was alone in the gloom—her children were lost. The cold chill of fear filled her soul.

A second, dark doorway stood directly in front of her. Still calling their names, she almost stepped forward, until she saw the black hole where rotted wood had given way and disappeared into nothingness. She paused, her heart beating loudly, hearing her own blood as it coursed through her body. The dark emptiness yawned before her, threatening her, summoning her, calling to her.

"No," she moaned. "Please, not down there."

The hole was old, the wood rotten, and it had splintered long ago, but she did not know that. In her panic and fear for her children—pictures of the worst possible tragedies came into her mind.

Tracie heard a sound behind her. A soft footstep? A creak in the wooden floor? She sensed a presence. Someone was there.

"Will?" she asked, turning around. There, silhouetted against the brighter sunlight, she saw the form of a man.

"Who-?" She never finished the question. Hands slammed hard against her chest, knocking her backward. She stumbled a step, then another step. The sound of breaking wood filled the dark interior. Tracie fell into dark nothingness.

CPSIA information can be obtained at www.ICGtesting.com
Printed in the USA
BVOW02s2019080416

443439BV00011B/50/P